GIDDAY.

READ THE PAPERS

EXCHANGE PROGRAMME

TREVS

Gidday. Now when it comes to discussing what to do
with our leisure time, and let's face it, it always does sooner or later,
the noble game of squash is always mentioned, ~~the instance~~

~~A~~ and the more scrutiny this activity is subjected to, the

Gidday. Have you ever thought about becoming a chemist. It
is the wish of the Fred Dagg Careers Advisory Bureau that
you do just that. I do not mean here of course the sort
of chemist who works in a laboratory developing nuclear
warheads, I mean the sort of chemist who works in a
chemist shop

Doctor
Architect
Engineer
Shearer
Film-maker.
Accountant
Dentist.

Tinkering

Also by John Clarke

Still the Two

A Dagg at My Table

The Tournament

The Howard Miracle

The 7.56 Report

The Even More Complete Book of Australian Verse

The Catastrophe Continues

A Pleasure to Be Here

Tinkering

the complete book of
John Clarke

Introduced by Lorin Clarke

TEXT PUBLISHING MELBOURNE AUSTRALIA

textpublishing.com.au

The Text Publishing Company
Swann House
22 William Street
Melbourne Victoria 3000
Australia

First published in 2017 by The Text Publishing Company
Reprinted 2017 (three times)

Sections of this book have previously been published in *The Fred Dagg Scripts*, first published by Thomas Nelson, 1981; *Daggshead Revisited*, first published by Thomas Nelson, 1982; *A Complete Dagg*, first published by Allen & Unwin, 1989; *A Dagg at My Table: Selected Writings*, first published by Hodder Moa Beckett, Auckland, 1996; and at mrjohnclarke.com.

Book design by Text
Front cover photograph © Stewart Thorn
Back cover photograph © Lisa Tomasetti
Typeset by J&M Typesetting
Illustrations on pp. 132–142 by Jenny Coopes

Printed and bound in Australia by Griffin Press, an accredited ISO/NZS 1401:2004 Environmental Management System printer. The paper used in this book is manufactured only from wood grown in sustainable regrowth forests.

National Library of Australia Cataloguing-in-Publication entry:
Creator: Clarke, John, 1948–2017, author.
Title: Tinkering : the complete book of John Clarke / by John Clarke ; introduced by Lorin Clarke.
ISBN: 9781925603194 (hardback)
ISBN: 9781925626247 (ebook)
Subjects: Clarke, John, 1948–2017. Comedians—Australia—Anecdotes. Comedians—New Zealand—Anecdotes. Authors—Australia. Authors, New Zealand. Wit and humor.
Other Creators/Contributors: Clarke, Lorin, writer of introduction.

Contents

What Thinkest
by Lorin Clarke

Some people's dads spend hours tinkering in the shed. Our dad, John Clarke, borrowed the word but required only a desk and 'gallons of tea' for the kind of tinkering he did.

After a day in his office on the phone, writing, chatting and reading, or, as he used to put it, 'bent over me lathe', Dad would snap open his laptop again late at night and 'tinker away' at his writing in some form or another—a script, his family history, an email, or an idea that might or might not develop into something.

He and I used to email each other drafts of our writing. He sent various things to my mum and my sister, too, and collaborators and friends. Most of those emails are timestamped after 11 p.m. 'Had a bit of a tinker since we last spoke. What thinkest?' the subject line would read. Or, at midnight, I'd send him something saying, 'Need to lose a couple of hundred words from this, what do you reckon?' Thirty seconds would pass. 'May I tinker?' would come the reply.

There were other shorthands, too. If, as is often the case, I can't find a draft of something Dad sent me, I just type 'Waddyers' into my search bar. Instantly, row after row of emails appear entitled 'Waddyers', a more economical form of the well-known Australian expression 'What do yiz reckon?'

In this way, despite his hyperbolic reference to his lathe, Dad's creative processes reflected not so much the industrial rigour of the factory as the natural rhythms of conversation. These little linguistic jokes proscribe any hierarchies or even formalities, suggesting a mutual adventure that might continue for some time. 'Writing another draft' sounds exhausting. 'Having a bit of a tinker' sounds delightful.

His tinkering, though, was forensic and, with his own work, from Fred Dagg to *Clarke & Dawe*, he confidently made the final call. This was, in part, due to his early work as Fred Dagg. When he first appeared on TV in New Zealand, television production tended to the rudimentary. He was not assigned a crew. He was given a camera. He took it, plonked it down on the ground near a field, turned it on and performed in front of it. It was a film camera, so he had to edit it himself later, using scissors. He always said that being required to engage in all these elements of production gave his writing and performance a discipline he might not otherwise have had.

It also meant that he valued all the creative aspects of production. He often said he learned to write partly by performing, and sometimes found himself performing his way out of a writing problem. Once, when he was directing *Stiff* for television (the diaries from which are included in these pages), he overheard the production manager fretting about the practical requirements of a complicated set. He asked what was complicated about it. She told him not to worry, he was the director, she'd deal with it. He asked her again what was complicated about it. She explained the problem. He opened his script and scribbled out the line describing the set. Always tinkering.

When asked what his influences were, Dad had a range of answers, but he always said the biggest influence on his writing and performing was talk. The adults in the next room talking at night, the way people spoke in shops, the wording of announcements over loudspeakers. If you listen to talk, you learn about tone, about speech rhythm, and, most importantly for Dad, about how important the form of delivery is to conveying (or avoiding) meaning. You can find him playing with all this in these pages—in the earnest authority of

Fred Dagg's advice to the masses, the religious theatricality of St Paul's Letters to the Electorates, the familiar format of the Letters from the School (applied not to children but to birds), the quiz answers (but no questions), and the reportage of industrial disputes pertaining to the tantrums of children (who bear no resemblance to any real persons past or present).

One can often identify in Dad's writing a form (like sporting commentary) from which he has removed key elements (any reference to existing sporting codes, for instance). This allows the form to be stripped of the cultural heavy lifting that gave it meaning in the first place. One of the best compliments he ever got from a member of his audience was someone who stopped him in the street and said, 'I like what you do. I watch your interviews with a straight face and then I laugh at the news.' Someone else once stopped him and said, 'What you do is a secret between you and your audience.' He liked the idea of that mutual understanding, that conversation between himself and his audience, recognising patterns of human behaviour together.

We had a term in our house for some of the more obscure jokes in Dad's work. They were 'one-percenters'. As in: one percent of your audience *might* get that joke, Dad. He loved those ones the most, because the audience had to work a little with him to get to the joke. Some of the writing collected here is reflective, some of it is funny, and some of it (like politicians' doorstop interviews reframed as poetry) is slightly surreal. There are one-percenters sprinkled throughout, and a lot of tinkering was done along the way to get here. Thank you for reading this book. Put the kettle on. It's probably best enjoyed with a cup of tea.

Origins

Eliza

The National Library of Australia is a large and impressive contemporary building looking out over Lake Burley Griffin in Canberra. Among the documents on display there at the moment are very early maps and atlases, Cook's *Endeavour* journal, records from Bligh's unusual voyage, the original sheet music for 'Waltzing Matilda' and the handwritten notes passed between Kingsford Smith and Charles Ulm in the loud and freezing cockpit of the *Southern Cross* as they flew across the Pacific in 1928.

Downstairs is a newspapers and microfilms reading room which holds millions of records. It's a researcher's dream and is full of people working on their projects. Some of the records are available only on site and among these is a copy of the New Zealand Electoral Roll for 1893. Not only do you have to be in the building to view this; you need to be on a particular computer. When I was there I went to this otherwise unremarkable device, sat down, opened the New Zealand Electoral Roll for 1893 and typed in the name of my great grandmother. Eliza Jane Fox. Up she came. Eliza Jane Fox. Waiapu electorate. Gisborne resident. Married. The 1893 New Zealand election was the first election anywhere in the world in which women voted. I can't tell you how pleased I am to have a runner in this event.

I also looked up Eliza's mother, Matilda Keys. Not there. No appearance, Your Worship. Matilda was also eligible to vote in this election but perhaps chose not to. Maybe it was all too modern for her. She'd crossed the world from Enniskillen, a perilous journey which took nearly half a year, she'd lived in often very tough circumstances, had five children, buried two husbands and had survived and made her own way, but perhaps voting was a bridge too far.

For Eliza, as for many of her generation of New Zealand women, suffrage was a significant advance but was only a beginning.

She was part of the effort to get a hospital for Gisborne and she later played a role in this and in other aspects of local politics. She came from immigrant stock and perhaps recognised the opportunity given to those who settle in a new land to define themselves in a context different from that of their parents. Eliza's parents were from the old world; she was from the new. They were formed and shaped and taught in Ireland; she grew up in New Zealand. Her parents were Roman Catholic; she was a free thinker who was married in the Knox Presbyterian church in Dunedin when she was slightly pregnant and she sometimes played the piano in a church in Gisborne which she refused point blank to join.

Eliza's life falls within other great patterns of her time. Born in the Victorian goldfields in 1862, she arrived in Dunedin as a baby when the Otago gold rush was attracting people from all over the world and at the age of twenty she married a man from Dublin who played rugby for Otago and Poverty Bay and was the New Zealand rowing champion. Together they brought up seven children, most of whom I knew.

If I were the New Zealand government I'd publish the names of all of the women who voted in the 1893 election. And I'd hope that anyone related to them or descended from them or living in the same area today would consider doing some research. What happened to these women and to their children? It's still only about a hundred years ago. These are the women whose sons went to the First World War. Eliza lost a nephew at Gallipoli. One of her sons was gassed in France. Her grandsons went off to the Second World War, one with the New Zealand Division in North Africa and Italy, the other a decorated pilot and the only survivor of his original squadron. Her daughters and granddaughters included teachers, writers and organisers.

If we don't do some work on our own history, our great grandchildren will have to pay to access it online or find it on a special computer in someone else's library. Most of the women who voted in

1893 would have been photographed. If we try really hard we might find images to match the names.

Neva

In 1944 our mother, Neva, was in San Spirito, in Italy, working at New Zealand army headquarters. During the Second World War, the role of women was changing. They began to do work previously done by men, in education, in health, in factories, in transport and on the land. These women often became more independent as their experiences took them beyond the lives of their own mothers. As the Irish poet Seamus Heaney said, 'in a life the nucleus stays the same but with any luck the circumference moves out.'

Not long before she was at the army headquarters, Neva was working as a secretary in Whakatane. Her boyfriend was a champion swimmer and they spent their weekends at dances and up the east coast. When the war broke out her boyfriend joined the air force and in 1942 he was shot down and killed over Benghazi, in Libya. In San Spirito, Neva was partly recovering from the trauma of losing her best friend and partly taking charge of her life.

Neva Yvonne Morrison was born in Gisborne on 20 April 1920. She had a happy, confident childhood and was bright and keen to do well. But times were tough and like many others she had to leave school during the Depression and find work. She learnt shorthand, became a virtuoso touch typist and could organise anything from a standing start. After the death of her friend, and partly as a response, she joined up for overseas service herself and, after training in Wellington, she arrived in Italy with the Women's Army Auxiliary Corps. In September 1944 the administrative headquarters of the New Zealand division was moved to Senigallia on the Adriatic coast and Neva was promoted to a position working directly for Major-General W. G. Stevens, the commanding officer.

The New Zealand Division, which was sometimes called the 2NZEF or 'The Div', had built its reputation through tough campaigns in Greece, Crete and across North Africa and was now part of the arduous and apparently endless fighting up through Italy. Thousands had been killed. Many of the men around head-quarters were on leave or were convalescing after being wounded. From them she heard of the battles and the terrible losses. She heard stories of men she'd known in New Zealand. Her sister's fiancé had been captured in North Africa and was in a German prison camp. Her cousin had come through the desert campaign in the infantry and was now part of the fighting in Italy. Another cousin was a decorated pilot with 70th Squadron, where life expectancy was somewhat limited. She herself was the victim of a sexual assault and was mentioned in dispatches for her actions in defending herself. On the other hand, there were good friends among the WAACs, beau-tiful beaches, historic towns, and there were dances. An Australian pilot told me, 'Your mother was the best dancer in the New Zealand army.' She also learnt enough Italian to make her way around and meet the local people, some of whom she stayed in touch with long after the war. As an Allied victory became more inevitable the WAACs took some leave and hitched rides in army vehicles going to Florence, Sienna, Milan, Venice or Rome. Neva also went hiking in the Alps and climbed Mont Blanc. Throughout this period she kept a diary in which she recorded her experiences and which was later published as a book, *An Angel in God's Office.*

It was at headquarters in Senigallia that Neva met our father, Ted Clarke, who was working there for a while after being wounded. Ted was from Wellington and was in the 7th Anti-Tank Regiment. He'd been at Sidi Rezegh, Ruweisat Ridge, Minqar Qaim, El Alamein, Tebaga Gap, the Sangro and Monte Cassino. Neva was keen not to become deeply involved with anyone, but she and Ted got on well and had a good deal in common. Both had parents with strong roots in Ulster, both were interested in the arts, both had a gift for language and they shared a sense of humour.

When the war finished Neva returned home via Britain and visited the place in County Down where her father had grown up. When she arrived at the railway station in Crossgar she approached a man with a horse-drawn taxi. 'Hello,' she said. 'I'm from New Zealand and I'm trying to find the place where my father grew up.'

'Is that right?' asked the man. 'What was his name?'

'William Gibson Morrison,' replied Neva.

'Right,' said the man. 'I'll take you up to the house. I was at school with him. How is he?'

'He's fine,' said Neva.

And that night she slept in the bed her father was born in.

A few months later she arrived back in New Zealand and was reunited with her family and friends. She quickly realised that she wouldn't be slipping back into Gisborne and continuing her old life. She applied to go to Japan as part of New Zealand's postwar presence in the region but was told they were only taking people who hadn't had the opportunity to go to Europe. She took a job in the prime minister's office in Wellington while she considered what to do. She and Ted had begun to spend some time together and he was thinking about the future. He had gone back to the job he'd had before the war with a national retail chain and had been appointed manager of the Palmerston North branch. After a while Ted was invited to go to Gisborne and meet Neva's family and on a fine summer's day in early 1947, in the garden of Neva's parents' house in Sievwright Lane, where we later spent many Christmases, Neva and Ted were married.

Neva was a modern woman. She was intelligent, capable, talented, ambitious and very employable. She had travelled extensively in Europe at a time when travel was generally available to few. Ted was a very good retailer and retail was booming, so he was quickly marked out for bigger things in the company. I was born in 1948 and Anna in 1951 and Neva was a very good mother. As for many women, however, being confined at home and deprived of independent income or social contacts was a gender-specific restriction. Despite her love for her children, the role of housewife in Palmerston North during the 1950s was not going to hold Neva's interest on its own.

She got involved with the local theatre group and began to appear in plays. The local repertory attracted actors from other towns, and for years afterwards I saw people in film and television productions who had been in plays at the Manawatu Rep. Sometimes they babysat us while Neva was at rehearsals or during the run of a play; Ngaire Porter, for example, who was from Napier and later played Irene in the BBC's production of *The Forsyte Saga* and Dennis Moore, who also went to London and became an agent and among whose clients were the members of Monty Python. They wrote a song about him in the manner of Robin Hood. It begins:

> Dennis Moore, Dennis Moore, Galloping through the sward.
> Dennis Moore, Dennis Moore, And his horse Concorde.
> He steals from the rich. And gives to the poor.
> Mr. Moore, Mr. Moore, Mr. Moore.

Dennis and I are still in regular contact and, despite the fact that he lives on the south coast of Devon, he still knows exactly what's happening in Palmerston North. Sometimes I was roped into actual involvement in one of Neva's plays. When I was about eight years old a boy called Bill Woollett broke his nose in a rugby match and I was blackmailed into replacing him at very short notice as Bob Cratchit's son in *A Christmas Carol*. Another time I was prevailed upon to stand just offstage in some production Neva was in and hand various props to an actor called Colin Watson, who later became a successful sculptor in New York. Colin was rather a physical performer and would dash into the wings, grab the prop and then bound back onstage, slamming the door so that the set heaved and rattled and the notion that we were in Moscow, which was already in some trouble, was briefly abandoned altogether. Brooms would fall over backstage and we'd fumble about in the dark catching cups and bits of lighting equipment in case the whole of Russia went up. I also remember an actress called Bunty Norman singing a song called 'Making Whoopee'. She was pretending to be drunk and I was aware that I was learning about something by seeing it exaggerated.

Neva was an encouraging and very amusing mother. She could talk about anything, and if there was nothing much happening she would help us to remember or imagine. 'Who is this man?' she would ask about a bloke walking up the street as we sat in the car. 'And what is he carrying in that bag? Onions? Fish? Has he murdered his wife and cut her up into very small pieces? And is that a limp or has he just got new shoes, and, if so, should he take them back and get some the right size?' She also took us to the A&P Show, to musical events, to visit her friends, to other towns and to shows by visiting artists. We went to the Opera House where we saw Joyce Grenfell, who was very funny and John Gielgud, who was very serious.

Neva also bought a typewriter and she began to write short stories. There were other writers doing this in the Manawatu and they met regularly. They were often women and they sent their stories away to magazine publishers. Before the arrival of television, magazines were king and some of the best writing anywhere in the world made its first appearance in periodicals. I remember Alice Glenday who became a novelist and Joy Cowley, who lived on a farm on the way to Ashurst and had a husband who could do somersaults on the lawn. I was deeply impressed.

Neva was sometimes ill in Palmerston North in the 1950s with various conditions we might these days see as at least partly psychological. The house was always clean and there was good food on the table but in emotional terms she was running on empty. She and Ted were drifting apart. Ted's business was expanding and he was at work a great deal of the time. There are photographs from this period in which we look like a dust-bowl family who have just lost everything in a tornado.

In 1960 Ted was promoted to head office and the family moved to Wellington. He had a senior position with the company and was going well. Neva loved Wellington and her illnesses disappeared immediately. There was quite an active arts community and she joined the Wellington theatre groups. She also joined the radio drama cohort and appeared in plays for broadcast. She took singing lessons from George Scott Morrison. But mostly she continued with her writing. She sold a great many stories to magazines and for the next fifty years she published stories, memoirs, wrote book reviews, appeared in theatre productions and on radio. She published a novel, she wrote histories and she still had a weekly newspaper column in her eighties.

During the 1960s, the sound we heard when we came in from school was the *clackety clack* of the typewriter. Neva would be perched somewhere in the house, often near a window where the light was good, and her fingers would be flying across the keys. She could type while looking at notes sitting on another chair or while saying, 'Hello boy who needs a haircut. How was school and why don't you put the kettle on?'

There would sometimes be a small gathering of writers in the house. I came home one afternoon and had quite an interesting chat with a man in the kitchen. He'd been working as a teacher in Malaya when he was diagnosed with a brain tumour. He was given a year to live and he'd always wanted to write a novel, so he set about it without delay. He finished it, got it published and when he didn't die, he wrote another one. He'd done this several times and had recently published a novel called *A Clockwork Orange*. His name was Anthony Burgess and he would live for another thirty years.

Another man called John A. Lee had published a memoir called *Simple on a Soapbox*. John had won a DCM in the First World War and had lost an arm. He'd been thrown out of the Labour Party for his socialist views and I gathered this had been a great scandal. He was a big genial fellow in a suit and he spoke in ringing tones in our small hallway as if he were addressing a large crowd in rather blustery conditions in open parkland.

For a while our postman was James Baxter, who had a beautiful voice and would often come in for a cup of tea and a chat with Neva about what was going on in the writing world. I also remember going to Barry Crump's house one day with Neva. I must have been about twelve and Barry was a hero of mine. I had first encountered him on radio, reading his early novels *A Good Keen Man* and *Hang on a Minute Mate*. It was the first time I'd heard fiction which caught the rhythm and tone of the New Zealand voice. Barry had overslept and was dressing as we arrived. He put a shirt on and pulled it down very firmly all around, which he referred to as doing the ironing. 'Come in Neva,' he said. 'I don't think you've met my new dragon.' And we peered into the gloom where a slightly horrified young woman named Helen Smith was gathered among the bedclothes. My admiration for Barry was tempered by my recognition that Helen would possibly rather be in Philadelphia.

In 1965 Neva became the New Zealand president of PEN, the international organisation of writers, and which over the next few years was instrumental in introducing public lending rights into New Zealand.

In 1971 Neva and Ted were divorced. Neva got a job running an employment agency, bought a small house and got on with her life. Within a couple of years both she and Ted remarried. Neva moved to the far north and settled at Coopers Beach with her second husband Len McKenna, an American ex-Lockheed executive who adored the bays and beaches of the far north of New Zealand as much as she did. They drove all the roads, walked all the beaches and swam all the waters of the place they called 'paradise'. Neva became the unofficial historian of the entire region and published books which are still among the best research ever compiled about the early days and places and people of the far north. Neva was awarded the Queen's Service Medal for this work, and if you go to Mangonui you'll see the boardwalk named after her along the beautiful foreshore.

Neva achieved a great deal in her life. She was creative, convivial, active and well organised. She had a strong personality and wherever she lived she was surrounded by friends and admirers. She travelled extensively overseas and established strong contacts with her father's family in Northern Ireland. She was interested in everything and she gave everything a go. She took up painting in her sixties. She was involved in a film in her seventies. She and the other participants went to Hollywood, met all sorts of people, had lunch with Phyllis Diller and enjoyed every minute of it.

Neva insisted she wasn't a feminist. Perhaps she thought feminism was inconsistent with motherhood and good housekeeping. Perhaps there were other reasons she didn't like the label. It sometimes seemed to us that, if she could see her personal history in terms of ideas rather than as narrative drama, she might have recognised the inequities she wanted addressed as those at the core of the feminist project. She fought some of them very early and some of them were very tough. Her grandmother had been a suffragist who lobbied for women to get the vote and had served on local bodies in the 1890s. Neva's determination to exist and succeed as an individual while providing life and support to others is a powerful legacy. Perhaps she inherited this determination. She has certainly passed it on.

In the last few years of her life, Neva lived in Hamilton, where Anna paid close attention to her needs as her capacities and her driving energy began to wane. In that time she loved receiving visits from her grandchildren, her great-grandchildren and her friends.

Until that time, Neva had an excellent memory and she always wrote things down. There were notes all over the house. Among some diary notes she made when she was in Wellington, she records a visit from Tom Seddon who lived up the road and was the son of Richard Seddon, who is still New Zealand's longest serving Prime Minister. The Seddons had been great friends of the Beauchamps and as a young man Tom had travelled from Wellington to Rotorua one day and had bumped into Katherine Beauchamp, who is better known by her middle name, Katherine Mansfield. When Tom saw her in Rotorua, she was sitting in a park in the rain, under a weeping willow. She had come up to Rotorua with a man and it hadn't worked out very well, which is why she was in a park. 'But...' she said to Tom. 'I've written a marvellous story.' The story was called 'The Woman at the Store' and Katherine said it was about a woman she had encountered on the way up to Rotorua.

'The Woman at the Store' is a well-known story and was published some years later in London. Katherine Mansfield scholar Lydia Wevers is interested in Katherine's conversation with Tom because it was not previously known. It suggests that the work was taking shape in Katherine's mind, and was possibly written in some form, years before it was published. It is typical of Neva to have written down what Tom had told her, and to have caught even in a diary entry the drama and value of a good story.

Neva Morrison Clarke McKenna (1920–2015)

Ted

Ted is our father. He and I had a few problems, but we'll let that pass.

Ted was born in Wellington in December 1914. His mother had just arrived from Ulster. Ted used to say he was designed in

Northern Ireland and assembled in New Zealand. Like many children of migrant parents, Ted was keen to fit into the culture of the new place. His father's instinct was to hang on to the old place. He thought nothing in New Zealand was good enough; the culture was no good, the politics were no good, the rugby wasn't a patch on British football. But as a boy, Ted wanted to be like the other kids. Ted played rugby. Ted was a New Zealander.

Quite early in his life, Ted developed a self which he presented to the world, partly as a way of fitting in and partly to put some distance between who he was and who he aspired to be. One characteristic of this developed self was a carefully edited history. Even people who met Ted in his eighties and nineties thought he was the product of an educated and rather comfortable English family.

The real story is considerably better.

In 1914, in the far north of Ulster, around Coleraine and Portrush, his mother Margot Hamilton, twenty-six, unmarried and working as a nurse, discovered she was pregnant and, with the First World War approaching, she left Northern Ireland and travelled alone on the long sea voyage to New Zealand. There is no evidence that any member of her family ever communicated with her again. When she arrived in Wellington she had little money, no work and she knew no one. When the time came she was admitted to the Alexandra Hospital for unmarried mothers, where she had an emergency C-section and was delivered of twin boys. The first boy was named after the father, whose name was Edward Clarke. The second boy was named Stewart, after the matron of the hospital, Miss Stewart. The births were not registered, a procedural slip which may have been finessed by Miss Stewart, and while the babies got a decent start and Margot recovered, Miss Stewart took the little family in. She had boarders at her house and she installed Margot as a housekeeper.

In 1919 there was a flu epidemic that killed more people than had just died in the First World War, and Margot caught it. The doctors told her to leave Wellington and move north, where she could get some sea air. So she moved slightly up the west coast of the North Island, the world capital of sea air, and Eddie and Stewart were brought up in and around Karehana Bay and Plimmerton.

After the First World War, when Ted was six, he was sitting on the verandah one day when a man came in the gate and Ted looked up as he approached the house. Ted always remembered seeing his father for the first time, from the shoes up. Edward and Margot were married at Miss Stewart's brother's house in Hawker Street, the births were registered, Edward got work as a carpenter and the semblance of respectability began to be constructed.

The boys went to the local school, the beach was only a few yards away and the family had a succession of dogs and cats. They didn't have any money but life was good. Ted's father was a fine fiddle player and people would often stop outside the house on their way home to listen to him. Ted had only a small repertoire of stories of his birth and childhood and they created only very general impressions. He spoke of his mother's family in England as if they were all close, despite the fact that they were neither close, nor in England. The facts were not the point. The point with Ted was always fitting in. Having the right effect. Creating the right impression.

Ted felt less in common with his father and he certainly looked like his mother and although he argued with her about politics (she was a socialist and he was pretending to be a free market capitalist) he never stopped admiring her determination, her stoicism and her dignity. No one knows where the boys' father was between 1914 and 1920. Ted always said he was fighting in the war but he couldn't remember where, and there's no record of him in any of the services. Stewart thought he was jailed for his involvement with the Ulster Volunteers in the sectarian violence of 1913–19 but there's no record of him either in prison records or in those of the Ulster Volunteers.

Margot and her boys and their friend Mary Stewart remained close and there are photographs of the boys with Miss Stewart until she died. When they were young they would sometimes go into town by train and stay with her for a few days and she would make a fuss of them and take them to see things around the city. For forty years Margot worked for the Red Cross and other charities which helped people in trouble. It had been tough but she knew she'd done well to bring herself and her boys to a new life in New Zealand.

The boys were bright, keen and talented, Ted was a good schoolboy sprinter and a very handy tennis and badminton player. Stewart, who had inherited his father's gift for music, wanted to be a concert pianist. But when they were fourteen, the world was hit by the Great Depression and, unless their families had money, teenagers had to leave school and get a job. Ted got a job at McKenzies, a retail company with branches all over the country. Stewart got work with Ballantynes, a large retail outlet in Christchurch where he worked for some years until after the war when Ballantynes burnt down, at which point he also got a job at McKenzies.

Ted was good at his job and during the 1930s he became a manager and began to climb from branch to bigger branch; Nelson, Timaru, Napier, New Plymouth, Gisborne and Auckland, before he was called up for military service in the Second World War. After training in Trentham and drafting into the 7th Anti-Tank Regiment, 66394 Clarke left New Zealand and arrived in the Middle East during one the great crises in the war. The North African campaign was beginning and the New Zealand Division was sent up through Palestine, Syria and Lebanon to defend the oilfields against a possible attack through Turkey, and then they were pulled back to defend Cairo from the German advance from the west which was occurring at speed under Rommel, and there followed, throughout late 1941 and 1942, some of the most significant battles of the war. Ted was in all of them: Sidi Rezegh, Mersa Matruh, Minqar Qaim, Ruweisat

Ridge, El Alamein, the Libyan and Tunisian campaigns and then up through Italy, the Sangro River and Monte Cassino. In the lives of anyone in the New Zealand Division in the Second World War, these years remained vivid. In his nineties, Ted could still describe in detail these events, his own actions, his feelings and his love and high regard for those who shared those experiences with him, Tony Ballard, Keith Garland, Maurice Spence.

Except when he was at home, where he often looked like a panto-mime lunatic, Ted was always well turned out. He wore good suits, brogues and a shirt and tie. He knew the prestige brands and he understood the value of a gesture which signified class and breeding. Eric Townley, another of his army friends, told me that all through the war, Ted was always clean-shaven, even in battle. 'Your father,' said Eric, 'was the cleanest man in the Western Desert.' One of the things Ted had with him during the desert campaign was a small book of poetry he'd bought in Cairo, and like a lot of the men he read and committed to memory large tracts of English verse. His standard greeting in the morning for the rest of his life was from the Rubaiyat:

> Awake for morning in the bowl of night
> Has flung the stone that puts the stars to flight
> And lo, the hunter of the east has caught
> The Sultan's turret in a noose of light.

He also loved Shelley's 'To a Skylark':

> Hail to thee, blithe spirit!
> Bird thou never wert-
> That from heaven or near it
> Pourest thy full heart
> In profuse strains of unpremeditated art.

(He loved that last line).

He also learnt, either from his father's repertoire or from troop entertainers, great slabs of British music hall and he could recite all that too. He had a good singing voice, kept perfect time and loved entertaining people. He knew bits of Sid Field, Flanagan and Allen, Arthur Askey and the Western Brothers. He sang 'Beautiful as a Butterfly' very well. He also recited a silly sales pitch he'd got from somewhere: 'All wool and a yard wide, this product is wiff-waffed on both sides and bevelled all around, has hot and cold folding doors, two kinds of water, clean and dirty, it's guaranteed not to rip, tear or bust. Recommended not by me; recommended by a better man than me. Recommended by the maker.'

On the way back to New Zealand after the war, the troop ship Ted was on stopped at Melbourne for supplies and anyone who wanted to go the theatre was invited to attend a performance free of charge. Ted put his hand up and that night he went to one of the big nineteenth-century theatres in the city. He couldn't remember what the entertainment was but, before it began, a man in a suit came out in front of the curtain and said, 'Ladies and gentlemen. We're fortunate to have in the audience tonight a party of New Zealand soldiers, returning from the war in Europe and the Middle East. You men are very welcome here, we hope you enjoy the evening with us and we wish you a safe trip home.' The audience then spontaneously stood and applauded.

Ted said this was the first sense he had of being home again and he never forgot it. Whenever he came to Melbourne he always went to the Shrine of Remembrance. He didn't go inside. He just wandered around the huge courtyard and stood by the eternal flame for a while and then he said, every time, 'They do this very well, don't they? They're very good, the Aussies. If you're ever in a war, try to make sure you've got the Aussies on at least one flank. They're very tough and very smart. I saw a lot of them in the desert and they're terrific in battle. They never give up. They never know when they're beaten.'

In 1944 in Senigallia, in Italy, when he'd been wounded and

TINKERING

was working at headquarters for a while, Ted met Neva Morrison, who was from Gisborne and was with the New Zealand army secretarial corps, the WAACs. Anna and I are the children of Ted Clarke and Neva Morrison. When we were growing up they were living in Palmerston North, where Ted was the manager of the McKenzies store. He used to tell the story of employing people on staff and if they were honest and responsible people he'd hire them but he always asked them one question. 'Who wrote Grey's Elegy?'

Once a bloke seemed confused and Ted said, 'It's not a trick question. An elegy is just a poem. It's like being asked, 'Who wrote Grey's poem?'

'I don't know anything about poetry,' said the bloke.

'No, you don't have to know anything about poetry' said Ted. 'Who wrote Grey's poem? Look out the door there. You see that shop across the square. What is it?'

'Hopwood's Hardware.'

'Right. Hopwood's Hardware. Do you know who owns it?'

'Mr Hopwood.'

'Right. Mr Hopwood owns Hopwood's Hardware. Who wrote Grey's Elegy?'

'Oh,' said the bloke. 'Mr Hopwood.'

He once got sent some kerosene heaters from head office. He'd asked for one. They sent him ten. They were terrible and they smelt and no other branch could sell any. Ted sold all of them. He put one out the front of the shop, turned it on so it glowed and felt warm, and he put up a sign: 'Limit One Per Customer.' He was a particularly good retailer.

Ted's brother Stewart went away to the Pacific War and had also come back into McKenzies and during the 1950s he was the manager in Rotorua. They were both pretty smart boys and in 1960 they were both promoted to head office, Ted as the buying controller and Stewart as the sales controller. Ted was on the board of Manakau Knitting Mills and other companies in the McKenzies group, and he travelled overseas in 1962, 1964, 1965 and 1970, when hardly anybody did, including going very early into China, buying merchandise in Europe and Asia (I think his favourite country was Austria). Business was good, the company grew and eventually the parent company, Rangitira, sold the McKenzies stores; the McKenzie Trust, which is an investment company, became the biggest philanthropic organisation in New Zealand history. The Clarke twins helped build this great enterprise.

Ted and Neva's marriage was not a runaway success and Ted buried himself in his work and for some years refused to acknowledge that he and Neva were effectively living separate lives. After their divorce they both remarried and Ted retired and took on some consultancy work.

When he had grandchildren, Ted gradually began to drop his guard. He managed this rather well and he was wise enough to recognise the benefits.

'These feminists,' he would say. 'Good grief.'

'I'm a feminist, Ted,' one of his granddaughters would say.

'No, no, no,' he would clarify. 'You're a very beautiful young woman.'

'Do you know what a feminist is, Ted?' she would say.

'You tell me,' he would reply, and he would then sit back and enjoy a small tutorial from which he would emerge wiser and smiling with pride. 'I just had the most interesting conversation. God those girls are intelligent. Absolutely wonderful.'

As he drifted through his eighties and into his nineties, Ted was sustained by his great love of the family, by which he meant a slightly fantastical skein of connectedness and common interests and ethics running from his mother, whom he adored, through his children and grandchildren. He also loved his sport and music, which he took up in a big way in retirement and from which he got a great deal of pleasure. He was a perceptive student of the human race. He had an excellent memory, a great gift for words and talk, an interest in world affairs and ideas and a very dry sense of humour. When he had an operation a few years ago to remove a cancer from his temple I rang him and said, 'How are you?'

'I'm good thanks.'

'Was the operation a success?'

'Yes. They seem very pleased.'

'Are you any better looking?'

'I don't know about better looking but I caught sight of myself in the mirror this morning and I can certainly see what the fuss is all about.'

Ted was a dignified, gifted and remarkable man. He started with nothing and succeeded in almost everything he did. He was interested in history, language and the society he lived in. A generation later and he'd have been at university and may have had some other choices. But Ted made the best he could of the situation he was in, as he saw it. He was unhorsed from time to time and there were difficulties. And he was troubled by these difficulties. He looked at these difficulties and in later years he tried to address them. If he didn't deal with them or didn't deal with them effectively, he would want to acknowledge his own failure. It was not because he did not want to. He was a loving, attentive and frequently hilarious grandfather and he said repeatedly in the last week of his life, 'When I go into orbit, I'll go into orbit with a smile on my face.'

Edward Alexander Clarke (1914–2008)

Ted's Advice

The following is the text of a lecture given to John by his father between 1948 and 2008.

Neither a borrower nor a lender be. Polonius said that. Shakespeare. Excellent advice. You young people; I hope you never have to go through what we went through. With any luck you'll be OK, you'll get some opportunities and you'll be able to grab them when they come along. We couldn't. I didn't even finish school. I had to leave. There was a worldwide depression. The stock market crashed. It was terrible. No one had ever seen anything like it. We had to leave school and get a job. My parents didn't have any money. We didn't starve but it was pretty tough. I was working at fifteen. I was lucky to get a job. You were lucky to get a job in those days. I had to leave school and get a job. I'd like to have gone on to university but it wasn't an option. Economics. I wanted to do economics.

Anyway, so there I was working. I was a manager at nineteen, different branches of the company, all over the country, then bigger branches, and then when I was twenty-five the war started and I got sent to the Middle East for four and half years. It wasn't exactly my idea. I didn't want to go. I didn't want anything to do with it. But you didn't have much choice. Anyway there we were, Egypt, Syria, Libya, Palestine, Lebanon, Iraq, Tunisia and then up through Italy. Sand everywhere. Battles all the time. We were artillery. Unbelievable noise. You can't hear yourself think. I'll never forget some of those battles. You wondered how anyone could survive. The Germans didn't seem to like us very much. They got particularly annoyed with me a couple of times. I don't know why. I hadn't done anything. They tried to kill me. Repeatedly. Repeated attempts to skittle Ted Clarke. It wasn't much fun. I'd rather have been playing tennis.

After the war we bought the house and had you monsters and I'll tell you something. The worst thing you can do is get into debt. It's a terrible thing to owe someone money. Never do it. They're making money out of you the whole time and, if you can't pay, they'll take everything you've got. That's how it works. If you don't owe anyone anything, you can hop into the cot at night and sleep the sleep of the just. Don't laugh. I've seen it happen. In the Depression. People had nothing. They lost everything. People were out on the road. Living out on the road. Literally. I had to leave school and go to work. I was lucky to get a job.

Look at all this credit these days. Lending people money to buy things they don't need. They don't need these things. Do you think people need a radio with buttons rather than knobs? What's the matter with knobs? Perfectly good knobs. You don't need buttons. Does Mrs Wheelbarrow need a new cake-mixer every five minutes? What's the matter with the old one? Nothing. And why are they lending Mr and Mrs Wheelbarrow the money? Because they're charging them interest. They're making money. That's what they're doing. And what are they producing ? Absolutely Fanny Adams. 'Usury', that's called in the Bible.

We could do that. We could go out and borrow a lot of money and say, 'Yes please. We'll live beyond our means. I'm a senior exec-utive in a big retail firm but yes, you're right, we don't have enough. A boat? Yes, that'd be fantastic thanks. Have you got a big one? A very new shiny one? It would need to be very bright and shiny because I've got plenty of friends I need to impress. Great. And has it got buttons on the radio? Good. Put it on the account, will you? We'll pay you later and yes, charge me interest, by all means. I realise the value of the boat will halve as I drive it out of the showroom and I'll use it three times a year but I've just recently arrived in the last shower and I have no brains at all and that'll be fine.'

And now we've got all these executive clowns paying themselves millions of dollars a year just for turning up. And you know what they're doing, don't you? John? Are you there? You know what they're doing? They're stealing money from their own shareholders. The company makes money and they're taking it out before it gets to the shareholders by paying each other in bonuses and golden handshakes. That's theft. And they're borrowing money to run the company. Why the hell do the shareholders let them do it? I'll tell you why. Because the shareholders are superannuation funds. The holders of the funds don't even know what they own. And as long as they're getting a return themselves they don't care. Well, I'll tell you what. It'll all fall over. You can't have companies borrowing these huge amounts and not have the bloke come round at some stage and say, 'We'll have the money now, thanks.' The whole house of cards will go over. You watch.

And I'll tell you another thing. The world is being destroyed by greed. And these people who are all opposed to regulations. They don't mind driving on the left-hand side of the road and they'll be the first people to call the police if they see some bloke coming out of their window with a video-machine under his arm. And this environmental disaster we've got on our hands. What's caused all this? Greed. Same thing. Capitalism. I was in business for over fifty years but I have to tell you this is wrong. They've destroyed their own system these people. I'm ninety-three now and I've never seen a bigger mess than this. This is a real mess. Somehow someone's going to have to make some rules and some of these clowns might find they have to take their rattle and go home. Someone should give them a lift. I'd do it myself but I'm a bit busy talking to my son.

Beginnings

The New Zealand Sense of Humour

Thinking about humour, I am reminded of an old army story. In 1945 the New Zealand Division fought a costly street-by-street battle against the retreating German army to take the city of Trieste in northern Italy. Once the city was secured, the Americans decided a victory parade was in order, to be headed by the elite US Marines. It was pointed out that the Americans had arrived after the battle had finished and that the fighting had been done by the New Zealanders. The Italian campaign was nevertheless being run by US Army command and the parade went ahead as planned. In front came the US Marines, with a large banner bearing their emblem and the words 'US Marines. Second to None'. Behind them marched the New Zealanders carrying a large sheet upon which was written the word 'None'. This squares my shoulders nicely. I'll have what they're having.

The New Zealand sense of humour is said to be laconic, understated and self-deprecating. Even if true this is not very helpful, as the same claim is not unreasonably made for the humour of the Scots, the Irish, the English, the Australians, the Russians, the Canadians and the ancient Greeks among others. North American humour rests on a writing tradition also rich in irony, laconic delivery and litotes. Mark Twain, Robert Benchley, Thurber, Dorothy Parker and Ruth Draper were all people whisperers. Dave Barry and many other writers enrich this tradition today.

In ancient Greece, irony was considered 'the glory of the slaves', suggesting that you can't have irony from above. How the world can consist only of underdogs is an interesting question. It may be that an ironical perspective emerges from the underclass of each society or in each of us, and that these are not national characteristics at all.

When my generation was growing up there was no television

and no New Zealand radio comedy. This was not because New Zealanders weren't funny. A lot of our parents had just returned from the war and if they had a gift for humour it wasn't much use professionally; it was just part of their personality. They didn't tell jokes, they just talked very well, often about local things. A man once described a friend from the hill country as having ears a bit further back than the rest of us. 'It's the wind,' he said, 'They get these very big westerlies. He had to go and get his wife from up near Opotiki the other day. She'd gone to hang the washing out. She still had the peg basket.'

The Second World War was the biggest conflict in human history. Seventy million people were killed. An important aspect of dealing with the carnage, the tragedy and waste was humour. It helped articulate what the Allies were fighting against and it fortified resolution and hope. There was humour in concerts for the troops, in books and magazines and there was radio. Humour that is identifiable as coming from New Zealand emerged at this time.

The most famous cartoonist in Britain was David Low. He reinvented the drawing style and purpose of the newspaper cartoon, removing crosshatching and class-conscious trivia and introducing bold lines and a moral stance on political issues. He spotted Hitler and the Nazis well before they came to power and portrayed them as liars, thugs and murderers. He opposed appeasement and was deadly and relentless in subjecting Hitler and Mussolini to continuous open mockery. His depiction of the Nazi Soviet Pact became one of the most celebrated cartoons of the century. After the war it was discovered that Hitler had prepared a list of the people he would kill when he conquered Britain. David Low, a Presbyterian socialist from Dunedin, was number five.

The most successful wartime radio show was *It's That Man Again*, broadcast by the BBC from 1939 to 1949 and featuring the comedian Tommy Handley. The show, known as *ITMA*, was the comedy equivalent of Vera Lynn and it sustained the civilian population through its dark night. It also changed the way radio comedy worked, establishing new forms to which the television sitcom owes a significant debt today. *ITMA* was written by Ted Kavanagh, from Auckland.

During the campaign through Greece, Crete, the Middle East and up into Italy the New Zealand Division experienced a steady procession of successes and setbacks, not always of their own making. One danger would be averted, one cock-up survived, one victory won, when a fresh disaster would arrive and all hope would seem lost. In response to this pattern the division adopted intelligence officer Paddy Costello's sardonic and perfectly balanced 'Hooray fuck'.

A major point of contact between my generation and these men and women was *The Goon Show*. It ran on radio through the 1950s but was essentially a Second World War show in which the madness witnessed by soldiers like Milligan and Secombe and the New Zealand Division was defused by logic disposal experts using surreal language and operating in a landscape of idiots, explosions and death. Only the British class structure held firm, just in case you didn't get the point that the system was absurd. I didn't know any of the history. I laughed at the jokes and the funny voices. Even when my father despaired of his children and had developed a rhetorical shaking of his head in disbelief while moaning, 'What have we reared?' we still laughed at the same bits in *The Goon Show*. We looked at each other and we smiled and laughed. When nothing else worked, *The Goon Show* convinced us we were related.

Television and the internet have not changed humour a great deal and we shouldn't expect them to. In writing about humour, Freud quotes a joke from Sophocles, which dates from as recently as about 400BC. A king is touring his kingdom and as he passes through a town he sees in the crowd a young man who looks very like him. He arranges for the man to be brought to him privately and he asks him, 'Was your mother ever employed at the Palace? Did she ever work at the Royal household at all?'

'No, Your Majesty,' replies the young man. 'No, she never did.' Then he adds, 'But Dad did.'

Paul Holmes

Early in 1970, when we were about twenty or twenty-one, John Banas, Ginette McDonald, Paul Holmes and I generated a series of late night comic shows at Wellington's Downstage Theatre, which then occupied the upstairs floor of a boating club. Our shows were presented on Thursday, Friday and Saturday nights after the main play had finished. We built an audience quite quickly and we wrote and added new material about every four or six weeks to keep them coming back. Some of the sketches parodied film and television but were filled with references to New Zealand life and politics. *The News in Briefs*, for example, which featured Holmes in his underpants reading the news and which the audience loved, was full of standard sketch material but with scurrilous references to prominent locals.

Holmes was a likeable and rather naughty boy from Hastings. I arrived to pick him up one night before the show. He was working as a waiter at a place in Oriental Bay and we were running a bit late and Holmes whipped a bloke's coffee cup away from him in his haste to clean up and leave.

'Hang on a minute,' said the bloke. 'There's still coffee in that.'

Holmes slapped the cup back down again and glared at the bloke. 'Well, fuckin' drink it,' he advised.

Paul and I had grown up with a lot of the same sounds in our ears and he was a particularly keen observer of the cadence and idioms in local radio. If you asked him the time he'd look at his watch, lower his voice slightly and say, 'It's Firestone Tyres time, 4.26, Clarkie. Firestone. Where the rubber meets the road.' John, Ginette and Paul were young Turks in the Downstage acting company but acting wasn't really what Paul wanted to do. He really wanted to be a radio. His special forte was racing commentators. In a previous show I'd written a piece for myself to do as the race-caller Peter Kelly and had established to my own satisfaction that it resonated with an audience and that racing and its language and associations worked as metaphor. When I met Paul I saw that he didn't do just Peter Kelly, he did Syd Tonks and Dave Clarkson as well and could confect a broadcast as all three of them. We would sometimes do this together, in pubs. We'd get an empty jug each (try this yourself; it's better into an empty jug) and we'd make up a race call, crossing to each other when we needed a break. Paul's favourite race was Peter Kelly's call of the 1970 Wellington Cup and he'd generally wind up with '…and with three great strides Il Tempo will take the 1970 Wellington Cup…' and the rest would be lost in delight and general uproar in the bar.

When I wrote a Kelly piece in those days I gave it to Paul to perform. He did them superbly. He would disappear into its rhythm, adding little flourishes and including people he saw in the room as part of the race-day atmosphere. It was a piece of idiosyncratic magic and was a joy to watch. The audience loved the sound. It was the sound of New Zealand on a Saturday.

That winter, we were asked to provide the mid-evening entertainment for the annual ball at Chateau Tongariro. We tailored the show for the crowd, lacing it with references to Griff Bristed and Grady Thompson and other citizens among the snow community. We had to make do with a very small rostrum for a stage and we changed behind a screen. There was nowhere else to go and as the lights dimmed we might have been Christians at the Coliseum. The crowd was very large and had been engaged in rutting rituals and wassail.

From the outset the show went beautifully and Holmes doing

Peter Kelly was a sensation. When he finished the racing commentary the crowd lifted the roof off. We looked at each other as they roared and whooped and it was pretty clear that he should repeat it immediately, in its entirety, which he happily did. The response was even greater this time because Holmes now relished something he knew was working, and he eased the throttle open and gave it the herbs. The crowd went nuts again when he finished and after we completed the show he moved away to the bar and did it a third time.

We were all feted afterwards but Holmes was the genius of the night and he was never the same again. He didn't go to bed that night and he didn't stop talking as Peter Kelly for the whole rest of our time at the chateau. He couldn't stop doing the thing they loved. He was captured by the audience's love for what he was doing and an addiction was born. Holmes could giggle about how silly it all was but these were the first steps towards a towering need and towards a belief that, if you get the voice right, it doesn't much matter what you're saying. My very fond memory of Paul tells me he didn't always agree with this rather dangerous proposition. He was a good fellow and a very gifted natural performer. He was full of affection for others, loved every bit of his life and at his best he was magnificent. We'll miss him.

> Happy the man, and happy he alone,
> He who can call today his own:
> He who, secure within, can say,
> Tomorrow do thy worst, for I have lived today.
>
> Be fair or foul, or rain or shine
> The joys I have possessed, in spite of fate, are mine.
> Not Heaven itself, upon the past has power,
> But what has been, has been, and I have had my hour.

John Dryden, Horace, *Odes* 3, 29

Paul Holmes (1950–2013)

Marcus Craig

Last weekend in a beautiful area just north of Brisbane, Marcus Craig died, aged seventy-three. Marcus and I worked together in the mid 1970s at a club in Auckland called The Ace of Clubs, an allegedly sophisticated barn in Cook Street run by Phil Warren. In business terms the stage entertainment was part of a smoke and mirrors argument designed to help obtain a liquor license. As I was leaving one night after the show, a quite small and very drunk patron was engaging in racial abuse and attempting to punch the very large and extremely sober bouncer. The bouncer, who had clearly dealt with sophistication before, grabbed the front of the man's shirt with one hand and turned it slightly so it became a handle and then he ran the surprised loudmouth about a foot and a half up the wall behind him so his feet were off the ground. 'Listen, mate,' he said softly to the man. 'If you hit me. And I ever find out about it. I'm going to be fuckin annoyed. Now, go home.' And he left the man to crumple gently on to the ground and consider the position in its many aspects.

Marcus was the main entertainment at the club in those years. He appeared in drag as a character called Diamond Lil, often with the excellent Doug Aston as his partner and a house band led by Doug Smith. When I was there the marvellous Bridgette Allen was also on the bill. Bridgette could sing anything and could still the room to pin-drop or light it up like a Christmas tree. Doug Aston came from a British music hall tradition and often added form and structure to what Marcus was doing. What Marcus most wanted to do was sing opera, so he'd get the drag schtick working and then repay himself with an aria so unrelated to anything else in the show or to the way he looked that the audience was delighted to find itself somewhere it had never been before.

Aside from being a terrific performer, Doug Aston was a caring and perceptive man who knew Marcus well and looked after him when he struck the occasional iceberg. For Marcus, the club and his work on-stage were life itself. He threw all his energy into it, his timing was fabulous, he was very generous on stage and he could really sing. Danny la Rue and many others specialised in glamorous costume changes and in Danny's case in representing a cavalcade of great female stars. Marcus simply went out as Lil, with the burners on high and the safety catch off. His costume and demeanour were exaggerated to a point where you wondered whether he was impersonating a female or impersonating a female impersonator. Whatever he was doing, he was very good at it and the audience loved it. I don't know when it all came to an end but sometime during the 1990s he moved to Sydney and after a period working at the Australian Opera Company, he moved to Queensland where he had a classical music show on Brisbane radio.

He remembered his days on stage with great fondness and with some pride. He was right to do so.

Shalom, Marcus.

Marcus Craig (1940–2013)

Bob Hudson

In 1976 I was in the vaudeville business. The odds against this were fairly high. It wasn't what I'd set out to do and I dropped stones all the way in so I could find my way back out.

Fred Dagg was working nicely on television but the going rate for two minutes of heroically underprepared material wasn't sufficient to trouble the scorer, despite having doubled from a base of $38 in 1974. In order to make a living it was necessary to tour the country, take in washing and live on what my father called 'a glass of water and a look up the street'. One night after a high quality workout at a cabaret in Auckland, I got talking to Bob Hudson, a boy of about the same age who'd been in the audience. Bob was from Sydney and had just had an enormous hit across Australia with 'The Newcastle Song', an ironical tribute to the city of his youth. We were both dealing with the Micawberish aspects of being writer/performers and we agreed to meet up again in Wellington the following week. Helen and I were considering moving our base from Wellington to Auckland at the time and we spent a couple of days driving around the beautiful Waitakeres imagining ourselves somewhere up there, in the bush.

When we got back to Wellington, Bob and I had various things to do and we arranged to meet after I'd finished doing a record and book signing at James Smith's. This was to be done in character so I was dressed in a black singlet and shorts, fashionable footwear of the period and a hat. Fred had a discerning audience of all ages and a large lunch-time crowd had gathered in the great emporium. After a while I noticed that Bob had found the place and it all seemed to be going gangbusters when the police arrived. Three policemen walked purposefully up past the queue of waiting citizens and directly to where I was sitting.

'John Clarke?' said one, a born leader of men.

'Yes,' I said.

'Step outside, please.' They waited for me to stand up, put down the tools of my trade and join them on a very public and completely silent walk out into the street. The population of Wellington quickly poured into Manners Street and watched as I was taken, in full costume, to a police vehicle for questioning. I'm pretty sure the crowd would have ruled out the prospect that I was a murderer. They were probably tossing up between sex crimes with small animals and some sort of tax fraud, possibly involving the $38.

'You are John Clarke,' checked one of the policemen.

'Yes,' I said.

'Thought so,' he said.

'What's this about?' I asked. 'I'm actually supposed to be in there doing a signing.'

'Are you the owner of a red Mazda car, registration number HRV683?'

'Yes.'

'Can you explain why your vehicle was seen last week in the Titirangi area driving very slowly and sometimes stopping in gateways and looking up driveways?'

'Yes,' I said. 'I was driving around Titirangi last week.'

'Were you driving slowly?'

'Yes, we were looking at houses.'

'Your vehicle was seen in that area at that time.'

'Yes. That would be right. That's where it was.'

'The vehicle was reported as behaving suspiciously.'

'Suspiciously?'

'Yes.'

'Who says?'

'The person who reported it. The vehicle was reported as behaving in a suspicious manner.'

'Couldn't you have rung me or written me a letter about this?'

'We read in the paper that you'd be here today so we thought it'd be a good time to pop down and clear this up.'

'Do you mind if I go back inside now and do what I came here for?'

'No, that's fine. Just checking. Thank you, Mr Clarke.'

I went back into the store and completed the signing, explaining to people that my vehicle had been behaving suspiciously the previous week in Titirangi.

I never heard any more on the matter.

Bob Hudson, who tells this story rather well but who requires oxygen around the bit where the police haul me out of the signing and question me in the street, had a radio show on what was then 2JJ in Sydney, and had been playing stuff from the Fred Dagg records, so when I was looking at working in Australia I found that he'd made me quite well known. A very smart and kind person, Bob has also given me very good advice a couple of times, and he and his wife Kerry opened their house to Helen and me when I knew no one else in Sydney and didn't know what I was doing. We worked together on various projects, notably writing material for Bette Midler's stage show. Bob later completed a PhD in Archaeology and now works at Sydney University, specialising in the mediaeval Buddhist period in Burma.

The Fred Dagg Advisory Bureau

Frederick, of the House of Dagg

Many older readers will recall an earlier time in New Zealand, a vivid and exhilarating time when a young nation, poised on the threshold of greatness, called forth from its ranks a natural leader.

From the starkly beautiful central North Island, erosion capital of the world and home of the Raurimu Spiral, came a figure uniquely attuned to the hour. No problem was too great, no matter so Byzantine in its complexity that he could not cut to its heart. He was fair-minded in all things, graceful under pressure and was capable of developing strong opinions unspoilt by knowledge or formal logic. He specialised in the common sense solution and the self-evident truth, and his language was that of Arnold, of Herbert and of Trevor.

His name was Frederick, of the House of Dagg. Born many years earlier, for reasons which need not trouble us here, he had undergone a comprehensive training in all aspects of farmwork and had then attended school from the age of five. His schooling was typical of its time and extremely effective in every way. The New Zealand Education Department had set rigorous standards. Fred learnt that the angles outside parallel lines were equal to the opposite ones inside the lines. He learnt the French for 'big absorbent bath towel'. By the age of seventeen he knew the valency of carbon and the German for 'I have fallen in love with the exit to the static air-display'. These skills have not been required nearly as often as the department led him to believe but there is still time and, should the need ever arise, Fred and a whole generation of New Zealanders will be able to calculate the compound interest on the square root of x, or the use of irony by Jane Austen, whichever is the lesser, and discuss its impact on the Chartist Movement. (30 marks).

As he obtained to the estate of adulthood, Fred was already

instinctively grappling with important issues of nationhood and philosophy. He supported the dropping of superphosphate on farms because he had a brother-in-law with a dung-dusting concern up the Pohangina Valley, but he was troubled by the realisation that the cobalt in the soil of the volcanic plateau was building up to a point where they would soon have to drop soil on it to prevent it from becoming a cobalt deposit.

Matters came to a head when Fred received a letter from his friend Bruce Bayliss, who was at that time a seasonal mutton-birder on Stewart Island. Bruce was not a man given to display but it was obvious that he had a problem. There was no work on the island and Bruce was obliged to pick up the unemployment benefit, which at that time was $137. There was no unemployment officer on Stewart Island and in order to obtain the benefit Bruce caught the boat to Bluff, travelled by bus to Invercargill, collected the emolument and arranged lodgings for the night since the next bus back to Bluff did not leave until the following morning. The next day he caught the boat at Bluff and arrived home in the middle of the afternoon. The total cost of this exercise was $138.

Bruce wrote a letter to the department. The problem with collecting the assistance, he pointed out, was that it was not commercially viable. The department replied that Bruce was the victim of an anomaly in the system. They thanked him for calling it to their attention. The reason there was no unemployment office on Stewart Island, they explained, was that for some time there had been no unemployment there. But since he was now unemployed and since he lived there, would he care to become the unemployment officer for the island? Bruce accepted the post and was sent a box of forms which were to be filled in each month, the top form to be sent to Wellington, the office copy to be filed alphabetically and cross-referenced as to date. At the end of the first month, Bruce sent off his first report stating that, since he was employed, there was now no unemployment on Stewart Island. As a result of this, the Department sacked him.

Fred decided at this point it was time to clear his throat and deliver himself of a few opinions. This book contains some of them. They wouldn't all fit.

The Socratic Paradox

Gidday. I'd like to have a word or two with you about the Socratic Paradox, which, without being too technical about it, is a paradox worked out by the late Socrates in order to explain some of the pitfalls involved in explaining things.

The argument says in essence that you can't learn things you don't already know, and given the widely accepted view that there's some difficulty to be encountered in trying to learn something you do already know, I'm afraid it's beginning to look as if the whole business of learning is largely overrated and should probably be left alone.

I personally have always held this to be more or less self-evident, although unfortunately my reasoning turns out to be a good deal less Platonic than I had hoped. Socrates argued that if you don't know something you probably wouldn't recognise the knowledge if it popped up in your porridge. And if you did recognise it then in some sense you must already have had the knowledge beforehand. And that, therefore, learning is merely a process whereby we recollect knowledge that is already in us.

This, of course, touches on the Fred Dagg Theory of the Human Memory and even though Socrates doesn't, so far as I know, have any real right of reply in the matter anymore, there are just one or two points I'd like to clear up.

Firstly, if the knowledge is in there anyway, at what stage was it put there and whose job is it to go about the place feeding knowledge in through people's ears before the memory takes over and renders the whole thing academic? As a matter of fact, I knew a bloke once who thought we were all born with a certain number of words in us and when we talked them out, we died, which impressed me as being fundamentally sound until I found out that he thought 'Portia Faces Life' was the story of a woman named Portia Face.

This knowledge represented the recollection of something I don't think Socrates has made enough allowance for, and that is that lack of knowledge or the knowledge of things that aren't quite right can be recalled just as easily and in some cases more easily than good solid everyday stuff like coming in out of the rain.

It's also possible to forget things and then forget that you've forgotten them. And then if you can recall the fact that you've forgotten something does this necessarily qualify as knowledge?

As a matter of fact I'll try to get back to you on this one. I'm a little bit confused at the moment and it's nearly time for my tablet.

Real Estate

Gidday. Now the Fred Dagg Careers Advisory Bureau has already done enough to secure its place in the social history of this once great nation but I think this report is probably among its more lasting achievements. In essence it outlines how to go about the business of being a real estate agent (and as things stand at the moment, if you're not a real estate agent, then you're being a fool to yourself and a burden to others).

Like so many other jobs in this wonderful society of ours, the basic function of the real estate agent is to increase the price of something without actually producing anything and as a result it has a lot to do with communication, terminology and calling a spade a delightfully bucolic colonial winner facing north and offering a unique opportunity to the handyman.

If you're going to enter the real estate field you'll need to acquire a certain physical appearance which I won't bore you with here but, if you've got gold teeth and laugh lines around your pockets, then you're through to the semis without dropping a set.

But the main thing to master, of course, is the vernacular, and basically this works as follows. There are three types of house: 'glorious commanding majestic split-level ultra-modern dream homes' that are built on cliff-faces, 'private bush-clad inglenooks' that are built down holes, and 'very affordable solid family houses in much sought-after streets' that are old gun-emplacements with awnings. A 'cottage' is a caravan with the wheels taken off. A 'panoramic', 'breathtaking', 'spectacular' or 'magnificent' view is an indication that the house has windows and, if the view is 'unique', there's probably only one window. I have here the perfect advertisement for a house, so we'll go through it and I'll point out some of the more interesting features; so here we go, mind the step.

'Owner transferred reluctantly instructs us to sell' means the house is for sale. 'Genuine reason for selling' means the house is for sale. 'Rarely can we offer' means the house is for sale. 'Superbly presented delightful charmer' doesn't mean anything really but it's probably still for sale. 'Most attractive immaculate home of character in prime dress-circle position' means that the thing that's for sale is a house. 'Unusual design with interesting and intriguing solidly built stairs' means the stairs are in the wrong place. 'Huge spacious generous lounge commands this well-serviced executive residence' means the rest of the house is a rabbit warren with rooms like cupboards. 'Magnificent well-proportioned large convenient block with exquisite garden' means there's no view but one of the trees had a flower on it the day we were up there. 'Privacy, taste, charm, space, freedom, quiet, away from it all location in much sought-after cul-de-sac situation' means it's not only built down a hole, it's built at the very far end of the hole. 'A must for you artists, sculptors and potters' means that only an idiot would consider actually living in it. '2/3 bedrooms with possible in-law accommodation' means it's got two bedrooms and a tool shed. 'Great buy', 'ring early for this one', 'inspection a must', 'priced to sell', 'new listing', 'see this one now', 'all offers considered', 'good value', 'be quick', 'inspection by appointment', 'view today', 'this one can't last', 'sole agents', 'today's best buy' means the house is still for sale and if ever you see 'investment opportunity' in the newspaper, turn away very quickly and have a crack at the crossword.

Sewing

Gidday. As anyone who's ever drawn a few stitches together will tell you, sewing is a major usurper of time and, in terms of energy, an afternoon of pleating buttonhole darts is about equivalent to running a marathon with a cast-iron stove strapped to each leg.

Let's just take a simple sewing exercise and see how the process operates. Let's say you want to do something fairly basic and everyday, like converting an old pair of jeans into a batik wall-hanging that doubles as a zip-up lampshade with pockets.

First of all, you'll need a sewing machine, so you locate that and park it somewhere good and central. Then you have a go at fixing whatever it was that broke last time and caused you to put it away when you were trying to make a shirt out of the curtains.

Once you've got the little light going, you can lay your material out, and start cutting it out into shapes that you think might be roughly suitable. Within a matter of moments you'll have most of the room draped in a solid ocean of fabric, you'll have lost the scissors somewhere back at base camp three, and you'll have to set out on a separate expedition to find the sewing machine. Everyone else in the house will have suddenly remembered they've got important things to do on the other side of the moon, and when you lift the material up you'll notice that you've cut enough carpet out of the floor to make a series of matching winter overcoats for most of the people you've met since you left primary school. Now you can get some of the hunks you've cut out and start trying to sew them together. You've got to be very careful at this stage, particularly with your foot. Unless you know how to work the accelerator properly, the machine will go into overdrive and sew a big line of blanket stitch through everything that's not bolted to the floor.

This doesn't last long, though, because in no time at all you'll break the needle and fill the insides of the sewing machine with about a hundred thousand kilometres of intricately knotted cotton.

At about this stage you should give the whole thing away and leave in disgust, pulling the sewing machine over and dragging the whole room with you, since by now you'll have sewn the jeans to the couch and the tail of your shirt and the only advantage is that it'll expose the floor again and reveal a zillion small pieces of cotton that you can spend the rest of the day cleaning up.

If you weren't present at the sacking of Carthage I recommend you have a crack at sewing. It'll give you an idea of what the place must have looked like afterwards.

Dreams

Gidday. Just getting back to the Socratic Paradox for a moment and the link sinclaired between it and the Fred Dagg Theory of the Human Memory, it's been called to my attention that if our knowledge is to some extent a function of remembering previous experience, one of the areas where the spanner might come into some sort of contact with the works is dreams.

If in order to have knowledge we must be able to recognise it, and therefore in some sense in order to acquire knowledge we must already have acquired it, and if we can have knowledge and then forget it and then remember that we've forgotten it, then it has to be decided whether or not the knowledge of lack of knowledge constitutes knowledge. And if knowledge of lack of knowledge or more correctly knowledge that there is lack of knowledge can be said to be part of life's rich tapestry, then the knowledge acquired by remembering what occurred in dreams must be admitted as evidence under sub-section four.

Now the nature of dreams must be discussed if we're to get anywhere at all with this line of thought. Some people say that dreams take place in the subconscious, but given that the knowledge of them doesn't exist until they're recalled and that the recalling of them must happen in a state of consciousness because if it happens later in the dream it's inadmissible on the grounds that we don't know what the state is, unless we're dreaming now, in which case we know a fair bit about dreams and nothing very much about anything else.

Sleep of course is the other important element in the relationship of knowledge to the memory and dreams. I read the other day that dear old Malcolm sleeps only very rarely and can get by on five hours a night, and about ten or twelve hours a day, which might explain why he knows so much, or maybe he's remembering things he knew in dreams, or perhaps he's only dreaming that he knows anything. I don't know. The country's a shambles. There's got to be some explanation.

Going to the Races

Gidday. If you're going to maximise race-going you'll need to get dressed up well beyond the nines and you'll need a couple of things to carry; binoculars are very good as they help to act as a ballast later in the day when the wolves are howling. You park your car about 800 kilometres away in a car park (which is Latin for 'expensive paddock') and by the time you get to the main buildings you should have built up a good thirst. Proceed directly to the bar. Do not pass go. Do not collect anything like $200.

Once you've had a few, you can move out to the gambling department and start whistling your fiscal toehold up the spout. The first race is easy. Anyone can pick the winner of the first race. The trouble with the first race is that no one's ever got there in time to bet on it. The first race finishes as you come out of the bar and the horse you were going to place your shirt on is on the board at a zillion to one and has just won the first race by ten lengths. Unfortunately in the second race you've got four gold-plated certainties all given to you by people who know the trainer's brother. So you stack your pfennigs on each of them for a win, and return to the bar and tell the barman you had the first race in your pocket if only you'd arrived early enough to bet on it. If his eyes glaze and he's obviously having trouble staying awake, don't worry, he probably had a late night or something.

If you go outside and peer through your binoculars now you'll see that there's a very big bloke standing right in front of you and if you listen carefully you'll overhear him telling someone that Mr Sandman will win the fifth race by a very long way indeed. So you shoot down and place a wager to that effect. Race Two has finished by now and the four nags you bet on had a great tussle in the run to the judge and eventually dead-heated for seventeenth. Race Three and Race Four seem to have gone, too. They always run Race Three and Race Four around the back somewhere and no one ever sees them, so you've got time for a couple of quick shots of juniper-extract before collecting on Race Five.

At this stage you'll run across a group of people you haven't seen for years because they've been in this bar together since shortly after the war. After a short time with your old friends you'll realise that the result of Race Five is not as important as the high harmony line in 'shenandoah' and your day at the races begins to take on a new character.

People who care about placings, dividends and quinellas will suddenly seem a bit on the silly side and, providing you've cancelled everything on your books for about four days into the following week, you'll find that the only drawback of the whole thing is that the sport of kings is the father of the prince of hangovers.

Teaching

Gidday. I think it's time I had a word or two to say about the teaching profession. Now look! Some of you people at the back aren't paying attention, and if you think…who did that? Come on, who did that? I can wait, I've got all day. I can just wait here until that person owns up. We can all just sit here and wait. What's so funny? What's that…no…perhaps you'd…you, you, no, next to you…you, no next to you…you …yes, you, yes, perhaps you'd like to get up and tell us all the substance of your very amusing little remark. I think we'd all like to hear the joke, wouldn't we? We'd all like to have a laugh. Yes I think we could all do with a laugh. Nothing? Oh, I see, it's not funny anymore. Well, isn't that interesting, the way jokes sometimes become a little less hilarious when we're asked to share them with our little friends.

Well, if I might be permitted to continue, I'd like to tell you about how to go about becoming a schoolteacher. Now, the first thing…stand up…stand up, you…no, behind you…no…behind you…yes, you, yes…stand up.

Well, Einstein, I take it that that magazine contains the answers to many of the problems we shall be confronting today. Who's that on the cover? I see, and who is Mr Travolta when he's at home? Oh, is he just? Well, I suggest that you put Mr Travolta away because you're not going to get anywhere in life by knowing a lot of nonsense about Mr Travolta. Are you listening to me? Are you listening to me at all? What did I say? What was the last thing I said? No, before that, smarty-pants! No, don't look out the window, don't look out the window when I'm talking to you. Look at me. Look at me. Look at me when I'm...I don't know why I bother. Who doesn't either? Come on, who just didn't either? Look, if people are going to 'didn't either', I think I've got a reasonable right to know who they are. All right! I've had enough of this. I want you to write an essay on what you did in the holidays.

Our Past Lives

Gidday. Now the last thing I want to be is an alarmist, but the other day I read the following: 'A Sydney hypnotherapist claims many of his patients recall past lives while under hypnosis. Is this positive proof of reincarnation?' The short answer to this, as St Thomas Aquinas was saying just this morning as we tethered the horses, is 'no'. I actually don't know who the Sydney hypnotherapist's patients are of course, or how many of them have actually recalled past lives, in fact I'm so silly I don't even know what a past life is, but the fact that you've got to go under hypnosis to recall one will give you some idea of the dire circumstances which prevail in this country.

For some time I held the Chair of Previous Existence at the University of Dubbo and I must say we had a good deal of trouble determining exactly what a past life is. There were those who said that the mind exists only in the present and that therefore the act of recalling a past life makes that life part of the present, or that if something occurs to the mind as being alien to the present, it needn't necessarily represent the past. It could represent the future.

It was even suggested that the past and the future were the same thing, and that as on the surface of things it would appear in the normal course of events to be impossible to recall the future, and we all freely admitted to great difficulty in recalling the present, perhaps our whole lives are being lived in the past, which would make recalling our past lives not a very tall order at all.

Of course ultimately this proved unsatisfactory because three entire departments of a tertiary institution would have had to stop putting in for a visual aids grant, and as a result I developed the Fred Dagg Theory of the Human Memory, and the rest, as they say in the motor vehicle industry, is bunk.

Membership of the Parliament

Gidday. Today I'd like to avail you of information garnered by the Fred Dagg Careers Advisory Bureau concerning the whys and wherefores of being a Member of Parliament.

How you go about becoming elected is up to you. It's pretty much anything goes in this area and there are very few whys and no wherefores, and I understand there aren't as many whithers as there were either. It's what you do once you're in there that's important, and it'd be just as well to sit the bureau's aptitude test right at the outset just to see if you're suited to it. So pencils out, please.

If someone asks you a question in the House, do you:

(a) accuse the other side of distorting the issue beyond all recognition and attempting to make cheap political capital out of something that should have been solved in the committee stages of the second reading of the recommendations of reports pursuant to amendments 129 and 130 of the bill as laid down in Standing Orders and held by the Speaker in

1893 to be the right and proper duty of the member intituled the questioner;

(b) answer the question; or

(c) do anything in the world except (b)?

The correct response here is either (a) or (c). In fact that question's just been amended and (b) isn't there anymore.

If a member from the opposite benches rises to speak to the motion, do you:

(a) go to sleep;

(b) shout 'rubbish', 'resign', 'sit down' and 'get out';

(c) stand up with nineteen points of order and then insinuate that the Honourable Member has been photographed at the Club Whoopee with his arm around a young woman of the opposite number; or

(d) do (a) and (b) and (c)?

Fairly straightforward that one; (d) is the one we're after there.

If somebody got up one day and made a brilliantly intelligent and thoroughly worthwhile speech, would you:

(a) understand it;

(b) understand it;

(c) understand it; or

(d) none of the above?

And here we're obviously looking for another (d).

So think about it, and if you've ever wanted to run away and join the circus, this could be the life for you.

The Two-airline Policy

Gidday. Now I'd like to have a word or two with you about the two-airline policy, which is in effect a long-standing arrangement to ensure that if the consumer misses one plane, he can be secure in the knowledge that if he'd got there five minutes earlier, he'd have missed the other one.

The policy is under a bit of a cloud at the moment because the two airlines involved have decided to compete with one another for business. It's a fairly pagan form of competition, but I think you'd have to say that in some sense it isn't *not* competition. Or at least it isn't entirely *not* competition in every respect.

The airlines are supposed to create the illusion of competition without actually permitting the competitive element to stand in the way of the fact that if one of them wins, it's a mountainous victory for all that's decent, and if the other one wins, they have to go back and start again.

What's happened recently is that everyone's gone out and bought the newest planes on the market, with great fats on the back and a big stripe up the bonnet, and each is accusing the other of having made a major miscalculation which is going to cost the people of Australia a fortune.

That is to say, a bigger fortune than paying for two half-empty planes to leave everywhere on the hour and near the hour, just about every hour, and follow each other to everywhere else, and use different car parks when they get there just to make it look as if free enterprise hasn't been delayed due to maintenance.

Personally, I hope that if there's been a mistake on the order forms, it hasn't happened in the white corner, because if it has, the boys in the blue corner will be brought back to the starting gates and forced to make a mistake of similar magnitude, just to give everyone an equal opportunity to take advantage of open competition.

That's the thing about the two-airline policy. It's got to be revised all the time in case it works.

Plumbing

Gidday. Now, of course, it costs a great number of ducats to get an actual professional plumber around to do your plumbing, so amateur plumbing has been thrust on the bulk of the populace and the sooner you come to grips with it the better. Obviously the only people making enough money to get professional help in are plumbers, so the people who really need to develop a reasonably impressive array of plumbing skills are those among us who are non-plumbers and I might say that, in non-plumbing circles, I am accorded the status of grand master.

Let's just take a simple everyday run of the mill plumbing problem and work our way through it until we've solved it, and I'm using the word 'solved' here for the metre. Let's say you have a dripping tap. Let's say it's dripping in the same way that, say, Niagara drips. The first thing to do is to turn the water off outside at the mains. For this you'll need a machete, about four day's rations and a good map. Next, you should unscrew the dripping tap. You'll find it's on fairly tightly and you'll have to belt it a few times with a big hammer. This'll strip the thread nicely and break the pipe off inside the wall.

I should have told you to let the surplus water run out of the taps once you'd turned the water off, but seeing you're wet now anyway you can really get stuck into it. Shove a few socks and newspapers down the pipe while you try to separate the tap from the bit of pipe that came off with it.

About now the build-up of water pressure will blow the shower nozzle off and provide you with a rather nice little soap recess about five metres up the dining-room wall, and you should find there's a fairly impressive geyser in the middle of the street. This clears most of the deposit out of the pipes and the only way to obviate the possibility of a series of ginger feature walls is to position yourself between the pipes and the walls in question. Once the surplus water has run out, you can chip the wall away and bend the broken pipe around so that it points outside.

Now you can turn the water on again and swim around making notes on what you'd like the plumber to do when he arrives. You've done most of the groundwork, you might as well get a professional in to provide the finishing touches. Anyway, you'll need someone to help you clear up before having the place relined.

Sitting on the Beach

Gidday. For this you'll need a beach, which is a long sandy arrangement somewhere near the sea, and you'll need something to sit on.

First of all, you should mention to everyone that you're going to just get away from things and let the wind blow away the cobwebs. Then go and find a beach with about a million people on it. If you're going to get away from it all you'll need to keep an eye on it all so you can keep your distance. Find yourself a piece of beach and get out your towel.

In front of all these people, and some of them were queuing on Thursday night for this, you've got to get out of your clothes and into your beach clobber.

Wrap the towel around yourself and slowly fumble away underneath trying to remove things as they come to hand, pulling each item out from under the towel and hiding it under some previous marginally less embarrassing item. And keep an eye on those people behind in case they rush you.

After a while things should be getting a bit sparse underneath, and about now you should break into a kind of carefree lunatic whistle to carry you over the last stages. When you've got down to the stage between phase one and Bob's your uncle, reach over and get your swimming gear, being careful not to move too rapidly or clap your hands above your head. You pull on your natty little summer sartorials and, with as much nonchalance as you can muster, you whip the towel away to reveal yourself, resplendent in beachwear, with the outfit on back to front and both legs down one leg hole. Don't let this worry you, just sit down fairly smartly and survey the scene.

While you were whistling, a gross of wet canines have come over and with any luck they'll shake about 400 litres of ocean all over you. This will cool you down nicely and you'll be ready for a bit of sunbathing.

Lie on your stomach and open a book. The book isn't for reading and it'll get sand all through it so take a book you don't want but one with a good title. If Tolkien had knocked out something on Wagner it would've been just the job. The sun will play about your person and the glare from the book will make sure your face gets plenty of good hot blinding rays and it'll reflect off that cream on your nose and you'll get some impression of what it must have been like to lose to Joe Louis after drinking Harvey Wallbangers for a fortnight.

My advice at about this stage is to go for a walk. Remember this is not just any old walk, this is a beach walk so you'll have to do your special unselfconscious body beautiful casual stroll. Fix your eyes on the horizon and command your body into position A. If the beach is fairly long you can relax every now and then and have a bit of a slouch but if it's relatively short and heavily peopled you'll need to hold yourself in the same position for the entire performance, so get comfortable and if anyone looks at you, just flex a couple of ripples and look as sensitive as you can without actually laughing.

By the time all this is over you'll need a lie down and you can have a bit of a look at other people walking up and down. Then it'll be your turn again. After each completed stroll, as you return to your towel, the judges will hold up the score cards, the lowest score is dropped and the average of the remainder is flashed up on a big electronic board behind the car park. If you want to save your big effort for the nationals, my advice is to whip away home as soon as you've notched up a personal best.

Character Analysis

Gidday. Now today's little lecture will concern itself with the analysis of the human character.

I remember some years ago when I was in London, taking the waters and some of the whiskies, I had my palm read by a charming woman who wore a red curtain and spoke with a series of very thick accents.

She told me I'd been on a long journey across many thousands of miles, and that I was in a new place, and had left my old place many thousands of miles behind me, and that I didn't have many of my immediate family with me, and that they were all away across the seas and the clouds and past many rivers, and were in a distant place a great many thousands of miles away, and that one day I would return whence I had come in the first instance, and it would be a journey of major proportions involving the traversing of many lands and kingdoms, to a distant place situated many thousands of miles away, and nowhere at all adjacent to where we were at the time, which happened to be just near the main entrance of the Highgate Cemetery. As you can see this is a fairly penetrating piece of divining and it affected me very deeply to the tune of £1 sterling.

Of course there are many other ways of ascertaining the nature of someone's character, and handwriting's one of the better ones.

If you write off about a ten-yard run-up, and you do huge swirling loops that knock the phone off the desk, and you can fit about three words of your neatest RSVP writing on to a sheet of foolscap, then you'll tend to be a relatively confident person; and you're quite possibly the sort of person who inspires either fear or laughter. If your writing is very small and extremely faint, and you write only because you're too shy to say anything, then you're probably a shy person and your handwriting will tend to be on the small side.

Now all this might strike you as being perceptive to a quite remarkable degree, but it's all there in the handwriting. I just read it; I'm only saying what I see.

You can also feel people's heads, although you will find that in a lot of cases people will want to feel yours back, and at about that stage it's a good idea to go on a long journey to a distant place many thousands of miles away.

A Nice Drive

Gidday. What you'll need here is a car, preferably one with a few major mechanical defects, windows that don't open properly without a hammer and ideally, of course, the car should be just a tiny bit too small for the number of people you've got to put in it.

For the sake of getting to the main business of the drive itself I'll ignore the many potentially charming aspects of the planning stages, the preparation of food and clothing for the journey and a fair amount of reasonably heated discussion as to exactly where you're going to go.

Around about five hours after you planned to return, you should be leaving. The day should be overcast, cloud down to about forty-five centimetres, visibility zero and falling. The temperature should be about 1000° Celsius on the Richter scale and the atmosphere would probably weigh in at around ninety-five percent water. You should have three in the front seat, or, if the car seats three in the front seat, you should have four in the front seat and in the back there should be a landscape of fairly small faces with perhaps a smattering of aunties, grandparents or some other mentally unhinged person with a bit of a death wish.

The boot should be burgeoning with beetroot sandwiches and spare jerseys and there should be tea in thermoses and at least an oodle of cold sausages and bacon and egg pie, so if the drive gets a little tedious you could conceivably have a crack at the north face of the Eiger.

You are now prepared and, as you leave home wondering about whether you turned the stove off and hoping the cat doesn't get accidental behind the fridge, you begin to feel free and hopeful. You look out the window and everyone says, 'Isn't this fun' and 'shouldn't we do it more often'. My advice to you is to enjoy this bit of the trip, savour it and let it linger on the palate. It's the last bit of enjoyment you'll have for a fair while.

When you're out in the unknown and the heat's appalling and you're up a side road that someone said was quicker but you can tell it isn't going to be, you should find your left back tyre's doing pancake impressions and it's a good thing you've got to pull over anyway because the temperature light's on, the oil light's flickering, the petrol gauge only works downhill and if the smell's anything to go by, part of the fuselage is on fire.

This is the highlight of the outing in several respects. You've got to get the food out to get to the spare and you can have a go at the prandials while you work out why the spare's only got one metric puff of air in it and who you lent the jack to. By now the weather's getting its eye in and the sandwiches have melted, the kids have collapsed and the top's blown off the radiator.

When someone eventually comes to the aid of the party and you limp home on one cylinder, you may not feel you've had the greatest time of your life. You might not even want to see anyone else ever again. But there's no denying you've given Sunday a run for its money.

Dentistry

Gidday. If you've ever walked into a room and had everyone in it try to get out through a very small air vent, you probably know what it feels like to be a dentist. You have to be a fairly resilient sort of character because you have to spend all day seeing people who don't want to see you.

Let's just take a typical dentistorial episode and give it the once over. You, the dentist, enter your surgery with considerable fore-boding and seated in the waiting room is your first patient, Mr Jones, hiding behind a big stack of *Illustrated London News*, with only his feet sticking out. You put on your white backwards-coat, and you go out and tell Mr Jones that he can come in now. Then you prepare your little glass tray full of instruments and you go out and tell Mr Jones that he can come in now. You should have a record card for every patient so you go and get Mr Jones's card, you have a look at it and you tell him that he can come in now. Then you go over to your nurse/receptionist and inform her that she can tell Mr Jones that he can come in now.

The patient will now look around the waiting room just in case there are some other Mr Joneses before him who've slipped down behind the heater and, having ascertained that he's the only major contender, he will eventually shuffle into your surgery and sit down. You can try to make conversation with him if you like. My own personal advice is to leave him alone and just sing to yourself while you look at his X-rays and mutter about his upper left five and the watch on his dorsal cusps. When you peep into his throat you'll feel the tension in his nervous system and you'll notice the perspiration roaring out of his forehead and running down into his ears, so get your repair work done as rapidly as possible or he'll short everything and blow your surgery into a less desirable area.

Once you've laid your cement you will have to leave him there until it dries, with his mouth open and the little bilge pump on overdrive. If you hide around the corner during this period you'll notice that he does things like trying to line his feet up with the new car park building, and inspecting your ceiling as if he's thinking of putting one in exactly the same at his place, or moving his head up and down so that the aeroplanes fly along in between the slats on the venetian blinds. The fellow's obviously a lunatic and you should get him out of your surgery as soon as possible.

That's the main trouble with dentistry: you meet a very strange class of person. Actually, I recommend you stay away from dentistry altogether. See you in six months.

Tennis

Gidday. Now today I want to waylay you with another suggestion about how to show the weekend who's boss. This method is safe, completely dependable and fulfils most of the requirements of a leisure activity as laid down in the Geneva Convention. It is time-consuming to a point where you can actually think you're busy, it's tiring, it involves special clothing and equipment and in general terms it's a 100 percent bona fide waste of time within the meaning of the act. I refer, of course, to the ancient and revered art of tennis.

First of all, you'll need a tennis court and, if you play your cards right, you can spend till about Sunday lunchtime waiting for one to be vacated by three or four big Brunhildes who've been whacking around on it since April, rallying for service. By the time you get a court it'll be raining and there'll be a Force 9 blowing leaves and silt in from Asia.

This will carry the ball over the net, the wire fence and a fifteen-hectare subdivision at the back. The net will have wound itself into a thin line of black string, so you can't tell whether your shots are going under it or over it, and you only find out where it is when you hurl yourself forward to smash a lob and it bends you over in the trousers and drops you on your back between the tramlines.

You should really wear whites and have a good racquet but, if you couldn't raise a mortgage in time, you can generally get away with an honest attempt. A pair of white shorts you once washed with some red curtains and now have a blotchy pink aspect to them and a painting rag with armholes is often quite acceptable, if you've got shoes the same colour and a good hat. A good hat is crucial and, if you can't get one of those visor arrangements from an old New York newspaper editor you might get by with a sweatband, which is like a sock you wear round your bonce to keep your brains from sliding out your ears. Always remember that the best sports gear has two stripes down it, so whatever you've got, get a good thick biro and plant a couple of stripes on it so you look like a pre-war postman and you'll be OK in the sartorial department.

The next thing is the game and, although it's the least important aspect of the whole exercise, it's as well to know a couple of the basic rules in case the Rosewalls on the next court ask you whether their last serve was a let or an inwards one-and-a-half with a degree of difficulty of 2.4.

The way to score is relatively simple and once you've played a few games, you'll pick it up, no trouble. The first person serves, which is called a double-fault, and so it goes on until you get to the point where all the balls are in the blackberries up behind the car park. Then the person to the left of the dealer says 'juice' and you all go and do that. From memory it's fun from there on.

Accounting

Gidday. If you want to become part of the modern world I recommend you become an accountant more or less immediately. First of all, let's just see if you're aptitudinally suited to this lofty calling. I'd like you to be so good as to answer the following questions.

Can you count to three? (You may use a calculator during the final stages of your working, although it's probably better to lease one than to buy one, because the leasing of business machinery can be deductible at full rate, whereas purchase price, although deductible through charges against the current account and again advantageous through depreciation, is ultimately going to show up as an item of capital expenditure, and the opportunity cost of such utilisation of funds is obviously going to be the possible write-back to standard value of any cattle purchased before balance date and held subject to fertiliser provided by the vendor with monies other than those already earmarked for consideration as possible year one and year two input figures for a forestry development programme with milling at year one plus twenty-three.)

Secondly, can you lean back in a chair, look out the window and demonstrate what's meant by the term 'a sharp intake of breath'? This is to be done whenever a non-accountant attempts to count to three so it's got to be mastered fairly early on. Of course, if you want to be a cost accountant or an auditor you'll also have to be able to put your hands together as if you're praying and tap your incisors with the nails on your two forefingers. But that's really fairly advanced and should probably be left till later.

Finally, and this is the real nub of the matter, can you draw a line down from the top of a piece of paper to somewhere near the bottom and can you count to three on both sides of the line? This is the very lifeblood of accountancy and if you can do that you're not only halfway there, you're halfway back as well.

The Diplomatic Service

Gidday. I'd like to have a bit of a nutter with you concerning the possibility that you could under certain circumstances consider the proposition that you might like to become a diplomat. Of course, I'm not suggesting that you're not perfectly happy doing what you're doing at the moment, and I certainly don't want to suggest that you're not very good at it. I'm sure you are; I'm sure you're excellent at it. In fact I'm told more or less constantly that without your steadying hand the whole place would fall apart. Neither do I mean to indicate that what you're doing is intrinsically inferior in any way to diplomacy. Very far from it. I know how valuable your work is and I hate to think what would happen if it wasn't done. The whole idea is absolutely unthinkable. And if anyone ever did anything to lessen the effectiveness of your work, I personally would release a decidedly cool statement, to be taken in the context of a joint communique which you and I would issue together, probably from a hotel foyer somewhere or with one of us at a lectern, confirming our mutual respect and reaffirming that our relationship can be expected to continue to produce ongoing dialogue of interest to all those with an interest in regional issues and in charting a viable course through the sensitive sargasso in which the Western power bloc finds itself at this difficult time in our history. Then we can hop out the back and I'll beat your face off.

If you're going to be a diplomat there's one thing you will have to face up to fairly early on in the piece, and that is that the human body can take only so much gin and tonic. You should probably work out your own capacity to the nearest bottle and have it engraved on a disc, which you can hang around your neck. In cases of dire necessity, when you've driven your Elan into a swimming pool, medical authorities can administer the relevant dose to bring you back up to a fully functioning quota. Otherwise you can get into terrible trouble. I knew a bloke once who drank too much goat's milk at a diplomatic ball and discovered next morning that he'd annexed the back of Raetihi to part of Persia in exchange for fifty-seven dozen pairs of sandals and a bathmat. So you'll have to watch yourself fairly carefully.

Of course, being a diplomat does involve a fairly comprehensive study of languages and you should probably have about half a dozen different languages up your sleeve. And you should have sufficient mastery of them that you can say absolutely nothing at all in any one of them. You should also study very closely the countries that you're working with, so that you can say absolutely nothing at all in the context of history. Familiarity with computer technology will enable you to transmit absolutely nothing at all at incredible speed directly on to someone else's hard disk and you should obviously have a reasonable facility in English so that you can say absolutely nothing at all several different ways at different press conferences and resist all attempts to trap you into saying anything other than absolutely nothing at all.

Television Drama

Gidday. I'd like to reveal to you one of the better guarded of the postwar vocational secrets, and that is how to write a domestic television drama. Before going any further I feel I should point out that, although there's a lot of public deprecation of the genre, this is largely an exercise in intellectual snobbery and in actual fact there's nothing wrong with it at all. It is a perfectly legitimate reflection of life as it is lived in the modern day and age and, although it is dramatised for maximum effect, it has more integrity than you could probably shake a stick at. It's all in the way you treat your subject matter. I'll just outline a simple plot which is not sensationalised and is true to life in every particular, just to show you that it can be done.

The show opens with the return home from university of a young man who's been away studying and who's come back because his father has unfortunately passed away during a break for station identification. When he arrives he gets a bit suspicious about the way people are carrying on and it dawns on him that his father might have been murdered by his uncle, a man named Claud. The uncle's actually not a bad bloke but he's always wanted the family business and in fact for some time he's been having the odd game of cachez le sausage with the young lad's mother. There are a couple of ghost scenes here where the lad talks to his father, but we can easily drop these if you think they're a bit unrealistic. I don't know that they work but the visual effects people won't let me touch them. Anyway, being a red-blooded young fellow, the student has a girlfriend and there are a few scenes here we'll have to drop, too, now I think about it; one in particular where he makes rather a lot of distasteful puns about her rural concerns and perhaps we could lose quite a lot of the audience if we're not careful. I didn't invite this and now I've come to read it properly I wonder whether it's suitable at all. It's Danish, as a matter of fact. Perhaps I should have gone for something else. Anyway, I'll see if I can clean that bit up.

Anyway, the young student then does what so many young students do these days, he has a sort of nervous breakdown, or at least he pretends to and he fools everyone into thinking he's a few coupons short of a toaster. There's no mention of drugs in the story but obviously his mother in particular is very concerned about the sort of life he's been leading and what manner of person he's been hanging around with. And, of course, as so often happens in circum-stances of this type, he has a series of very dramatic scenes with his girlfriend and he hurts her deeply. So distracted is she by his strange and possibly drug-crazed behaviour that she goes away and drowns herself in a river during another break for station identification. Then, of course, her family gets really quite litigious and her brother decides to nail him and there's a bit of a punch-up at a rather suspect dinner party organised by the mother and this Claud rooster.

By now of course the young shaver's got his hands full because, aside from everything else, he's killed the girlfriend's father by stabbing him up the arras. We'll have to position about ninety-seven cameras all over the studio because just about everyone gets finalised in one slightly ridiculous final scene.

The one big disadvantage of the story is that, although it's no more ludicrous than any of the other daytime TV plots, there aren't going to be enough characters left over at the end to get you into the second episode.

But give it a go anyway and if the public likes it I've got another little humdinger here about a very high-up black government official who snuffs his wife out because he thinks her handkerchief might have been carrying on with another bloke, and there's a beauty here about a crippled king and another little cracker about a transvestite lawyer and old man who bleeds when you prick him and goes to court over a meat deal. So if the TV industry runs out of unlikely plots for soapies there are acres of them in this book I've found.

Writing a Novel

Gidday. In the following little bagatelle I'd like to have a few words with you about becoming a novelist. I address myself to this subject in response to many zillions of letters I've received from persons claiming to be latent or potential novelists. Here's a sample, just to give you an idea of the type of thing we're knee-deep in down at the bureau.

'Dear Fred. I think I have a novel in me. I think perhaps we all do. Signed, Budding Novelist.' Here's another one: 'I've always wanted to write a really good novel. At the moment everything

I do is just a little bit boring. I hope this comes right with time. I'm writing this for a friend. Signed, P. White.' And thanks very much Perce and, of course, there are countless others along similar lines.

Clearly there are many novelists out there fermenting and just waiting for the muse to spirit them into print. So I think this is probably a suitable moment to whistle through some of the more fundamental dos and don'ts of the novel-writing caper in general.

The first thing to decide is what sort of novelist you'd like to be: a tall novelist, a short novelist or a novelist of medium stature; a modern novelist, a neo-classicist or a pastoral stream-of-consciousness gothic feminist. And once you've made this decision you're halfway there, really.

Next, of course, you've got to sit down and pound out your actual novel, beginning each new sentence with a capital and numbering the pages very carefully. There's nothing more frustrating to the reader than getting right through a novel and then discovering that it was read in completely the wrong order.

You'll need a main character (a protagonist will probably do if you don't mind cutting a few corners) and you'll need a plot of some sort. This is really just a device to give you something to write about while your main character's in the toilet or changing hats or something. And once you've got your plot worked out you'll have to develop some manner of style.

Now when it comes to style in the novel, it is instructive to browse through history and see what's available. First of all there's the first person, which is 'I', or in this case 'you', which is the second person, and 'he', 'she' or 'it', which are the third person, except 'it', of course, which isn't a person at all, and whatever you're having yourself. The novel was begun in a hotel called The Mists, which is just outside Antiquity. It was begun by several people and Richardson was one of them. Samuel Richardson his name was (he's probably dead now, he was a very old man when I knew him) and he wrote a thing called *Pamela*, which established two great strains which run through all subsequent history of the novel: the use of the narrator and boredom. The story was fairly simple and it concerned promiscuity, attempted rape, submission and other burning issues of the day. It was basically a diary and the style was a good example of what scholars refer to as 'awful'.

You could, of course, do worse than emulate the style of Dickens, who wrote mainly for periodicals and, as a result, has a fair number of his characters down a snake pit on a rope which is being burnt with a fire by a man-eating tiger at the end of each week's little capsule. This gives his novels more climaxes per chapter than most novelists could handle, and it embodies Dickens's claim to be 19th-century literature's equivalent of *Neighbours*.

Then you've got your Tolstoy, of course, who came from a small village in England called 'Russia'. He experimented with the novel to see how thick it could get. And he discovered that with proper attention it could get very thick indeed. And he sold the film rights and died in his own personal railway station.

D. H. Lawrence should not be imitated without medical supervision as he was captain of the Nottingham raincoat brigade, and in later life had a brush with an outfit called the Bloomsbury Set, who make Liberace look like a football team.

James Joyce is really the prince of style and, if you're looking for a style for yourself or perhaps a nice little style for a friend of the family, I recommend that you look very closely at James Joyce and Walt Disney.

By now your novel should be coming along quite nicely and in the interests of artistic integrity, which is basically a marketing concept, it's probably time to address yourself to the difficult task of injecting local flavour into it because, of course, the greatest possible achievement for the scrivener is to come up with The Great New Zealand Novel.

In this pursuit there are several cardinal rules. Firstly, if you've got any interesting characters in mind, drop them immediately or you'll ruin everything. If there's one thing that The Great New Zealand Novel should not have under any circumstances whatsoever, it's an interesting character. By all means have a main character, but ideally he should be a character of unexampled tedium. In fact, he should never actually do anything. Things can happen to him by all means, but he's a victim at all times and never an initiator of an action. And the things that happen to him should, so far as is possible, be boring.

If you find that for some reason or other you do have an interesting character, have him shot about halfway down page one by a boring character. Make it obvious that the boring character didn't actually decide to shoot the interesting character, he was forced to do it by the crushing heartlessness of the postwar fusion of urban and rural society, in which process the doctrine of free will is emasculated by the power of capital and the stark hostility of the land itself (I'm sorry, the stark hostility of the very land itself). Of course, the main character should be a testament to the alienation of mankind from the pantheistic subtleties inherent in his world. And he should demonstrate with frightening clarity the tragedy of self-deception and man's inhumanity to woman.

Have your novel published by some university in the Chathams in a run of a couple of dozen and if nobody reads it you'll be up there with the giants.

The Perils of Air

Gidday. I presume you're all well aware, in fact it's my devout hope that you're acutely aware that I don't want to be alarmist about this. But, on the other hand, there's no point in hiding behind a bushel and pretending everything's perfectly all right when really we all know very well it isn't.

I've warned you off the bicycle, which I always thought was only a passing phase anyway, and I've recently revealed in the public forum the horrifying dangers of lip gas; and with any real luck you're now philosophically prepared for the startling disclosure that getting up in the morning can kill.

I'll tell you basically how this happens. There's no point in going into it too deeply as it's actually a little bit frightening and needless scientific detail will probably serve only to worry you. You will appreciate that during the night, as we scientists call it, the atmosphere has a chance to settle down. During the day it is subjected to the injection of industrial fumes, germs, toxic gases and, on occasions, balloons; and during the night it sorts itself out into basic elements, hydrogen, nitrogen, earth, fire and water. And in order to do this it requires absolute absence of artificial stimulus; the wind is all right, the process can cope with wind, wind is a natural force and as such is an integral part of the wonderful jigsaw of microscopic life, but the movement of people through the realigning gases while they're actually in the process of realignment is extremely dangerous. This is why people who come home at half past four in the morning look so terrible the following day. The realignment has been disturbed by the passage of their bodies and has wrought a terrible havoc upon their persons, particularly around the eyes and in the back of the mouth. Any movement, and getting up in the morning is a good example, disturbs the natural regrouping of the gaseous elements and, instead of walking into a fresh revitalised atmosphere, you're likely to stroll into a big pocket of incomplete air, and the effects of this are horrendous. I've done it several times. The lungs and the spleen are the first to go, and after that you'll be all over the place.

Stay in bed, that's my advice to you, and if possible stay asleep.

Swimming the Ditch

New Zealand, a User's Guide

New Zealand is the most beautiful country in the world, as is clearly stated in the UN Charter. (I think it's in Article Seventeen.) The land is nourished by warm sunshine each morning and receives the benediction of good rainfall around lunchtime. It is an egalitarian nation made up of well over four million rugged individualists and naturally gifted sportspeople and is run on alternate days by the government and whoever bought the national infrastructure.

Like Australia, New Zealand was established as a colonial economy by the British. This meant they bought our wool and our meat, although not for our benefit. It was purchased from the farmers by British companies, shipped on British ships and processed in British factories before being sold in British shops in British currency. The money then went into British banks. I think we can probably all see the problem here. The British made more out of New Zealand than the New Zealanders did. This changed slightly in the early 1970s when Britain went into the Common Market. Kids had been doing school projects about this throughout the 1960s but it came as an enormous surprise to the New Zealand government and it has taken them some time to adjust. The principal business in New Zealand used to be sheep but the country has now moved into milk in a big way and if you'd like to enjoy the beautifully clean swift-flowing New Zealand river system, you should make every effort to get out there before the dairy industry gets any more successful. New Zealand also produces a large quantity of fruit, wine, fish, coal, wood pulp, flightless birds, cups of tea, middle-distance runners and other people's film industries.

Before the British, the Maori people arrived from Hawaii in the year 1273, at about quarter past four in the afternoon. There were allegedly people here before that, called the Moriori, and there may have been people even before that. Harry Armitage has been a stock agent up around Raetihi for at least that long and he tells me his father had the pub at Te Karaka.

Like most of the world's major democracies, New Zealand is run by international capital and a few local big-shots who tickle the till and produce a set of annual accounts in a full range of colours. There is a national parliament in Wellington, which looks like the hats in the Devo clip 'Whip It', although very little of any importance has ever occurred there. The country works a lot better during the weekends than it does during the week, there are no states and the senate voted itself out of existence after the Second World War. When the Lower House eventually follows its excellent example, constitutional experts agree the next step will be beers all round.

In 1893, women in New Zealand were the first in the world to get the vote and in more recent times women have had a run as prime minister, opposition leader, chief justice and governor-general. Even the queen is a woman. The country's most famous pop singer, best known opera star, most famous short story writer, greatest novelist and most consistent world champion athlete are all women. They're not allowed in the All Blacks as yet, but don't be fooled. It's just a matter of time. New Zealand women are stroppy, imaginative and a major strength in both the Maori and Pakeha cultures. In some New Zealand families, women are practically running things.

During the 1970s, New Zealand was confronted by very serious economic and political crises, although, according to police records, there's some suspicion these were both inside jobs. During that period New Zealand rugby administrators were ex-forwards who looked like spuds in their jackets and when they announced that they were sending an All Black team on a tour to South Africa, there were suggestions it might be time to go and get some new spuds, and maybe some who'd played in the backs. At this stage Nelson Mandela had served about ten of his twenty-seven years in prison and the rest of the world took the radical left-wing position that democracy might be worth a try in the region. New Zealand Prime Minister Norman Kirk went to see the Rugby Union.

'I'm the prime minister,' he explained.

'Is that right?' said the spuds. 'Take a number.'

'We'd rather you didn't go to South Africa,' said Norman. 'It will look like an endorsement of the white supremacist policies of the South African government, to which we are opposed.'

'So what?' said the spuds. (I'm summarising a bit here, obviously.)

'So it's not going to happen,' explained Norman.

The spuds were furious. They saw this action by the government as a direct threat to the way the country was run and, after a smaller prime minister had been elected in 1975, the tour went ahead. As a result of New Zealand's endorsement of the white supremacist South African regime, the Montreal Olympics in 1976 were boycotted by twenty-six African nations.

'So what?' said the spuds and the smaller prime minister.

And so it was that the return Springbok tour of New Zealand in 1981 was a famous disaster, for the spuds and the government did not have the support of the people and the nation was divided and brother spoke not to brother, nor sister to sister, nor yet generation to generation, each of its kind. And there was a gnashing of teeth and the scribes were thrown into a great confusion and there came a heavy sadness upon the people and upon the land, and upon the face of the deep.

The economic crisis of the 1970s occurred over the issue of debt. Was the New Zealand economy borrowing too much overseas? While this question was being considered by economists, a Debt for Equity Swap was organised by a group called 'I Just Drove the Getaway Vehicle'. At the time government policy had not yet been outsourced; we still owned the infrastructure, the power, the gas, the water, the phones, the post office and the national airline. The Bank of New Zealand was still a New Zealand bank and one or two of the newspapers were still owned in the country. During the early 1980s, however, the New Zealand economy was put in the hands of finance ministers due to a filing error, and authorities are still looking for the black box. A social democracy with only one previous owner was asset-stripped and replaced by a series of franchises. Even rugby sides stopped being called Canterbury, Wellington, Otago and Auckland and were instead given the names of animals, colours and weather conditions. The next thing anyone knew they'd appointed a currency dealer as Prime Minister and the equities market became a place of worship.

New Zealanders don't have much trouble working out what they think. It's the next bit that might need some work. In 1969 I was standing in a pub in a country town in Otago. They'd run out of Speights and we were drinking a beverage produced in the north. The man next to me was deeply unimpressed and made a number of uncharitable statements about the quality of what was on offer.

'You don't like it?' I said.

'I don't,' confirmed the man. 'It's bloody terrible,' he said. He then thought for a moment and resolved the matter in his mind. 'This is the worst beer I've ever tasted,' he said. 'I'll be glad when I've had enough.'

This probably wasn't the answer. Complaining about what's wrong but not taking action has the same effect as not noticing what's wrong.

Incidentally, New Zealand remains the most beautiful country in the world. There's no question about this. You can go to any part of it with confidence, at any time of year, with the possible exception of Hawera at Christmas, Otautau in August and Taihape in a stiff westerly.

Hands Across the Tasman

My first contact with Australians was in London, where I was living during the early 1970s for tax purposes. At one stage, seeking a career in retailing, I wrapped mail orders at the back of the book department of Harrods. Each volume was placed on a piece of corrugated cardboard and the cardboard was then manipulated until the book was no longer visible. A skill I have never lost.

Across the bench from me was an Australian who called everyone Bruce. He pointed out a friend of his in the sports department. 'See him Bruce?' he said. 'He's a professional tennis player.'

'What's he doing working in the sports department of Harrods if he's a professional tennis player?' I asked.

'He's no good,' said the Australian.

I lasted three days at Harrods, but my Australian friend lacked my persistence and was impeached on the second afternoon for putting a famous sign on the main stairs. It was made out of corrugated cardboard and said: harrods, no farting.

It was at this point that I recognised the shared perspective of Australia and New Zealand on matters of international significance. The question is whether or not this communion of subversives can be converted into export dollars.

Closer Economic Relations will do much for the exchange of ideas among business people of course, although it should be remembered that there is really only one idea among business people and exchanging it is an achievement of only modest dimensions. It must surely be possible to develop something more worthwhile than the intercourse of moustachioed primates in Flag Inns all over both countries.

A new nation should obviously be forged, combining the two in such a way as to maximise the contribution of each. Australia would grow fine wools, beef and trees for Rupert's newspapers.

New Zealand can provide dairy products, coarse wools and trees for Rupert's other newspapers. Bob Hawke should head a government, possibly in Brisbane where there hasn't been one for a while and where it will have novelty value.

Roger Douglas is an automatic selection as minister for finance. Someone would have to explain the job to him, but once he understood it he'd be hard to hold. He is dedicated to excellence in all things and is apparently a delightful person. His appointment would also eliminate the need for the portfolios of health, education, social welfare, housing, agriculture and the arts.

Paul Keating is the best treasurer in the world and could run an expanded banana republic with his eyes closed. Indeed that might be where he's going wrong at the moment. New Zealanders will have to get used to the idea that the stock market crash was 'a correction' and that it confirmed the brilliance of Paul's mid- to long-term thrust, but this shouldn't be a problem. The correction was almost terminal in Wellington and drove at least one correctee to camp in a Sydney living room with twenty-seven journalists and a change of tennis socks.

David Lange would be Speaker. He has been trying to curb this tendency lately but there seems little point and a man who only shaves because it provides him with an audience has much to offer an emerging nation. If the post of governor-general is available I would suggest almost anyone except Alan Jones or Kylie Minogue and I submit the following changes to the governmental structure of all states in the new federation.

The bicameral system obliges the government of the day to deal with vestiges of the last government but three. The same thing happens when cousins marry and quite clearly there should be one house, as is the case in New Zealand, with the proviso that the power should be retained by the states, as is the case in Australia. This will allow for spirited debate and important pronouncements which have nothing to do with the running of the country and will accommodate both the New Zealand yearning for regional independence and the Australian desire for a perpetual Constitutional crisis.

The new Parliament House in Canberra can then be turned into an all-weather sporting complex, thereby satisfying the only genuine interest of the entire population of both countries.

Spot the Deliberate Mistake

In response to questions from confused members of the Australian public, many of whom are known to me personally, I've embarked on a programme of national education.

Too little is written about the ignorance of the Australian people. There is, by way of contrast, too much written about their intelligence. Their resourcefulness, initiative and fearless traditions have been set to music in order to sell a wide range of foreign products; the Anzac spirit is evoked by no one more beautifully than American fast food chains, and the chairman of Australian Steel has been made a Sacred Treasure by the government of Japan.

The problem of educating the Australian population is clearly urgent and must be addressed on a scale never before contemplated. We've started at a very rudimentary level with a massive television campaign designed to teach people what a Post Office is. We've tried to do several things at once, which is a sophisticated concept, but one we like. We're explaining:

(a) What a Post Office is.
(b) Who those people are, in Post Office uniforms, who deliver your mail.
(c) What those things are, that are put in your letterbox (through a slot in many cases) by the uniformed artisans mentioned in (b).

(d) What those boxes are. (The ones in which articles are placed by the liveried representatives of the essential service industry alluded to in (a).)

(e) That when it's raining, the mail is delivered in the rain.

(f) That during periods of intense sunshine, the mail is not delivered in the rain.

(g) That in order to effect delivery, some postal employees use bicycles, although on very steep hills, particularly when the mail is not being delivered in the rain, the bicycle may choose not to be ridden but to be pushed.

We've referred to the Post Office throughout as 'Australia Post', a catchy name meaning Post Office. In fact, we've been even cleverer than this would imply. We've decided to improve our logo. Initially, I wasn't sure this was possible. The old logo has ben extremely successful and, despite claims that it was unnecessary and meaningless, research has demonstrated that many people realised eventually that the logo had something to do with Australia Post, which, of course, they associated with the Post Office. Aside from these practical considerations, the logo is very appealing to the eye and is a fine example of Australian design at its triumphant best.

There is no limit to the amount of money we're prepared to spend on developing a new logo. The cost is simply not a factor. The stakes are too high for petty mercantile considerations to be of any significance. What we'd like to do is annihilate our competition so comprehensively that it will be almost as if it hadn't existed.

I know this all sounds new, but we've done something very like it before. We ran a visually very satisfying campaign some time ago explaining to people what a telephone is. (In effect, a telephone is a thing that rings in the mountains of southern Europe, and the ringing stops if you pick it up and cry into it.) It worked better than we dared hope, and at the time of writing there is now only one organisation operating nationally as a provider of telephone services.

In some countries, of course, both Telecom and the Post Office would be owned by the state, and the millions spent on advertising would be wasted on improving services and lowering costs.

So buoyant did we feel after all of the above, and such was the feeling around the office, that we decided to keep going. Gamblers will know what I mean when I say we felt we were 'on a roll'. It was resolved on a show of hands that we adopt the suggestion made by the young work-experience person, and change the name of TAA. We tinkered briefly with the conceptual work and decided to call it either 'Australian Airlines' or 'Australia Post'. We eliminated 'Telecom' because we wanted to avoid imagery of mountains and crying and making expensive telephone calls to women who live alone in Surrey. After a heated lunch we also ruled out 'Australia Post' because despite the many common elements (uniforms, rain and sunshine), aeroplane travel and group cycling are fundamentally different. We felt this difference demanded expression. Very few of the sample group associated the name 'Australian Airlines' with the Post Office, and TAA is, as everybody has known for years, an Australian Airline. Simple really: 'Australian Airlines'.

But how to sell it, how to market this intricate and yet muscular idea. The answer was, of course, again, Educate the People. Paint all the aircraft, order new badges, new paper, new hats, new buildings, new front doors for the vans (the cost of all this to be charged against 'Improvements'.) Follow this with a massive multi-media campaign, trumpeting the arrival of a completely new airline that no one has ever heard of, and which only a small number of people will think of as the Post Office. I have seen criticism of our decisions, but it is petty and ill informed. I will not dignify it with a response.

Helpful Suggestions

I don't mean to harp on about this, but there still isn't anything like enough public money being syphoned into the advertising industry. There are plenty of government-owned bodies spending virtually nothing on nebulous ideas and anthem quality statements of the obvious.

I exclude the Post Office from this. I know I've been critical of them in the past, but my hat is now raised in a gesture of respect. Their television commercials have made them the market leader right across the country.

They have filleted the competition to the point where, I believe I am right in saying, in some areas the Post Office is now the only Post Office still operating as a Post Office.

I also have only the highest regard for the millions sensibly invested by Telecom in establishing that a telephone can be used for making telephone calls. I may have oversimplified this. The commercials actually indicate that a telephone can be used for making overseas or interstate phone calls. There is no suggestion that it is possible to make local calls, but there is probably a reason for this. Perhaps the phone is out of order and no one can look at it before Wednesday, or maybe all the phones in the whole area are out and nobody knows why, or it is possible that the phone has been cut off because the user is too poor to go on helping with the TV commercials.

Neither do I intend any disrespect to the airline that used to be TAA. Their work in establishing whatever their new name is has been without parallel in the history of image-based money-flushing, although they didn't have it all their own way. The Buy Australia Campaign must have given them an awful fright.

This was a benchmark effort. It pointed out that people should not buy Australian products just because they were Australian.

This broke down the old, stereotyped idea that a commercial should achieve what it set out to do. The Buy Australia campaign depended for its success on the ability of the buying public to reject the advice of its advertising. I'm presuming here that the aim of the campaign was to encourage people to buy Australian products, supposing such a thing were possible.

It would be unfair to ignore also the spectacular media-spending embarked upon in the name of the Priority One campaign. It would not be at all appropriate to remember the campaign itself, but the figures involved were very reassuring.

For the Bicentennial one can have only the most open-hearted admiration. Not only are they currently funding about a quarter of the world's shipping, but the plan to sail the *Deficit* around Australia during the summer months is well advanced and the television campaign is on air, even though it obviously isn't quite finished yet. There is a song about all of us doing something without hands. I'm sure it will all become clear once it has been edited.

It is what is called an 'awareness' campaign. It doesn't sell anything or provide any actual information. Its main aim is to be on television. It can then be demonstrated that a number of people might have watched it. They will be 'aware' of it.

Whether or not the Bicentennial can recover from this advantage remains to be seen. There can be little doubt, however, that so far they are doing everything expected of them.

What I want to know is, where are the other government departments? Where are the awareness campaigns for the Weather Bureau and the Official Receiver? Should their Australianness not be celebrated?

Would not the romance of Soil Erosion lend itself to the screen? It is Australian Soil Erosion, after all. It is the best bloody Soil Erosion in the world and it wants to tell its story. A more natural subject for a song would be difficult to imagine. It has everything;

wind, rain, floods, the pitiless heat of the sun. Perhaps the Weather Bureau could be part of it. The Official Receiver should also be approached without delay.

There are others of course. The Albury–Wodonga Development Corporation, for instance. Isn't this the sort of dream that sustained the lads in trenches all over France and Belgium? Is there an Australian heart that does not quicken at the mention of The Inspector of Inflammable Liquids or the Department of Lifts and Cranes?

These people cannot be expected to continue unless their work is accorded the simple dignity of being described within an inch of its life and sung about by groups of white Australians who are not hanging from prison ceilings.

Farnarkeling

Farnarkeling is a sport which began in Mesopotamia, which literally means 'between the rivers'. This would put it somewhere in Victoria or New South Wales between the Murray and the Darling. The word 'farnarkeling' is Icelandic in structure, Urdu in metre and Celtic in the intimacy of its relationship between meaning and tone.

Farnarkeling is engaged in by two teams whose purpose is to arkle, and to prevent the other team from arkeling, using a flukem to propel a gonad through sets of posts situated at random around the periphery of a grommet. Arkeling is not permissible, however, from any position adjacent to the phlange (or leiderkrantz) or from within fifteen yards of the whiffenwacker at the point where the shifting tube abuts the centre-line on either side of the thirty-four-metre mark, measured from the valve at the back of the defending side's transom-housing.

Dave Sorenson: The Early Years

Dave Sorenson was the product of the union of Brian Sorenson and Mary Shannon. For them, as for so many others, the postwar years represented a period of rebuilding.

Brian had returned after five years of active service pitted against the might of the Nazi war machine in North Africa and the Levantine and another demanding period turning back the Japanese menace in the Asian theatre. He elected not to follow his father and his elder brother Geoffrey into the family's well-credentialled footwear-wholesaling concern in Melbourne's Ascot Vale, but instead to seek a future in the Australia he had heard other men talk about, the Australia he had read about in books, the real Australia.

With his bride of only three weeks, he purchased from the late Jimmy Cobden a 140-acre vineyard, six and a half hours' drive due west of Brisbane, in the heart of the inhospitable blanket of territory that runs from the Queensland border in the south through to the Gulf country at its northern extremity.

Mary Shannon was a fine, tall woman with a cascading laugh and an inner faith. She had the charm of the Shannons, and from her mother had learned the fierce dedication of the Busbys. Intelligent, quick, both in anger and forgiveness, she had played hockey for the New South Wales B side and had beaten Frank Sedgeman's father at tennis. It was Mary's determination and cheerful disposition that qualified her uniquely for a shareholding in Brian Sorenson's dream.

Brian himself was a quiet man, a dreamer, perhaps even a mystic, a man who once left a tractor running while he travelled to Adelaide to attend the wedding of a younger sister.

When David, the third child, was born, the farm was not going well. Conditions were as unfavourable as anyone could remember. Rain, the life's blood of the vintners' trade, was not forthcoming.

For nearly eight years, the district had insufficient rain, and the little vines shrivelled and burned in the pitiless sun. A series of crippling loans were negotiated. Still no rain. Irrigation was planned, but the government containing the neighbour's brother-in-law was swept from office. Brian retreated further and further into himself, at times becoming completely inaccessible to rational discourse, entering the house only to consult almanacs and tell the children stories about Crete.

The damage done by the 1959 floods was devastating. From Ningham to Wollawolla, almost everything was lost. Even the soil was lifted from the Sorenson property. As the family vacated Brian's vision in a makeshift raft with what personal effects they could carry, the young Dave swore that this sort of thing would never happen again. Not to him anyway.

Within a month, they were resettled among the saltbush of the South Australian cattle town of Wyhoonoria, where Mary's brother Vince was the farrier and assistant librarian and where the Sorenson children could recommence their schooling. On 24 April 1961 a barefooted eight-year-old lad was ushered into the single classroom. The teacher bent slightly and extended his hand. 'Good morning, Dave,' he said.

History records that the man's name was Dieter Togbor, arguably the greatest arkeler of the pre-war period and certainly the best mixture of height and length ever to come out of Europe. His stamina, his speed and his ability to feign movement in one direction while proceeding in another had made him almost impossible to out-manoeuvre. In the 1934 World Championships, he had an average of 16.8, despite playing with a pinched nerve in his elbow and a greenstick fracture in the clavicle as a result of the attentions of the Welsh in the first round.

Mr Togbor moved to the blackboard, while appearing to move towards the door. The new boy walked to a vacant seat, while appearing to feed the fish. Togbor liked the young boy immediately, and so began one of the great sporting apprenticeships in history.

Australian Farnarkeling Back in Business

Finland. Wednesday.

Last night the national side staged an amazing comeback to retrieve the fat from the fire at the last minute in the second half of injury time in the group 1 quarter finals of the European championships being played at the indoor farnarkeling centre in Helsinki late last night, Australian time.

The Australians came from fifteen arkles two tackles and a bracket-and-a-half down, to get up off the paving and defeat the highly credentialled and very well-performed Scotland who are ranked second in the world and haven't been beaten on a European grommet in nearly four years.

The Australian side, undermanned since its much-vaunted backline drove a small catering van into a water hazard at a charity equestrian event on Saturday, has had it all to do since arriving here for the European campaign. Already troubled by lack of form in recent outings and in particular by lack of drive in the centre where both Graeme Graham and the evergreen Dave Sorenson have been sidelined, Graham with extenuated shoulder ligaments and Sorenson with a corked thigh, the team arrived in Budapest a fortnight ago to find that their equipment was sitting on the runway at Broome airport due to a filing error.

When it arrived two days later it was found that the material in some of the flukems and the outside ends of the boot-wafting had been altered by exposure to temperatures in excess of the boiling point of some of the carpet nails used in the construction of the upper sections of the transom-housing. Replacement equipment was sent for but, as far as team officials were aware when I spoke to them a few minutes ago, it isn't here yet.

Australia went into last night's affair with most of their gear borrowed from the Canadians and with the dorsal hinges and much of the scrotal padding borrowed from the South Koreans.

In the event it was nip and tuck all evening, Australia mounting good attacks, principally up the right wing where Neville Dorf was as fluent as we've ever seen him, and in the centre where thrust was coming from Lo Bat, the Chinese boy from Port Adelaide.

Australia's finishing was not good, however, and too many opportunities went begging to arkle from quite handy positions. It wasn't until Plinth was taken from the grommet with what looked very much like a nasty knot in the clavicle that Australia began to regroup up front and go about the business of actually building a total.

Dave Sorenson is one of the great converters of the postwar era, although he hasn't arkeled at the top level for quite a few seasons now and when he was dragged out of retirement for this tournament there were plenty of those who thought he'd never be able to keep up with the modern game and, when he came on last night just before the umlaut, I have to say he looked in all sorts of trouble. He was slow. He was sluggish. At one stage he tried to turn while moving laterally across the back of the cotyledan and if he hadn't run into the side of one of the hospitality tents he may well have sustained permanent damage to the entire upper part of his person.

This seemed to steady him, however, and within moments he began to arkle with all the authority of a master. He notched up three or four absolute beauties before the Scottish coach shifted Fergusson and put the Quinn brothers in around Sorenson like a blanket. In the next six minutes Sorenson arkeled fifteen times and took Australia from nine behind to full of running and in front by two.

It was this passage of play that altered the nature of the fixture and, although Scotland jumped away again in the latter stages, Sorenson pulled one out from well behind the tripod and the Quinn brothers, who must have thought they had him, were completely outflanked. By the time they looked up the gonad had reached its cruising height and there were Australians all over the ground swinging towels round their heads and enhancing the air with well-meaning obscenities.

Perhaps out of this Australia have sensed that this thing is possible over here. They withstood wave after wave of attack in extra time to hold the plucky Caledonians out and they looked a very determined outfit at the after-match function.

The cost of this victory might well prove to be catastrophic. Tragically, Dave Sorenson may take no further part in proceedings following an unfortunate incident on full time when he arkeled successfully but lost control while attempting a reverse hasselblad and caught part of his lower mandible on a heating fan. Surgeons are non-committal about his condition but are apparently quietly confident they can get him down out of the roofing by Friday.

Australians Hit their Straps

Korea. Thursday.

The Australian farnarkeling team gave every indication on Friday night that it might be running into form at the business end of the season as it accounted for Italy in a majestic and confidence-building first-round display at the world championships being contested in somewhat balmy conditions under lights here in Seoul.

The programme for Australia's defence of the bevelled orb has been the subject of some scepticism in recent months as the troubled national squad has registered a string of lack-lustre performances against often boisterous but fundamentally inferior opposition sides drawn principally from the rest of the world.

When they arrived in Seoul there were immediately problems. The hotel had double-booked four floors and there was no possibility of getting in anywhere else as the whole town was packed to the gunwhales and it was past three in the morning. Ian Geddes and Stewie Davidson slept in a telephone booth in the hotel car park. Neville Dorf spent his first night on foreign soil in a goods lift with his feet in the ashtray and his head in a potted plant. Dave Sorenson, whose pelvic brace wasn't due to come off until the Thursday, slept standing up in the foyer and woke in some surprise to find that he was holding nearly two dozen umbrellas and a fair range of gentleman's millinery.

It was a somewhat bedraggled sight which met the eyes of team management as they arrived for breakfast fresh from a working session on threats from some of the Western Bloc countries to pull out of the championships unless the playing surface at the Hyperbowl was changed.

There had actually been suggestions as late as mid-morning Thursday that the Astro-Arkle© surface, which is not universally favoured by the players, might be replaced by Flexi-Gromme©, the rather more spongy substance developed by the Swedes in order to cope with variations in temperature and atmospheric pressure.

In the event, organisers decided that the surface was playable as it was and the festivities got under way at the appointed time as per the attractively designed brochure. The Italians began confidently and displayed their traditionally well-balanced combination of strength and speed with perhaps a slight tendency to waste opportunities out wide where Bartocelini was giving away a metre or two to the rapidly improving Graeme Graham and where Australia consistently found an overlap by running one player through the bracket and another down the back of the shifting tube. There were seldom fewer than three Australians to the left of the hasselblad and by the midpoint of the second warble Sorenson was arkeling with ominous authority.

The Italians made a surprising tactical error shortly after the umlaut by concentrating their defensive effort on the unlikely Dorf. Dorf had intercepted a pass from Martinetti to Rossi and the Italians obviously assumed the interception to have been intentional. As far as coach Donnatesto was concerned, Dorf was the danger man. This left Graeme Graham to roam the circle and he fed Sorenson with good gonad until Boreo was shifted forward and the Italian reassessment of Dorf began to make its presence felt.

Australia had the fixture parcelled up by that stage, however, and it was encouraging to see the defensive operation knitting together so well after all the problems of recent months.

The next encounter will be with either Peru or the Ross Dependencies who saw Denmark off in an elegant affair late on Wednesday. Unfortunately, Sorenson pulled a bank of lockers down on top of himself while grabbing for his towel in the ablutions facility and it will be another few days before the power of speech is revouchsafed and he can comment on his condition. Australia can ill afford to be without him for long in this class of competition.

Australian Farnarkeling at Crossroads

Colombo. Monday.

Australian farnarkeling was rocked to its foundations this week. On Tuesday, a seemingly aimless Australian side containing no fewer than seven of the world championship players was humiliated for three warbles by the Zambian Under-19s, and only a purple patch from the still-injured Sorenson prevented the team from bowing out of the competition altogether and heading homewards before the commencement of the second round. It was an unfortunate exhibition, and some very serious thinking is necessary at selector level if further catastrophe is to be averted.

The Australians were especially poor in defence, which allowed the agile Zambians (particularly Kwee) to carve out huge tracts of territory at will, operating from the centre and exercising complete control of the flanks. And big Stewie Davidson must be wondering why he came here. He was left standing by little Ngawa, and the only thing he did properly all afternoon was consume half an orange.

Other big name players to be completely eclipsed were Leslie Stavridos, Robin Wylie and Neville Dorf. On one memorable occasion, Dorf had only to stroke the gonad slightly forward of his own feet in order to set up a cascading Widdershins Pincer involving three players and salvaging a tincture of self-respect before the umlaut. In fact, if he had made any proper contact at all, the rest of the manoeuvre would have looked after itself. But for some reason not apparent from my point of vantage, Dorf chose this moment to deflect the gonad backwards into the path of Nriwi, whose alacrity had been a feature of proceedings, and who arkeled without slowing from a curving run that finished in front of the main stand with the delighted crowd rising in its place and calling his name. Dorf claimed later that he had failed to allow for the wind. When told that the wind was recorded at zero, Dorf said that he had possibly failed to allow sufficiently for a lack of wind.

The young Zambians lack cohesion, but their arkeling has a wonderful spontaneous quality, and there can be little doubt that Tuesday's final score flattered the victors. Nriwi, particularly, is a player of whom we shall hear more.

This was not the first close shave for Australia in recent days. The Cubans came within a blither of a famous victory in Perth the previous Thursday. Had Sorenson not been moved into the centre in the final minutes, and had he not imposed his authority on the fixture by peeling off three arkles of surpassing subtlety (one of them while lying down as his thigh was being strapped by a handler) and had he not neutralised the hitherto devastating Tostaro, the result would undoubtedly have favoured the visitors.

Of the leaden performance against Scotland on 27 October, enough has probably already been written. It is easy to find fault with the players, and certainly on the grommet, where it counts, mistakes have been made. Of course they have. No one would deny it. Wylie's lateral traverse against the Cubans opened up the entire left-hand end of the splicing zone. Dorf's almost complete loss of confidence in his teammates and the team's nearly total loss of confidence in Dorf are possibly driving a wedge between Dorf and the rest of the side.

Things are not good and the players will need to find something if their world ranking is to be retained. But it can't all be put at the door of the players. The decision by the world farnarkeling body to ban Australia from further competition after the next world championships has had a very debilitating effect. Players who used to train for hours with smiles on their faces now sit and look out the window. The talk is of retirement and of the past. The Australian government's attitude to Aboriginal policy is well known, and it is difficult to see any softening of their position.

The South Africans have proposed a tour and have outlined a programme of encounters between the two nations beginning in January and running through until somewhere in the second half of April but, with the exception of Dorf, the players have declined the offer. Sorenson is said to have been offered $250,000 to take an unofficial invitation team called The Official Australian Farnarkeling Team and appear in selected cities for three weeks. Three weeks is known to be a bad time for Sorenson, and he is not expected to accept. The standard of play by the national representatives has fallen off by all means, but it is a difficult and very disappointing period for them.

What they need at the moment is support and encouragement and what they do not need is Cyril Dorf writing to the newspaper with his unusual interpretation of international politics. Cyril Dorf, it should be remembered, led the movement against the introduction of the fifty-three-metre penalty line because, he said, it punished initiative and favoured players with frizzy hair. He also appeared on 'Have Your Say' and argued the point with Evan Harrua and Grgtrt Ydklg. The spectacle of members of the federal executive sniping at each other on national television was a lasting embarrassment to the code and not one to be repeated. Cyril has a son in the Australian squad and a daughter in Telecom and should be well pleased. He must consider the consequences of his actions, however, and those members of the press who seek to fan the fires should study their history. The last time Cyril Dorf turned up at an after-match function an incident occurred which reflected badly on the character of the louvre windows and obliged Sorenson to miss the game against Honduras.

Challenge Round Wide Open at this Stage

Tuesday night.

Ideal conditions prevailed in Perth late yesterday for the staging of the first two fixtures in the regional section of the challenge round build-up for the world championships currently expected to be decided in either Rangoon or Amsterdam in early August, Australian time.

In a fast-moving and very enjoyable curtain-raiser, the gallant Nepalese went down to the more experienced Canadians, but not before giving the Great White Northerners a little something to be going on with. Lacking the height or the reach of their opposition, the Nepalese brains trust had worked out a series of well-prepared running moves, particularly through the centre and down the right-hand phlange, playing mainly to Nanyad, the deceptively fast utility back whose dominance of McSixpack will surely have the Mounties in the back room grouped in a circle.

The second encounter was delayed for forty-five minutes when it was discovered that the clock was running forty-five minutes fast and that to start on time would therefore be to begin forty-five minutes early. The committee decided that rather than start on time and be forty-five minutes early, they would start forty-five minutes late and be on time. As a result, the radio broadcast of the main fixture was replaced by an announcement that because play had already finished, the live commentary would be transmitted as soon as it hadn't started yet. There followed some light music and a list of river heights.

In the event, Australia came from behind to edge out a determined Poland in an evenly contested and free-flowing affair from which the home side can take some satisfaction but from which it must also learn. The Poles, notably Katjscinski, Wotjekzniski and the evergreen Witold Osip were very strong in the flanks and around the whiffenwacker, and their consistent ability to run the gonad out of defence and take the Australians by surprise meant that both Stavridos and Wylie had to be moved into the plonking box, and the Australian frontal attack was left in the unlikely hands of Neville Dorf and Stewie Davidson. Dorf's inclusion in the side had been openly questioned by many experts, including most of the capacity crowd. (The publication of his book, *The Genius of Neville Dorf*, after only two appearances for his country, had led to suggestions that his commitment to the team was perhaps less than absolute, and his only significant performance had been against the Madagascans when Australia had an insuperable lead and Dorf arkeled by accident while attempting to hit the opposing captain in the ovipositor while the referee was unavoidably detained underneath a pile of other contestants.)

He and Stewie Davidson posed no threat to the Poles. Davidson seems to have lost a metre or two of his pace and by the look of his fuselage he had a particularly enjoyable Christmas.

As expected, the focus of the match was the tussle between the dangerously fit Wojek Conrad and the very remarkable Dave Sorenson. Conrad had got away from Sorenson several times early in the second warble and seemed poised to take command, but Sorenson, who had been on antibiotics to clear up a blockage in the Eustachian tubes that had caused him to surprise himself while sneezing, proceeded to take the initiative and turn on a display of arkeling that will linger in the memory. The crowning achievement was probably the Inverse Blither he performed while running backwards by reversing the position of his feet and by leaping both up and sideways as the gonad was intercepted and despatched at apparently different altitudes simultaneously. The wall he hit will be shifted before the second round of matches beginning on the twenty-fourth.

Standings after Saturday: Group 1: China 1, Burma 1, Peru 1, Singapore 1, Norway 1, Angola 1, Tanzania 1, Canada 1, Zambia 1, Australia 1, Corfu 1, Hungary 1, German Democratic Republic 1, Italy 0, France 0, Nepal 0, South Korea 0, Sudan 0, Algeria 0, Poland 0, Uruguay 0, Vanuatu 0, Laos 0, England 0, Portugal 0, Ross Dependencies 0. (Mexico had a bye.)

The Run Home

Australian farnarkeling received a much-needed shot in the arm with the news that Australia has eliminated Sweden in a nip-and-tuck affair in sub-zero temperatures at the all-weather Farnarkeling Centre in Gottenburg earlier today, Australian time.

Dave Sorenson, the Paavo Nurmi of Australian farnarkeling, was prominent throughout and set Australia up with a powerhouse display in an explosive third warble. The axiomatic Sorenson, who was cleared to play only moments before the phlange was lowered, was all over the opposition until a spring went in his knee and he lost all feeling in the hormones. Sorenson is now in doubt for the semi-final against either Scotland or Taiwan and it will be tragic indeed if they can't unscrew him before the weekend.

Australians into Final

Farnarkeling history was made last night in Madrid when Australia confounded the experts and bundled Scotland out of an incident-packed semifinal in front of an estimated crowd. In near-perfect conditions on a beautifully prepared grommet the Australians began well and wore the plucky Caledonians down with a combination of accurate lunging and superior fitness. Once again the very dextrous Dave Sorenson dominated the attacking phase and, after a short time, was arkeling from all points of the compass. Unfortunately, he suffered a spectacular mishap in the middle of the fourth warble when he dislodged a pinion in the goalpost-housing and impaled himself on the southern wall. It'll be tragic indeed if he can't be prised off the facilities in time to take his place in the side for what promises to be the final against the East Germans in Moscow next weekend.

Historic Victory

The Australian farnarkelers were literally on top of the world last night following their epoch-making victory against the formidable East German farnarkeling machine in a closely contested final at the People's Farnarkeling Centre in light drizzle and heavy security in Moscow.

The ruthlessly professional East Germans began strongly and had the Australians reeling from a series of quite obvious and very brutal personal fouls. But just after the leiderkrantz it became obvious that the continually impressive Dave Sorenson had weathered the bone-crushing first warble and was prepared to take the fixture right up to the East Germans after the umlaut. The turning point came in the third warble when the oleagenous Sorenson arkeled from behind his own goal line despite being held by both opposing fullbacks and a small ice-flattening machine he'd inadvertently backed into during a lapse in concentration. Unfortunately, only moments later, he struck an overhead light with a wet knee and short-circuited his trousers. It'll be tragic indeed if he can't be deionised in time to return home to what promises to be a hero's welcome in Sydney on Tuesday night.

Conquering Heroes Return

The victorious Australian farnarkeling team returned home in triumph last night with the bevelled orb safe in their keeping until the challenge round in late July, Australian time.

Team members were fulsome in their praise of the running of the championships and are approaching the government to get an arkeling grommet of international standard built in Canberra so overseas teams can provide much needed competition here during the northern summer.

The heavily bandaged Dave Sorenson, who aggravated a thigh injury with a heavy fall from the aircraft while deplaning before the ramp was in position, reacted strongly to suggestions that corporate sponsorship is poised to take farnarkeling into commercial television.

Proposals are already with the governing body to introduce a solid programme of one-day farnarkeling fixtures under lights with edited highlights between the warbles and a viewer competition tentatively called 'Classic Arkels'.

Major manufacturers have already come up with what they claim is the definitive farnarkeling shoe, and T-shirts and initiatives in fast food are already in the pipeline. The well-credentialled Sorenson said he would have nothing whatever to do with what he described as 'A ridiculous farnarkeling circus' which he claimed would turn the game into some kind of joke. Although he did admit he had been approached.

It will be very unfortunate for arkelophiles if Sorenson's assault hearing coincides with the exhibition match in Perth next Friday.

A capacity crowd was treated to a display of champagne farnarkeling in an exhibition fixture run in Perth on Friday to aid world famine relief.

In an all-star engagement the victorious Australian world championship sidelined up against a composite invitation team from other farnarkeling countries. The national side quickly demonstrated its total mastery of the code and pulled out every type of arkel from all parts of the grommet and seemed to have the flukem on a string, particularly when moving forward in defence. The very dextrous Dave Sorenson, who seems to set new standards every time he steps onto the sward, was in inspirational form and the game has never had a better ambassador. He was instrumental in one almost magical arkel just before the umlaut when he notched one up from well outside the whiffenwhacker by deflecting the gonad with his foot while being tackled. He was later involved in an unfortunate altercation with a section of wire netting at the southern end of the concourse and it'll be tragic indeed if he can't be disengaged in time for the Sportsman of the Year dinner, where he is the red-hot favourite to pick up the big one.

Sorenson Honoured

Dave Sorenson was named Sportsman of the Year at a well-attended post-prandial black-tie wallop in Sydney earlier this evening, Australian time.

The heavily bandaged but very dignified Sorenson, the Mick Young of Australian farnarkeling, was given a standing ovation as an edited sequence of some of his more spectacular arkles was projected on to a makeshift grommet positioned in the ceiling at the back of the transom-housing.

Unfortunately, Sorenson suffered a catastrophic personal mishap while mounting the podium to pick up the sculpted tribute. He hadn't looked well since the soup and it was no surprise to onlookers when he fell through a rostrum interstice only seconds later while raising the golden artefact and thanking his immediate family.

Organisers said that this was the first time since the function's inception that the award had been taken internally and it'll be tragic indeed if the accoladectomy can't be performed in time for Sorenson to attend the launch of the farnarkeling federation's new televised drive for popular support.

The Resolution of Conflict

*In which a mature understanding is brought
to certain delicate questions and from which it
may be deduced that a fat lot of good it is too.*

Industrial Unrest Crisis Point

An uneasy truce, in existence since members of the Federated Under Tens' Association accepted a package of long-term benefits and returned to work a month ago, is showing signs of fraying at the edges.

The Massed Five Year Olds have grown in strength, having changed jobs this year, forgoing a part-time casual consultancy, pasting pieces of refuse together and reassuring one another as to the circular persistence of the wheels on the bus, in favour of a full-time tenured position painting themselves green and hanging upside down from garden furniture.

The curfew introduced in early February, as part of a range of initiatives designed to improve operational standards following the annual break, has not been accepted at all well. The Federated Under Tens were known to be opposed to curfews and a rather inept and politically dangerous attempt was made by management to introduce one without calling it a curfew.

The FUT read the mood of the meeting beautifully, and boldly decided that the correct response to something that was pretending to be a curfew was to pretend to accept it. This prevented the problem from emerging as a theoretical discussion and consequently a number of hours are now being lost through regular tests of muscle and endurance on the evening shift.

The moment of curfew is in effect, the trouble begins. Within minutes, as if by prearranged signal, one of the delegates is located in a restricted area. Offenders are frequently apprehended carrying contraband goods, impounded literature or rolls of Sellotape, which they are believed to be storing somewhere, possibly in an underground warehouse.

On one recent occasion, a delegate was found holding down the flushing mechanism on a toilet in order to simulate ablutionary activity while another delegate was pushing a member of the Australian Association of Dogs around in a cardboard box. When asked to explain the merits of this exercise, one of the delegates described their purpose as being in some way related to dental hygiene. The AAD made no official comment, but its representative was clearly embarrassed and will perhaps not be so easily coerced again.

This followed a heated exchange in mid-February when authorities investigating unusual sounds were surprised to walk in on a trampolining contest in what was listed as a dormitory zone. This had obviously been in progress for some time as those involved were perspiring freely and the area had sustained serious structural damage.

Government stepped in. The position was said by government to be one of the utmost gravity. Safety standards were being jeopardised, product quality was down. Such privileges as had previously been negotiated would be subject to immediate review, said government, if this sort of thing did not stop forthwith.

The following night an office-bearer in the Massed Fives was found to be conducting a series of command-style raids on the food refrigeration facility. The facts were difficult to obtain in this instance because the accused was wearing a stackhat and could not hear the carefully worded questions of security personnel.

Other outstanding disputes include the long-running controversy about the clothing allowance, which is said by the FUT to be completely inadequate and which ministry representatives have described as 'very generous indeed'.

Regulations currently in force lay down parameters for the cleansing, refurbishing and replacement of suitable clothing to reasonable levels. It is this last phrase upon which the disagreement pivots. For example, regulations express a need for two socks per person per day, such to be returned. The FUT wants 'unless lost' to be added to this requirement, and it wants the number increased from two to twenty-seven.

The Massed Fives are pushing for alternative legislation providing for a particular set of clothes, deemed ideal for prevailing conditions, to be cleaned daily and not varied by management without the express written consent of the wearer; any variation or other breach of this understanding to be met with instant withdrawal of all services by the Massed Fives, and any attempt at arbitration to be rejected well above acceptable noise levels.

The overall position is considered by experts to be about as average as anyone can remember. No one can remember a time when the overall position was less perfectly normal than it is now. All parties are said to be hopeful of an early settlement and are planning to meet first thing in the morning provided they get enough sleep.

Entire Country Held to Ransom

Australia ground to a virtual halt on Tuesday when the Federated Under Tens' Association withdrew services, stating that in their view it was an unreasonable demand that they wear a sun hat in the sun. They further suggested that the placement of sunscreen lotion on or about their persons was an infringement of basic human rights and was 'simply not on'.

A compromise was reached when it was conceded that they should not come over here and do it, but that someone would go over there and do it, and that, yes, they could go to Timmy and Simone's afterwards.

Wednesday saw the dispute widen when an affiliated body, the Massed Five Year Olds, showed their hand by waiting until the temperature had built up and management had about a hundred-weight of essential foodstuffs in transit from supermarket to transport and then sitting down on the footpath over a log of claims relating to ice cream.

The Federated Under Tens, sensing blood in the water, immediately lodged a similar demand and supported the Massed Five Year Olds by pretending to have a breakdown as a result of cruelty and appalling conditions.

The problem had been further exacerbated by a breakage to one of the food-carrying receptacles and some consequent structural damage to several glass bottles and a quantity of eggs, the contents of which were beginning to impinge on the wellbeing of the public thoroughfare.

Government stepped in. Government expressed itself in the form of a brief address. Ice cream would be provided, explained an official, but not simply because it has been demanded. This was not the way to achieve results and no repetition of this sort of thing would be tolerated.

A highly ranked source in the Under Tens said: 'We regret that we have to take this type of action. Believe me, we tried reason.'

'Strawberry,' said someone from the Massed Fives, 'with pineapple and blue heaven.'

Relations seemed to have stabilised by Thursday following substantial reorganisation along the lines of a collectivist approach to decision-making. The Federated Under Tens and the Massed Fives were awake to the possibilities here and by block-voting and the use of secret hand signals they dominated meetings and might have taken complete control of policy formation had it not been for an unfortunate incident in which an office-bearer in the FUT was arrested for the attempted murder of the National Secretary of the MFYO in an internal disagreement about Textacolour ownership.

An attempt to establish clearly marked territories and separate job definitions was unsuccessful as it was the preferred option of each group that it should have the territory and the other should have the jobs. The matter was deadlocked at tea and a cooling-down period was necessary before negotiations could continue.

The evening was passed quietly except for a near tragedy when the local representative of the Australian Association of Dogs upset the fragile ceasefire by sitting on the Ludo while nobody was looking.

Friday was a lay-day as the site was visited by independent authorities from the National Union of Grandparents, a benevolent organisation thought to be funded by the tea industry.

Differences were forgotten and any slight flare-ups were resolved by the laying-on of hands or in one rather more passionate instance, by the laying-on of feet.

By mid-morning on Saturday, interest rates were improving and both major industrial groups seemed happy with production levels and working conditions. At 1100 hours sun hats were provided and a protective lotion was distributed to all personnel. At first there seemed to be no objection. Then the FUT refused point-blank to put them on or to handle them in any way and the MFYO, in flagrant contravention of previous undertakings, demanded ice cream and plenty of it.

Prospects for the rest of the year look a little bleak from here. I can only wish you well.

Winter of Discontent

There is a feeling in the market that during recent months the unions have quite consciously prevented disputes from flaring up in a random and isolated fashion, and have instead been stockpiling ammunition for a comprehensive showdown. It promises to be a top-of-the-range affair and tickets should be booked early.

There are several very major problems. The Federated Under Tens' Association have had a range of grievances festering since early in the June quarter, when new clothing regulations were introduced. The Under Tens were known to be against regulations of any sort and their reaction to the provision of compulsory wet-weather gear was predictably hostile, despite the fact that the principal reason for the introduction of wet-weather gear was the wetness of the weather.

All personnel were issued with the standard kit consisting of 1 × raincoat, 1 × warm hat, 1 × pair of gumboots and 1 × pair of warm socks.

The Federated Under Tens saw this as a calculated attempt to subject them to ridicule and further worsen their standing in the community. The Massed Fives were frankly insulted by the whole business. Stripped of its fancy language, they said, it meant that their members would be asked to accept sub-standard garments which had been discarded by members of the FUT. Such garments were quite obviously second-hand, very old, extremely unattractive and according to a highly placed source in the Massed Fives, this was 'typical'. It was suggested that management was favouring the Federated Under Tens by attempting to co-opt them into a sweet-heart deal with the promises of new clothing.

Management denied this ludicrous charge and initiated discussions with the Massed Fives to see whether or not they could be attracted into a sweetheart deal of their own relating to some new socks. This rather messy and ill-advised approach backfired immediately. The Massed Fives made it clear that any settlement would have to include a new hat, a new coat (of a type specified by the delegates according to taste), a proper pair of boots and ideally a book about dinosaurs.

Independent tests were conducted by the National Union of Grandparents, a charitable order made up of ex-management personnel who had a pretty easy ride while in office, but whose ability to deal with trouble-makers is sometimes uncanny. They monitored a senior delegate from the FUT for a trial period of a week.

On the first day the delegate began the morning shift in the full kit as detailed in the regulations, although at close of play the raincoat was left at the worksite because in the estimation of the delegate, it wasn't raining.

The rest of the clothing was dried during the evening as reports continued to come in of state-wide flooding. Several towns had been washed away and many people had been tragically buried by hail-stones. On the second morning, management provided another coat from a secret supply in the boardroom as driving rain was still falling and only the tops of the trees were visible. Although it touched the ground and was described by the delegate as 'a hideous boring tent', the coat looked well with the hat and it also matched the one boot that was found.

By the beginning of day four, the boot position had been clarified to the point where each foot had a boot and one of the boots bore the name of the delegate. Another boot was found in the delegate's bag but even the National Union of Grandparents couldn't work out whose it was or how it had got there. An office-bearer in the Massed Fives suggested that the boot may have been put there by Martians, as apparently something very similar had just happened on television.

A marked shortage of socks on the fifth morning occasioned a search of the dormitory zone. Those involved are still only learning to talk about it. Things were seen which beggar the imagination and reveal much about the so-called 'dark side' of the human soul.

On the plus side, the second coat was found rolled up under a bookshelf and inside it were two pairs of socks, a yoghurt container full of deceased moths and an apple which has been carbon-dated to the early 1520s. The matter of the bicycle wheel and the object which may have been a sea anemone was dealt with separately and I'll say no more about it here. It has not been an easy time for us and it is with high heart that we anticipate the prospect of spring.

There will be more rain of course. Farmers need rain. And it affords the Massed Five Year Olds a wonderful opportunity to get out in their new hat, new coat and brand new gumboots; especially now they've finished the dinosaur book.

AUSTRALIAFORM

Answer ALL questions.
You have three hours.
You may start writing NOW.

AUSTRALIAFORM
1 July 1989 to 30 June 1990

Specify period if part year or approved substitute period.

Post or deliver the return by 31 August 1990 to a Taxation Office in the State in which the income was derived or was last seen.

This document must be carried at all times whilst the driver is in charge of a car on any public highway.

IMPORTANT

Please complete Section [A] before moving on to Sections [B] [C] [D] and [E].

You must answer one question from Section [B] or [C] and one each from Sections [D] [E] and [P] before returning to the Optional Sheet [attached].

If you require more paper, raise your hand and asked the supervisor.

You may start writing now.

SECTION [A]   ▲
SURNAME . . . .
GIVEN NAME . . . .
(If Keating, move to Section [F])
Personal tax number (Confidential) . . . .
[Will not be revealed to anyone who does not already have it]☆ ☆ ☆ ☆ ☆ ☆

Name of spouse . . . .
Maiden name of spouse. . . . .
[Where applicable]   ■ ■ ■ ■
Does/do Spouse/es Fill in His/Her/Its/Their [if more than one] Form or does/do Spouse/es consent willingly and/or freely to his/her/its/

their [if more than one] details being included herein. Such consent to be represented by the affixing of his/her/its/their [if more than one] signature/s [if more than one].

Names of children . . . .

Your own children. Do not attempt to be amusing in any way. ▶

ADDRESS. . . . .

Address to which bills and court summons may be sent.

Occupation (if any) . . . .

Other occupations . . . .

Occupations not mentioned so far . . . .

▼

Have you had anything to drink in the last 4 hours?   YES/NO

Are you a member of an approved superannuation scheme?   YES/NO

Well don't worry, we'll get you anyway.   □■

INCOME   ▲

What was your income during the year to 30 June? . . . .

How was it obtained? . . . .

Where is it now? . . . .

Who touched it last? . . . .

Have you conducted a thorough search around the home? . . . .

What did it look like? . . . .

Have you reported the loss? . . . .

Was your income gross? . . . .

VERY □   UNBELIEVABLY □   I AM DOCTOR □

Enter subtotal here

Carry forward amount [G] net of depreciation

Add on Items 7, 18, 26 and Part xxi from Heading M

Attach sheets 8–34

Pin tax stamps to back of earning statement and retire to safe distance

Show accrued yields from all interest sources as per Section T

Add money left in other trousers, down back of car seat, in jar on mantelpiece, glove box, other [specify]
Imputed amount for enjoyment of garden or reading
Express checkout: eight items or less ◀◀◀

SECTION T ▲
Income from other sources
Name Race Meeting . . . .
Date of Race Meeting . . . .
Nature of Investment . . . .
State Odds . . . .
Did you witness race in Question? . . . .
Why not? . . . .
State name of brother-in-law . . . .
Amount consumed . . . .
Furnish recording of brother-in-law singing *Danny Boy* ◀————

SECTION [B] ▲
Company return . . . .
Address of registered office. . . . .
Company file number . . . .
[Cannot be used except by persons who read this document or data sourced from this document. Staff of the Taxation Office and their families are not eligible to enter this competition.]

i] What books of account, if any, are kept by or on behalf of the taxpayer? . . . .

ii] By whom are these books kept? . . . .

iii] Where is he? . . . .

iv] Would you recognise him if you saw him again? . . . .

v] Is the return in accordance with those books? . . . .

vi] If the return is not in accordance with those books, which books is the return in accordance with? . . . .

vii] Have the film rights been sold? . . . .

viii] If this return has been prepared by an Accountant, has this Accountant ever won a major award for Fiction? . . . .

ix]   Is the Accountant in Jail?.............................

x]   Why not?..

LIST OF SHAREHOLDERS   ■ ■ ■

Living.....................Non-living ....

Other ....

WHERE WERE YOU ON 17 OCTOBER 1987?

OK LET'S TALK ABOUT SOMETHING ELSE   ✪

LEAVE BLANK

APPROVED DEDUCTIONS   ▲

Office Expenses, School fees, Travel and Accommodation, Equipment,
Stationery, Depreciation, Furniture and fittings, Sex, Bribes to Law
Enforcement Personnel, Wastage [Ariadne Shares, Liberal Party
Donations, etc.] ....

Other...

See Box [7] Under GENERAL   ⑨

DO NOT WRITE IN THIS BOX   →

OR THIS ONE   ←

Key to symbols

AO Adults Only

PGR Parental Guidance Recommended

G General Viewing

ABC Repeat

SECTION [Y]   ▲

Indemnity

IS THE ABOVE A VOLUNTARY STATEMENT? ....

HAS ANY THREAT, INDUCEMENT OR PROMISE BEEN HELD OUT

TO YOU TO MAKE THIS STATEMENT? ....

DO YOU SEE THAT MAN IN COURT? ....

DO YOU WISH TO HAVE THE CONTINENTAL BREAKFAST? ......

SECTION [F]
To be completed if your name is Keating.

Name ....

Last return lodged ....

PLEASE BE SERIOUS ....

Address ....

Other address ....

DO YOU THINK THIS IS FAIR? ....

SCORE THE FOLLOWING STATEMENTS IN ORDER OF PREFERENCE
1–5

I enjoy the company of others

I enjoy the company of some others

I enjoy the company of other companies

I find it difficult to build up a rapport with others

By and large people give me the squirts

☐   ☐   ☐   ☐   ☐   ■

The Trickle-down Effect is: ●

a] A process whereby money given to the rich trickles down to the poor.

b] A process whereby instructions given by the rich trickle down to the government.

c] A code name for the Trickle-up Effect.

ACCOUNTANTS

If you are filling this form in for a client or friend, should you have one, you must complete this section.

Name ....

Name of person for whom you are filling in this form ....

Is he/she in the room with you? ....

What fee are you charging? . . . .

Pardon? . . . .

Will you get away with it? . . . .

Have you got away with it before? . . . .

How many times have you got away with it? . . . .

Sorry, I can hardly hear you.

Is your client sane?	**32u**
	□□□

Part 4[b]   ▲

If you answered 'yes' to question 20 or 'don't know' to either question 17 or 24 [in section 12 on P.5] complete the following very carefully.

i]   Is the discharge coloured? . . . .

ii]   How many sex partners have you had in the last month? . . . .

iii]   Name them. Male . . . . Female . . . .

Other [specify] . . . .

Extra space is available on the reverse . . . .

iv]   It's for their own good . . . .

v]   Look at the photographs in Schedule 9 . . . .

vi]   Memory perked up a bit now has it? . . . . :

vii]   Cough . . . .

viii]   Do you suffer from any of the following . . . .

Hepatitis, Gall Stones, Corked Thigh, Pulled Giblets, Dipsotryponia, Telecom Business Services, General Anxiety, Hearing Voices, Paranoia.

SECTION J

G   What City does the World's Greatest Treasurer live in?

E   What remarkable May Economic Statement dominated 1988?

H   Who is the Longest Serving Australian Labor Prime Minister?

A   What are The Arts?

SN   What Rainforest has a new road through it?

SL   What famous golfer is Prime Minister of Australia?

SECTION K ▲

Did you get a pension during the year to 30 June? . . . .

Type of Pension? . . . .

Which war? . . . .

Do you think anyone cares? . . . .

We need names . . . .

Can you walk? . . . .

Well can you hop? . . . .

Do you think complaining is part of the Great Australian Tradition? . . .

Goodness gracious me.   ©

Words fail me.

Carefully insert flap [f] into socket [j] folding along line p–q to meet at housing [d] and invert reverse section at [t] to rest on pinion [h] using tube of glue provided.   ☐

DECLARATION

I declare that the particulars in this return are true, certainly as true as anyone else's, and that they provide a fair to reasonable impression of the overall picture taking into consideration a margin for error and not counting the odd thing I may have overlooked in the rush to get this in on time, or very nearly. I am over eighteen or accompanied by an adult.

Signature . . . . Date . . . .

REGARDLESS OF YOUR TAX OBLIGATION, DO YOU WISH TO MAKE A DONATION ANYWAY?

Yes . . . . No . . . . Other . . . .

[specify]   **3n**

THINK ABOUT IT

I understand that I pay NOTHING for six weeks but that after that I'll be peddling like a duck.

CUSTOMER SERVICE DIVISION
Helping us to serve you

1. Where did you first hear about the Australian Taxation Office?

- ■ Read an advertisement.
- ■ Saw one of your boards on a building.
- ■ Was told about it by friends.
- ■ Attended a mortgagee sale.

2. How would you rate the service you received?

- ■ Excellent.
- ■ Fabulous.
- ■ Friendly and helpful.
- ■ Post-modern.
- ■ Refreshingly efficient.

OFFICE USE ONLY

Customer description:

- □ Compulsive liar.
- □ Muddler but not criminal.
- □ Unctuous buffoon.
- □ Complete mongrel.

Action taken:

- □ Cleaned him/her out.
- □ Summons issued.
- □ Other [specify].
- □ Other [specify].

89/90

Golf

A series of golf lessons with the Great White Whale, one of the true legends of the game. As a player he thrilled a generation, playing shots of astonishing power and virtuosity, many of them unusual and some of them not previously thought possible.

Hi there! I thought we'd begin with a few general things which might be of use to the weekend golfer because, when you think about it, most golfers are simply people who like to get out and hit a ball.

It's a great game, as we all know. Let's see if we can improve our performances by remembering a few basic rules. I can't offer a guarantee, of course, but these are the questions I'm most often asked about.

Playing the Shot

It is important to lift your head as you hit the ball. This ensures control and frequently improves distance. Also, if you keep your head down you won't see where you have hit the ball. The result is that you will lose the ball and of course you can't play the game without one.

I played with a young fellow recently who kept his head down for every single shot. He literally never knew where his ball had gone. Fortunately I was able to find it for him quite often on the green or in the hole, but what he does when I'm not there I shudder to think.

Stance

Very important. The correct stance is obviously crucial. The exact position is up to you. Make sure you are comfortable.

Although don't make the mistake of sitting down.

There are two main positions relative to the ball:

(a)   Too close, and

(b)   Too far away.

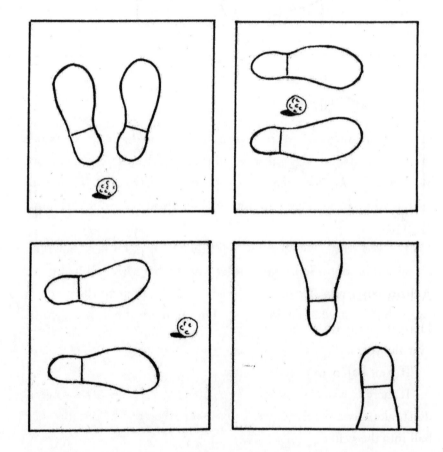

Many experienced players combine them. They stand too far from the ball, hit it, and then find that they are standing too close to it.

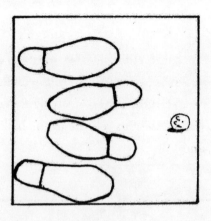

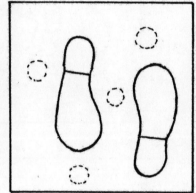

A Few Simple Tips

Here are some little pointers which I have found to be very helpful over the years.

If your ball is in trouble, shift it.

If there is water to the left of the fairway and safety to the right, don't take silly risks. Pull your front foot back about 18" and hit your ball into the water.

When you fail to get your weight through the ball properly, get your confidence back by banging the club repeatedly on the ground.

Putting

Putting is a separate game and there are as many putting styles as there are individual players. My own putting action might not work for anyone else. It doesn't work for me. Why the hell it should work for anyone else I can't imagine.

PUTT-ING ON THE RITZ

Scoring

Don't worry about how you are scoring. Why put pressure on yourself? Just concentrate on your shots. At the end of the round, look over the card and score yourself along the following lines.

A drive which hit a tree, second shot never found, a couple of other shots and four putts: Score Par.

A good drive, a second shot which would be on the green if the wind hadn't hauled it on to the next fairway, two third shots and an approach to within forty feet of the flag: Score Par.

A magnificent drive, long second shot into light rough, short third into heavy rough, a bit of tidying up, some approach shots and a few putts: Score Bogey (the penalty for a lapse in concentration).

LITTLE WAY   FAIR WAY

Twelve shots to the green and one putt: Score Bogey (good recovery).

Hit the green in one, eight putts: Score Bogey.

Hit the car park in one, took a drop, shanked ball into nearby lake, took a drop, drove beyond the green, missed it coming back, overhit gentle pitch-and-run, misread difficult lie down bank and lofted ball into sprinkler-housing on adjacent fairway, took a drop, missed ball altogether, moved it with foot, topped it into long grass, took a drop, troubled by low branches affecting swing, threw ball on to green, hit green with second throw, missed long putt by centimetres, missed next two attempts and tapped in with toe of shoe: Score Double Bogey. Make mental note to be careful on this hole next time.

WATER HAZARD

Enjoy Your Golf

One of the great things about golf is the opportunity it affords to simply get outside and enjoy the world we live in. The best time to appreciate the world we live in is about halfway through your down-swing. As you feel the club head beginning to accelerate towards the ball, pull your face up and have a good look at the surrounding countryside. Some regular players have trained themselves to study cloud formations as the ball is actually being struck.

The Grip

Many players have a reasonable swing but they throw it away with a bad grip. A hook or a slice can often be traced to a grip problem.

The correct grip is the Double-Lattice Multi-Stress Underlap grip in which the fingers of the left or leading hand are wound beneath the thumb of the right hand at the point where it crosses the apex of the shoulder at the top of the backswing, although obviously you do that the other way round if you're left-handed, and of course you reverse that if you're not.

The grip should be firm. There's nothing worse than playing an important shot and looking up to see your club disappearing over a big clump of conifers because you weren't holding on to it properly.

Your arms should feel nice and strong, there should be plenty of tension across the back of the shoulders, your hands and wrists should be rigid with that potential energy and strength and you should be able to see your knuckles going white with exertion and concentration. If your knuckles aren't white, perhaps golf isn't your game.

Imagine the Shot

Many famous golfers recommend 'picturing' each shot; imagining a 'film' of the shot being played. This is a useful technique and should be adopted whenever possible. Look at the shot. Imagine it being played. 'See' it in your 'mind'.

Then go home. Do not attempt to play the shot.

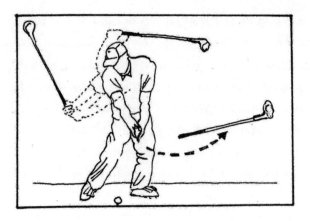

Bunker Shots

Don't 'psyche yourself out'. Assess the position carefully, with a positive outlook and a specific aim. Work out where you would like the ball to land. Then take a sand wedge, work your feet into the ground slightly to give yourself some traction, take a couple of practice swings and then pick the ball up and throw it on to the green.

Club Selection

It is important when selecting a club to be aware of the distance it is designed to hit. Let's have a look in the bag. Let's say you're playing a relatively standard par 4; it's about 450 yards from tee to green with bunkers left and right at about 260 yards, water down the left side and a forest to the right containing a number of tigers.

From the tee you'll need distance. A driver, a 1 wood or a 2 wood should get you over most of the trouble; ideally over the bunkers although personally I'd be just as happy to be over the water or over the tigers. As long as you get over something.

Your next shot, not counting a bit of cleaning up here and there, your next shot of any real importance, is very often a remarkable recovery shot and frequently requires a good lusty whack of about 200 yards. There are two ways to approach this: you can try to get to the green with, say, a 3 iron, or you can pull out the fairway wood and lay up, leaving yourself a pitch of about 186 yards.

Around the green the sand wedge comes into its own. This club is particularly useful for players who enjoy looking at flags. Get the flag lined up properly, try to guess how far away it is, and whether the fact that it's fluttering has anything to do with the wind. Look up at it and shift your feet a few times, then look at it again in case it moved while you were shifting your feet, now shorten the backswing slightly and play a fairly simple little pitch, looking at the flag as you commence the downswing. Don't worry about the ball, you can find that in a minute, it won't have gone far.

One further word about clubs: two of the most valuable clubs in the game, you have on your feet. You can very often solve quite difficult problems, which baffle less skilled golfers, by playing a judicious pitch with the foot iron. You will sometimes see a golfer standing under a low branch of a tree, bent double and with no room for a backswing, or obliged to chop a ball out of some grassy hollow with no view of the green. These golfers are only fooling themselves. Believe me, there are no shortcuts; if you want to play the game properly, you need the right equipment.

Here are the distances you ought to be looking for with each club in your bag.

Driver:—Anywhere from 1 to 500 yards in pretty well any direction.
3 wood:—14 yards.

DRIVER   WOOD

IRON

SAND   WEDGE (N.Z.)

1 iron:—There is no such thing as a 1 iron.

2 iron:—Difficult to tell. No one has ever found a shot hit with a 2 iron.

3 iron:—180–200 yards in regions where there are no trees.

4 iron:—Exactly the same as a 3 iron or a 5 iron.

5 iron:—140–600 yards, mainly to the right.

6 iron:—For playing a 5 iron shot with the wind behind you or a 7 iron shot which you wish to hook into oncoming traffic.

7 iron:—150 yards. Annually.

8 iron:—130–145 yards unless there is water within 20 ft.

9 iron:—Just short of any distance.

Pitching wedge:—See Driver.

Sand wedge:—3–5 inches.

Practice

How often do I practise?

I don't, but of course I'm not typical. I've reached a kind of Zen plateau where I no longer need to practise. I have a couple of general swings on the first tee with one of the longer irons, just to get the feeling back in my joints, but otherwise I seem to be beyond the stage where mere practice is of any real use.

I do sometimes practise an individual shot. For instance if I detect a slight swing-fault with my driver, the first ball I hit is frequently a practice shot and I don't start scoring until I get my rhythm right and hit a decent one.

In the case of chipping it is sometimes necessary to hit three or four practice balls before getting one to work. Obviously if the first ball runs up to the hole nicely there is no need to improve the shot and you should simply move on.

Putting practice can improve your score by several strokes and I recommend it be incorporated in every golfer's routine. The best time to practise your putting is immediately after you have putted, while the fault is still fresh in your mind. Put another ball down and have another try. Many golfers practise putting BEFORE THEY START PLAYING. I have never seen much mileage in this, since it is not clear until you are playing your round exactly what the fault might be, if any. Why sap your confidence by assuming that some of your putts won't go in? I stand up to every shot on the course believing in my own mind it will go in the hole. I don't play a shot until I am convinced in my own mind it will go in. I hate to think what my score would be if I faced reality prior to making contact with the ball. I may well go to pieces.

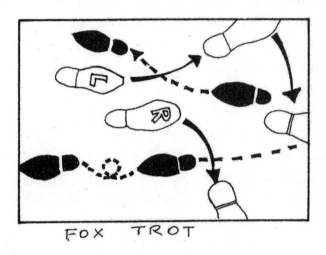

FOX TROT

The Tempo of the Swing

The rhythm, or TEMPO, of your golf swing is crucial. If you are rushing your shots or trying to force the ball, the chances are control will be lost and your game will deteriorate. Each player has a different swing and no two TEMPOS are the same. In fact, I quite often use a different TEMPO for every shot. I have been asked about this many times and although I have never listed my various TEMPOS before, it may help some struggling golfers to know that I have at least five main ones:

1. Very slow and deliberate takeaway, holding the club at the top of the backswing for a moment to steady the shot and then

swinging through the ball at the speed of sound. Useful in all conditions and a TEMPO I personally favour.

2. Beginning the downswing before the backswing is completed and stopping the club head as it hits the ball. This eliminates the need for transferral of weight and minimises the importance of club selection.

3. Extremely long takeaway forcing the upper part of the body well back so you can almost see underneath the ball, and then, at some instinctive signal from the brain, jumping into the shot and driving the club head powerfully up the front of the ball and into a follow through of astonishing velocity.

4. Lifting the club away more or less vertically and then slamming it down on to the very back of the ball and through the layers of rich loam which lie many hundreds of feet under the earth's surface.

5. Taking the club head away inside the line and starting the down-swing with a forward thrust of the hips and a simultaneous lifting of the front shoulder which takes the club back outside the line from the top of the swing but inside the line again once the drive from back leg pushes the hands ahead of the ball with the un-cocking of the wrists, and the acceleration of the club head itself pulls the hands, the back elbow and the ball into alignment for the moment of impact. This tempo is not easy to repeat at will and I personally have only ever achieved it once. I was attempting a number 1 but was surprised by a sprinkler system at an important point in the downswing.

Now go out and shoot a sixty-three.

What you do on the second hole is up to you.

Australia and How to Repair It

In case of fire break glass.

Operation Manual

Congratulations. You are a part-owner of 'Australia'™, a fully serviced time-share resort and manufacturing centre set in the attractive environs of South East Asia. (Still Selling but Hurry.)

We trust you will be satisfied with your 'State'™ and that you have noted the names of participating dealers in your 'City'™.

Despite the best traditions and the highest standards of design and maintenance, management wishes to advise that owners may experience some minor problems. 'Australia'™ is still in the early stages of development and many teething troubles require constant attention.

During the past year for instance, head office has been inundated with calls from people complaining that they had been charged for a Bicentennial but had not received one. In fact only the 'Sydney'™ Model was fitted with a Bicentennial money-tap and the function has now been discontinued for obvious reasons.

A slight fault in the wiring of the Economics display screen has been discovered and it is with regret that we announce the overall position is somewhat less attractive than we may have indicated. Notice the position of the mustering station nearest to your seat.

Due to an increasing number of calls to our offices, it has been decided to produce a guide to the Use and Care of 'Australia'™. May we suggest you keep the guide near the unit at all times.

Should a problem emerge, refer to the guide and apply the remedy outlined in the handy-to-use table. If pain persists, see a doctor.

Troubleshooting

Problem	Probable Cause	What to Do
GRAUNCHING SOUND COMING FROM TREASURY	Balance of Payments valve clogged.	This problem may be accompanied by sparks from the back of the main panel and an increase in the Hawke sports-photograph syndrome. Turn unit off at wall. Check use-by date on budgetry estimates. Place bucket under explanation printout tray, opening Keating filter and leave overnight. Have area sprayed in morning.
SPORTING RESULTS NOT WHAT THEY WERE IN THE 1950s. VERY COMMON COMPLAINT IN THE HOSPITALITY INDUSTRY	It is the 1980s.	Come to terms with Probable Cause. Have a nice day.
GREENHOUSE EFFECT	Greed.	Nothing.
THE ARTS	Need to keep unemployment confined to lower section of batting order.	Spend small fraction of cost of National Tennis Centre. Make speech: 'Vital We Retain Distinctive Cultural Identity'. Give money to Bureaucrats.

'AUSTRALIAN LITERATURE'™	Misreading of Handbook. 'Australian Literature'™ is not a Pleasure Function. See Bourgeois.	Plug the Old Friends and Relations Pin into the back of the Funding Network Job Inventor. Fold results back into Private Production Opening. Suck gently on Literature Board Valve until flow is regulated, then direct into Publishing Output Mode. Pull Premier's Award Knob until fully extended and allow Favours and Tradeoff Sacks to empty. If Loss Quotient unacceptable, push Tax Flusher and open Development Grant Function. Key in Personal Bank Account Digit Number. Enter Password. (Try 'Quality and Innovation'.) Put name at bottom of list and send to four people you went to school with.
THE ABC	He's just popped out for a moment or two. He was here a minute ago.	Someone will get back to you later today. Friday. Monday at the very latest.
BANK PROFITS AT ALARMING LEVELS	Secrecy screen not working. Truth leaking through code de-scrambler. Check Hawke posturing switch.	Increase Home Lending rates. Slap thigh.

Problem	Probable Cause	What to Do
LIBERAL PARTY FAILS TO OPERATE, EMITS CONTINUOUS MOAN	Howard-eject button jammed.	Locate wiring to back-up decoy. Re-route power lead to spring-loaded hinges on far right of central dingbattery. Pull Chaney-supply cord from upper housing and plug into lower socket. Cross fingers. Guess own weight.
THE PRESS	Too great a diversity of Ownership.	Open back of Government section. Pull out Media Legislation panel. Take central decision-making mechanism and plug into money-fellation unit. Obtain paper through completely independent paper-supply feeder at rear of money-fellation unit. Enter facts into PR convertor attached to money-fellation unit. Read printout into money-fellation recorder. Caution: if competition indicator blinks, turn off immediately and replace roll.
TELEPHONE SERVICES CHARGED FOR BUT UNAVAILABLE	Loose connection between Telecom profit accelerator and actual usefulness counter.	Call service department. Please enjoy the music.

CPI SENDING BACK PHOTOGRAPHS OF OTHER SIDE OF MOON	The industrial output flow-pipe has been wrongly labelled in the manual of the Keating Delux model. Subsequently redesignated '24-hour constant industrial in-flow tube'. This was not picked up earlier due to a distortion in commodity prices. We apologise for any inconvenience. If the unit was purchased from 'Creans' (The Working Man's Friend) it is unfortunately out of warranty.	Whistle.
QUEENSLAND	Unknown but it looks bad, Your Honour.	500 units. Detective Sergeant Simpson. Race 4.
HOUSE PRICES	Share prices.	Share houses.

Problem	Probable Cause	What to Do
JOHN DAWKINS	Liked his education so much he bought the company.	Answer all questions. [1] If a student cannot afford his/her university fees he/she will: a) Take in washing. b) Mow lawns. c) Pick up a little babysitting work. d) Sell drugs. [2] The drugs will be sold: a) Around the family home. b) Around the House of Representatives. c) Around the Mulberry Bush. d) Around the university. [3] Make up own question. Mark out of 100. Enclose fee.
CHILD POVERTY	Adult poverty.	Bob will eliminate child poverty by 1990. Please enjoy the music.

Warranty and Conditions Attaching to Citizenship

The CITIZEN hereby warrants that any or all complaints referred to herein are genuine and bona fide and have been witnessed by authorised persons or their agents.

All information provided hereintofore is fair and reasonable and all goods were checked by suitably trained artisans upon despatch and/or transmission.

No CITIZEN will at any time speak in a manner likely to bring discredit or opprobrium on this his/her native/adopted/wide/brown/ other [specify] land in any wise and in any capacity unless said person is an imbecile or a member of Her Majesty's Opposition.

The penalties for abuses or breaches of this or any other Regulation in whole or in part shall be those laid down in *The Crimes Act [Sundry Complaints Division] 1927* (and subsequent amendments) taking into consideration those writs in accordance with Normal Redress in Matters of Umbrage, Dudgeon and Righteousness, the Treatment of Pelts by Minors, Claims against the State by Individuals Not Yet Born (R v. Jung), the Statutory Maintenance of Sealanes and other concerns bearing in the material detail on the case WITH THE SINGLE EXCEPTION of Writs in Fee Complicit. These shall be deemed to include: Claims by a Shire against itself, Claims by Drivers against Roadways and Sidings (SRA v. Moss), Claims by Buildings against Architects or their agents, and Claims involving two foreign nations (W. Indies v. Pakistan), where the State Boundaries are those determined by Ordnance Survey No. 73982 and $\pi = 22/7$.

Those CITIZENS sniggering at the back will stay behind afterwards and see Mr Richardson.

The CITIZEN agrees that this country (hereinafter referred to as The Entire Joint) is in GOOD and CAPABLE hands and is superbly managed in every way and that any problems and/or breakdowns due to equipment failure or negligence of any type whatsoever are THE SOLE AND COMPLETE RESPONSIBILITY of the CITIZEN and are nothing to do with the government and are specifically nothing to do with Robert Jesus Lee Hawke, THE PEOPLE's CHOICE [all stand] who has at all times struggled to carry the difficult load of office and has done so most NOBLY under very bloody difficult circumstances.

The CITIZEN furthermore warrants and UNDERTAKES TO KEEP WARRANTING that whatever the apparent failings of Paul Keating

WHICH ARE ONLY VERY SLIGHT IF THEY EXIST AT ALL, there is and can be no doubt whatsoever in the mind of a reasonable person that he IS VERY GOOD AT WHAT HE DOES. The names of the people he has done it to can be inspected during normal business hours at the office of any Parisian tailor.

Someone will get back to you. Please enjoy the music.

Itty Bitty Litty Critties

Hamlet by William Shakespeare

Boy returns from university to find father dead, mother married to uncle. Takes it out on girlfriend. Can't decide what do to. ('To be or not to be', etc.) Kills girlfriend's father by accident. Girlfriend suicides. Girlfriend's brother wants revenge on account of family disappearing. Hamlet by now existentialist, allows himself to be tricked into showdown in which everyone not already accounted for dies. (Big finish.)

Othello by William Shakespeare

Iago (archetypal shit with nothing better to do) convinces king that queen is having affair on circumstantial evidence involving handkerchief. King kills queen. King realises he has been complete tool. Complicated by race issue. (See *Machiavelli*.)

King Lear by William Shakespeare

Ageing father devises pompous test for daughters. (Declare love for me or suffer consequences.) Cinderella speaks truth, ugly sisters profess unconditional devotion, etc. Stupid king rejects Cinders, takes up with Edmund, husband of ugly sister (it's a man's world), goes mad and finds himself in blizzard with blind Edgar. (Some kind of mixup here.) King realizes, too late, love of Cinders worth having because real.

Pride and Prejudice by Jane Austen

Elizabeth Bennet (mother obsessed with marrying daughters off, father amusing but not very helpful) dislikes Mr Darcy because he is too PROUD. She becomes PREJUDICED against him and even likes one man (Wickham) because he speaks ill of Darcy. Her life is occupied with sisters Jane, who is calm and loves Bingham, and Lydia, who loves soldiers (Wickham) and who brings family into disrepute (Wickham). Elizabeth inadvertently discovers that Darcy is UNBELIEVABLY RICH. They marry immediately. Mother knew best.

Emma by Jane Austen

Beautiful daughter of silly old fool has nothing better to do than manipulate and matchmake in snobbish rural society. Behaves very stupidly and messes up life of Harriet Smith, a harmless woman who should obviously marry local farmer. Eventually marries best friend Mr Knightley, the resonance of whose name she had previously failed to notice. (See *Clueless*.)

Persuasion by Jane Austen

Featuring Anne Elliot (plain, educated, sensitive, wise, family down on luck). Father and spoilt sister go to Bath for society, Anne to another sister, selfish, stupid, married to cheerful farmer. Children get sick, Anne tower of strength. Visited by Cpt. Wentworth. (Naval man at time of Trafalgar = national hero.) Wentworth and Anne have met before, have loved, and Anne has rejected Wentworth's proposal of marriage but heart not still. Farmer's sister falls off seawall and Wentworth realises he's an idiot about Anne. Hooray!

The Count of Monte Cristo by Victor Hugo

Edmond Dantès (France, corruption, treachery) is wrongly imprisoned for life. Old prisoner tells him of a great fortune in a cave on an island and when old dies, Dantes sews himself inside dead man's body bag, is removed from prison and escapes. Makes way to island, gets treasure and returns to France representing himself as the Count of Monte Cristo. Gets stuck right into enemies who put him in jail. Ruins some. Kills others. No beg your pardons whatsoever. On for young and old. He had a long time to think about it and he gets right on with it. Revenge in spades, on all fronts, and no mistake.

David Copperfield by Charles Dickens

Fatherless boy rises above bullying by stepfather, enjoys seaside with Aunt Betsy and lovely Mr Dick. Marries silly girl with annoying dog. She dies. (But wait, there's more!)

Moby Dick by Herman Melville

Man meets whale. Man loses whale. Man tries to kill whale. Man loses leg. Whale finds man. Man loses marbles. Whale kills man. (Metaphors all over the place. Man v. Nature, Life v. Death, Dark v. Light, Christian v. Pagan, Arsenal v. Manchester United.)

Great Expectations by Charles Dickens

Boy (Pip) helps escaped convict (Magwitch) on marshes. Spends childhood happily with blacksmith Joe and land-girl Biddy although is sometimes invited to big house (Miss Havisham: old, loopy, cobwebs everywhere, clocks in house all stopped, etc.) to play with rich girl, Estella. Pip informed he is to become a gentleman at expense of mysterious benefactor. Pip becomes gentleman and snob, believing Miss Havisham to be benefactor and expecting to marry Estella. Benefactor turns out to be Magwitch (Australian connection here) who also turns out to be Estella's father. Bad spell of Miss Havisham on Estella broken by Pip's love. About time too! (All stand.)

Anna Karenina by Leo Tolstoy

Married woman (Russian, upper class) is in love with man not her husband. Completely absorbed in her love for him to exclusion of all else. Cannot concentrate on other things at all. Tries really hard but simply can't. Ends in tears. (See *Magritte*.)

Tess of the D'Urbervilles by Thomas Hardy

Poor, rural, Tess Durbeyfield is raped by rich distant cousin D'Urberville, has baby, which dies. Tess cuts off hair and works as milkmaid. Educated rich man (Angel Clare) falls in love with her and they marry. He confesses a day of sexual debauchery with another woman. She forgives him and tells him about her baby. He does NOT forgive her and leaves for South America. Years later he returns and they meet at the house where Tess is living with D'Urberville. Tess goes into the house briefly, murders D'Urberville and then leaves with Angel. They wander through the countryside, doomed, happy. (See *Bonnie and Clyde*.)

Heart of Darkness by Joseph Conrad

Man is sent to Africa to take over from Mr Kurtz, who is branch manager. Trip rather dull. Mr Kurtz dead on arrival. (Conrad was Polish.)

Ulysses by James Joyce

Formative modern work. Entire novel set on one day. Classic outsider Leopold Bloom (Jew, advertising, sensitive, Irish, cuckold) attends funeral, pub, brothel, with young man. Wife has last word (husband not as good as boyfriend, psychology of marriage blighted by death of infant child). Wife's monologue caused book to be banned. (See *Catholic*.) Thought by male academics and critics to be great expression of woman's thoughts. (See *Sluts*.)

The Fortunes of Richard Mahony
by Henry Handel Richardson

Man (dreamer, hoper/hopeless, author's father) emigrates to Australia, goes to goldfields, fails, goes into business, fails, returns to Britain, fails, re-emigrates to Australia, practises as doctor, fails, concentrates on marriage and family, fails, attempts to keep mind in order, fails. (Wife a tower of strength.)

Nineteen Eighty-Four
by George Orwell (Eric Blair)

Novel written in 1930s (cf. Stalin) suggesting powerful and unscrupulous interests will work to obtain control of democratic process, orchestrate media, institutionalise 'freedoms' and crush opposition in name of nation and people. Couldn't happen here.

Lord of the Flies by William Golding

English public schoolboys cast adrift on island behave badly or well or neither. Those who behave badly kill those who behave well, leaving future to be determined by those who behave badly and those who can't decide. (cf. England.)

Voss by Patrick White

Doomed explorer whose name isn't really Voss embarks on doomed attempt to cross Australia. Expedition marred by fact that both explorer and enterprise are doomed. Perhaps whole country is doomed. (Discuss.) Surprise ending in that explorer doesn't die earlier than he does.

Owls Do Cry by Janet Frame

The Withers family live in New Zealand. Mum Withers, Dad Withers, everybody Withers, the children Wither, the dog Withers. Get it?

Stiff,
Director's Diary 2004

Sometime in 2002, it was decided to make a pair of movies based on Shane Maloney's first two novels, Stiff *and* The Brush Off. *The arrangement was that Sam Neill would direct one of these films, and I would direct the other. Sam selected* The Brush Off, *which is set in the art world.* Stiff, *the one I'm directing, will be made first. Next slide please.*

The central character in the novels, Murray Whelan, is a natural for film and television. He is a slightly shambolic middle-range political advisor with a healthy scepticism, a gift for pressing on regardless and an interest in attractive women with nice personalities. His boss, the demanding Angelo Agnelli MP, is a government minister whose smooth administration is unhorsed, in each story, by the sudden appearance of a dead body. Detective genre without the detective.

David Wenham likes the novels and will play Murray. In terms of confidence-building, this is up there with the invention of the wheel. I haven't met David before but have observed his career with admiration and we are certainly paid more attention in restaurants than has hitherto been my personal experience. In script discussions David is astute, generous and relaxed. His suggestions are excellent. He thinks, for example, that instead of a briefcase, Murray should carry his stuff around in a plastic bag because he's that kind of guy and David says he will make this look completely natural. When asked why he is so confident about this, David says because he carries all his own stuff around in a plastic bag. David's instinct in such matters will turn out to be a matter of some significance. Later, during filming, when dangerous things happen to Murray, David will seldom use a stand-in. Once he has got Murray right, David will back himself in.

A full cast read-through gives the performers and the crew their only chance to see the whole story. After this, the filming process is fragmentary. The story is scheduled and shot in a completely different order. I enjoy our read-through and David hides the comedy so well he looks as if he's being funny by accident.

Because of the relatively low budget the movie must be shot in twenty days (a normal shoot here would be about two months and in the US movies are known to take hundreds of years to shoot), so we will need to box exceeding clever. At one stage of the movie, Murray Whelan's car must be driven off the road at high speed at night in heavy rain and dropped in a lake. The art director, Chris Kennedy, who can process his own weight in information every four seconds, gets a piece of paper and draws the sequence: driving rain, oncoming vehicle, lights, pumping brakes, car skids off road, turns upside down, car crashes into water. 'Excellent,' I say. 'Is all that possible?' 'Yes. Should be,' says Chris. 'Where will we be able to shoot all that?' I ask. 'No idea,' he grins, giving me a copy of his drawings. Laszlo Baranyai, who will shoot *Stiff*, is another who can think fast and deep at the same time. He and I go through the script and discuss the feeling we need from each scene and where the rhythm is in the story. There's not much Laszlo and Chris don't know about where we're going and I make a mental note to maintain eye contact with both of them at all times.

Day 1

Seven a.m., we're filming at the old Four and Twenty Pie factory next to the railway line in Kensington and Laszlo is beaming from a crane because it is raining. Much of the film takes place in heavy rain and this is a handy start. By mid-morning we are upstairs in an industrial office with David and actors Susie Dee and Denis Moore. I'm crouched in a low scrum in a room about the size of a stamp, watching 'the split', which is a little video screen showing what the camera is seeing. At one stage David as Murray picks the phone up, does something he doesn't like, stops, puts the phone down, picks it up again with his hand and head in exactly the same position, does something he does like and continues with the scene. This not only saves us the trouble of starting again but indicates that David can concentrate on his performance in the context of an editing process which won't occur for a month. The scrum freezes. We look at each other. Did we just hear him do that? The continuity was perfect. What is this? There is a very good feeling in the room.

After two days at the factory, Laszlo and the crew have lit and shot forty-nine setups and we've completed nearly twelve minutes of finished screen time which, as Damon Runyon would say, is by no means hay. My brilliant first assistant, Annie Maver, has a cascading, peeling laugh which lifts and builds and then reaches a cruising height and ultimately decks the halls with boughs of holly. People who have never previously encountered this machine of delight normally need a couple of days to acclimatise. This, too, is going well.

Day 3

We're in a restaurant in Federation Square, shooting scenes with Murray and Agnelli, including their crucial early meeting and the final scene in the picture. While we're here, in order to help suggest Agnelli's rise through the ALP, Barry Jones, John Button and Joan Kirner have generously agreed to appear in some scenes with the excellent Mick Molloy, whose Agnelli slips straight into gear.

Day 5

This morning David has to be chased up a laneway by a car and hurl himself into a large pile of rubbish before belting back to another location and peeling off several pages of fairly subtle dialogue with Sam and Mick in a room whose temperature would ripen tomatoes at sixty paces. David does the running himself, of course, avoids the speeding car and hurls himself into a vast pile of rubbish to applause on all sides. Back in the office location the difference between the light levels outside and those in the room require black film material to be put on the windows. We then put a dozen people in the small room and begin to rehearse. It is by now very hot and lesser talents would melt. David, Sam and Mick, however, are superb and these scenes will be among the strongest in the film.

Day 6

Today is Deb Kennedy's first day and it's good to see her. We were married in *Death in Brunswick* and although she's one of the best actors in the country she's probably best known for squirting the words 'not happy, Jan' through a small hole at the bottom of a window. Her voice is rich and her eyes can fill with enormous patience and deep disdain at the same time. We also spend some time in the Turkish Welfare Centre, which Chris Kennedy and his team have constructed inside a voluminous hall and where we are greatly helped by the actor Ramez Tabit, who lights up on camera and becomes the soul of the place.

Day 7

On Day 7 we shoot a scene in which a man called Memo confesses to a murder. George Prataris, who plays Memo, does it beautifully. As we leave, Annie and I are invited into the camera truck, whose name is Pearl. Laszlo and Miranda solemnly draw out two cardboard boxes bearing the names of film stock manufacturers; one is marked Kodak, one Eastman. The Kodak box contains red wine, the Eastman white. As we sitting there drinking Kodak after a good first week, I ask Laszlo about the big accident sequence. He tells me not to worry about it. Chris's drawings are right. It won't be easy and people will say it is impossible, he says, but it will all come together. We have some more Kodak.

Day 9

Trouble at mill. We're filming above the roof of Murray's house when the remote focus breaks down. This slows us and will require a rescheduling of the shots we've lost. We can't really afford this and must make time by shooting other scenes faster. Inside the house, there are about four thousand of us in three rooms. This is actor Darren Casey's first day. He has one scene. He is quite worried. He arrives, gets it right first time and leaves.

Over lunch there is a meeting about getting the roof to come off Murray's house in post-production by shooting the preceding scene in a particular way and then taking the shots into a computer environment and using animatronics. I nod a fair bit and maintain eye contact with Laszlo and Chris. They seem happy so I relax and have a cup of tea with the gaffer, Darryl, who has subjected his best boy, the noble Anthony, to continuous low-level flak over the performance of the All Blacks in the World Cup. The Wallabies/All Blacks semifinal is on this weekend. Ant and I look forward to it. Bring it on. Let Darryl's humiliation begin.

Day 12

The result of the rugby is not important. It is a childish game which has never really interested me. More pressingly, as we are getting the shot of the house that is required in order to do the computer whizzbangery with the roof, an enormous storm hits and we rethink the afternoon so we can use the rain. It's always messy to change the schedule on the run and I'm sure there are problems but no one complains and what we get is very good indeed, with David inventing his dialogue as he goes. We may discover something David can't do but it hasn't looked like happening yet.

Day 15

On Day 15 we shoot Darren's first scenes in the office. He has five of them. He is quite worried. He arrives, gets them all right first time and leaves. Deborah and David agree to shoot three scenes in one great sweeping progress featuring three separate arguments and using the full length of the office. They eat it alive and it is not until the following day we learn there is a hair in the gate. This means a strand of hair has been caught in the camera as we were filming. The footage is unusable and we must reshoot it.

In the afternoon we're in a hotel in Clifton Hill shooting a Labor Party branch meeting, a Beckett scene, rich in boredom. Chris has hung a large yellow tarp up behind the stage with 'True Believers Karaoke Night' on it in red, David sits on the stage and Laszlo has put the camera down low to David's right, looking up. It's a beautiful shot and I wander over from the split and tell Laszlo it looks great. 'When I was a young cameraman in Budapest,' he tells me, 'that is how you had to shoot the Russian leaders. It makes them look big, strong, important.' I compliment David on his playing of the scene and his eyes soften: 'My father was a friend of Fred Daly,' he says. 'I grew up licking envelopes in Fred Daly's electoral office. I've been to meetings like this since I was a kid.'

We finish early today so David can go the AFI Awards where he is the red-hot favourite to be named best actor for his remarkable performance in *Getting Square*. Like many of us in the industry, David is concerned about the likely effects of the amusingly named 'Free Trade Agreement'. I flick the tellie on when I get home and see him mention this in a gracious acceptance speech.

The following morning we reshoot the 'hair in the gate' shot. One of the actors asks if he can have his photo taken with David. 'I'm sorry to have to do this to you David,' he says as they pose. 'But I work in the building industry and nobody believes I'm doing a film with David Wenham. I got time off to do this scene the other day. But when I said I had to come back and do it again because there was a hair in the gate, no one knew what I was talking about. So this will prove I'm actually doing a film.' After shooting the studio parts of the roof scenes at Murray's house, we go outside and shoot Angelo Agnelli taking a call from Murray in the company of a young bit part actor called Steve Bracks who moonlights as the Victorian State Premier.

Day 19

On Day 19 we shoot the enormous accident sequence. We start at dusk. We have agreed to get certain parts of the job done by certain times, so as not to inconvenience nearby horse stables, residents and local businesses, so the logistics are somewhat character-building. We have tall water towers and tankers for simulating the rain, we have two yellow Renaults, both expendable, a massive crane to drop one of them into the water, a team of police divers to go down and re-attach the car so it can be pulled back out again; we have two cameras, lights on both sides of the river, we have the art department dressing ramps and bits of ground and cars. And we have Chris's dog Ethel who will feature as the stray dog who sticks with Murray through the rest of the film.

We drop the car in the water. Great. Move on. Our guide is still the drawing Chris did in the office. Laszlo works out how best to shoot these sequences and all night we shoot the various parts of the accident. It is nearly dawn and Chris is walking Ethel toward the car as David tiptoes along in clothes dripping from the river. Ethel walks gently and cautiously, listening to Chris but completely in sympathy with Murray as if taking her cue from David. When they get to the car and the sense of danger has lifted, Ethel jumps in and sits in the offside driver's seat. The car drives off. Perfect. The big impossible night-shoot is all done and we've got several extra shots which weren't in the schedule. This is a remarkable outfit.

Monday

I go into the editing room where I sit with Wayne Hyett, who has been joining the footage up day by day as we've been shooting and already has an assembly which currently runs 103 minutes. We'll need to take about ten minutes out of it and we have a couple of problems but they're addressable. When Murray swims to shore and scrambles up the bank to safety after his car accident, for example, we need to shorten the sequence slightly and this is hard to do because there's nothing else we can cut to. We can't cut from David coming up in the middle of the water to David reaching the shore. We can't cut from David getting out of the water to David at the top of the bank. We need a couple of extra shots of Ethel to give ourselves something to alter the pace with, and we're still waiting on the computer miracle whereby the roof comes off the house. The shots we need after shooting officially finishes are called 'pickups'. These are scheduled and shot. Ethel looks great in the new shots and we can redesign that section of the film.

We meet with the post-production sound team and with Jeremy Smith, who will write the score. Jeremy was previously a Hunter and Collector and has already begun beavering away at Murray music in the basement of his house in Fitzroy.

Wayne and I begin to whittle. The odd scene disappears altogether. Sometimes we don't need the beginning of a scene. Sometimes we can get out a bit earlier at the end. We try some things, find they don't work and have to put humpty dumpty together again. We get the duration down to about ninety-four minutes and we show it to a few people and listen carefully to what they say. We also show it to the investors, to Channel 7 and Southern

Star, to the Film Finance Corporation and to Film Victoria. Wayne starts taking out the temporary music he has been using as a guide, and putting Jeremy's music in. The post-production schedule is being run by Colleen Milling, who should be running Telstra. The service is excellent, the technical backup is immediate and the customer is always right. The computerised removal of Murray's roof works brilliantly, Jeremy gets his final music cues done and suddenly we're in a sound suite mixing the final picture.

Sunday 18 April

We have hired one of the cinemas in the Australian Centre for the Moving Image in Federation Square and have invited the cast and crew to a screening. The screening turns into a very satisfactory afternoon in fine company.

Sunday 30 June

Stiff goes to air and wins the ratings.

Letters from the School

MEMO TO ALL STUDENTS FROM THE HEAD

I don't know how many times I have to say this. The playground equipment is there for exercise and for fun. But, as I have repeatedly said, care must be taken or serious injuries will result. This sort of thing, for example, is simply not on. Hanging off the bars with nothing between you and the ground is an accident waiting to happen.

I've spoken to Laurie Keete about his irresponsible actions in this instance and he has accepted that, if something had gone wrong, he might have broken his neck.

Matron is particularly concerned that she might not have the resources if someone sustains a major injury. She has only one part-time assistant two days a week.

For goodness' sake. Grow up. Enjoy yourselves by all means but try to stop short of idiocy.

Dear Mr and Mrs Keete,

I have had occasion recently to talk to Laurie about irresponsible behaviour in the playground. He may have mentioned this. It was in relation to hanging upside down on the bars, a dangerous practice and one which is strictly forbidden. Laurie made the point, in our refreshingly honest discussion, that he is a talented all-round sportsman and can perform tricks which, were others to attempt them, would lead to serious trouble. This is precisely the point. If others tried to imitate Laurie, I shudder to think what might happen. Laurie must be conscious of his important role as a leader in encouraging others to operate within their limits.

On another matter, it has since been drawn to my attention by one of the senior teachers that Laurie has been dyeing his hair blue. I wonder if there is some reason for this. He has not received permission from anyone here. There were some hijinks at the school swimming sports on Friday and we do turn a blind eye to some larrikin tendencies in regard to the displaying of house colours, especially in relation to support for the relay teams. It is now Tuesday, however, and Laurie's hair is still a very vivid blue. In fact, his appearance is rather peculiar. At his age, of course, they think this sort of thing is clever, but unless he actually wants to look like a rainbow I suggest he present himself more in line with regulations 4–12 in the school handbook.

Thank you.

Louden Clearmessage
Deputy Head
St Expensives

Dear Parent or Guardian,

I regret that some slight concerns have emerged in relation to aspects of Book Club. Many of you will be aware of this important initiative, begun in response to declining levels of literacy and very well supported by the English staff. A reading programme has been worked out, featuring works designed to stimulate young minds and to encourage an interest in ideas. Despite the best efforts of organisers, however, Book Club is often regarded as just an excuse to fool around, a problem which the facing image demonstrates very clearly.

Many of these students have obviously not read the book. There is inattention. There is chatter. There is complete disregard for the nature and purpose of the exercise. No benefit can accrue from this programme unless students seize the opportunity presented to them. This is not a time for immaturity, for lack of interest, or for wasting everyone's time.

These students are not just letting the programme and the school down; they're letting their teachers down, their parents down and their friends down. But more importantly, they are letting themselves down.

I expect some improvement over time but so far this is a disappointing response.

Starling, second from the left, bottom row, come and see me afterwards.

Iva Krapp-Daley

Iva Krapp-Daley
Co-ordinator
Book Club

The Secretary
The Wodda Packer-Galahs Institute
Wodda 3082

Dear Madam,

As you know, we have quite a number of your charges in the school. The association with your boarding establishment is one we value greatly and, as you know, some of our best students have come to us from a Packer-Galahs background.

Unfortunately, I write to outline some worrying developments in the school, which we think may perhaps originate in the home.

We have seen evidence for some time of collusion during tests conducted in the school, particularly in the maths and sciences area. Answers are often identical and even errors are sometimes replicated faithfully over entire classes. It is very difficult for us to assess the individual students properly in this atmosphere, and our claim to inculcate a strong sense of responsibility and self-sufficiency is consequently in some jeopardy.

I wonder if I could prevail on you to have a word with the students at your earliest convenience, and impress upon them the need to think for themselves, to finish their own work, and to compete against one another. This is the basis of our education system and, indeed, of our entire society.

Security cameras recently picked up the image attached, of one of our better female students talking to a male student during an algebra test. The boy, pictured right, who has hitherto proven rather a slow learner with an attitude problem, nevertheless appears to have topped the state in trigonometry, an honour he shares with the girl (left). This result, while gratifying, is of some concern given that collaboration is clearly at epidemic levels.

Yrs

Sue Pervisor

Sue Pervisor
Curriculum Planning
St Expensives

Dear Mr and Mrs Kiddner,

As you may be aware, some gym equipment has gone missing in recent weeks from the storeroom at the rear of the pavilion. One of your sons was seen attempting to break into the storeroom, and I'm afraid that when questioned about what he was doing (he was supposed to be at orchestra practice) he said he was looking for ants. Why he would come up with such a pathetic explanation for his behaviour is not obvious to us. I've spoken to other staff members and no one reported any project involving a need for ants. When asked why he thought there might be ants under the storeroom, your boy said, 'I could smell them.'

You may care to discuss this with us. The pilfering of school equipment is a very serious matter indeed and the ants story, which your young bloke seems to be sticking to, is little short of ludicrous.

Jim Teacher
Head of Phys Ed.
St Expensives

The Howard Apology

Delivered by John Howard on 3 July 2000 on The Games

Good evening. My name is John Howard and I'm speaking to you from Sydney, Australia, host city of the year 2000 Olympic Games.

At this important time, and in an atmosphere of international goodwill and national pride, we here in Australia—all of us—would like to make a statement before all nations.

Australia, like many countries in the new world, is intensely proud of what it has achieved in the past 200 years. We are a vibrant and resourceful people. We share a freedom born in the abundance of nature, the richness of the earth, the bounty of the sea. We are the world's biggest island. We have the world's longest coastline. We have more animal species than any other country. Two-thirds of the world's birds are native to Australia. We are one of the few countries on earth with our own sky. We are a fabric woven of many colours and it is this that gives us our strength.

However, these achievements have come at great cost. We have been here for 200 years but before that, there was a people living here. For 40,000 years they lived in a perfect balance with the land. There were many Aboriginal nations, just as there were many Indian nations in North America and across Canada, as there were many Maori tribes in New Zealand and Incan and Mayan peoples in South America. These indigenous Australians lived in areas as different from one another as Scotland is from Ethiopia. They lived in an area the size of Western Europe. They did not even have a common language. Yet they had their own laws, their own beliefs, their own ways of understanding.

We destroyed this world. We often did not mean to do it. Our forebears, fighting to establish themselves in what they saw as a harsh environment, were creating a national economy. But the Aboriginal world was decimated. A pattern of disease and dispossession was established. Alcohol was introduced. Social and racial differences were allowed to become fault lines. Aboriginal families were broken up. Sadly, Aboriginal health and education are responsibilities we have still yet to address successfully.

I speak for all Australians in expressing a profound sorrow to the Aboriginal people. I am sorry. We are sorry. Let the world know and understand, that it is with this sorrow, that we as a nation will grow and seek a better, a fairer and a wiser future. Thank you.

Doorstop Poems

A series of poems made from verbatim transcripts of interviews given by the nation's leaders. These are best read between the lines.

John Howard

The Tao of Howard

Look, I have said all
I am going to say
About that.
            Don't ask
The same question
Fifteen different ways.

18 September 1997

Alexander Downer

My Greatest Hero

I don't know.

Isn't that
An incredibly difficult

Question?

It would have to be,
You'd have to ask
Yourself the

Question:

Who is the person
Who's had the most positive
Influence on the whole of the

Millennium?

And,
You know,
It is tempting to say

Don Bradman

But I think the honest
Truth has to be somebody like
Caxton
Who developed the printing press because without

Printing

Then the whole of civilisation would have turned out to be
Completely
Different.

30 December 1998

Philip Ruddock

A Plea for Understanding

If desperation
Is born out of a desire
To achieve a migration outcome that you're not entitled to,
We're dealing with
Desperate people.

Let's understand
What we're dealing with
Here. We have a group of people who go out there

To release people who are lawfully detained,
To breach our laws,
They take children with them and
They hold themselves out to be fulfilling some
Public duty,
Under the name of 'There are no borders'
Or like euphemisms.

30 March 2002

Simon Crean

If…

Well, they
Shouldn't be there,
That's the starting point.

And if
Labor was in office, they
Wouldn't be there.
This war is wrong, and we
Shouldn't be part of it.

And if
I was Prime Minister today,
I would bring them home.

But
The reality is,
The reality is
I'm not the Prime Minister…

27 February 2002

John Howard

The Explosion of the Water Tank

Another lady
Who I embraced
Said—
We've lost our house but
We're all safe
And sound and we can rebuild it,

We're all safe.

A man,
A veteran
Of World War II
Showed me his charred
Medals and we
Sort of
Resolved to make certain that he got some new ones

And he got them replaced. There were many stories
That are so touching.
And freakish stories

Of one house under an ember
Attack
And somehow
Or other
It led to an explosion of the
Water tank,
Which put
The fire

Out.

19 January 2003

Quiz Answers

January 2010

We had an excellent response to last month's quiz and we congratulate everyone who entered. The winner was Robin Vale of Robinvale. For the record, the correct answers were:

1. Climate Change. (We'd also accept Global Warming, John Howard, Eleven Years, Nothing.)
2. Punt Road. With a huge international effort and determination on all sides, there is some prospect of a solution in the Middle East.
3. 'To be or not to be' (Shakespeare), 'I have a dream' (Martin Luther King), 'This was their finest hour' (Churchill), 'The budget's buggered' (Wayne Swan).
4. Stage three and a half water restrictions. Peter Pan and the unicorn are imaginary figures for children.
5. Brendan Nelson. He was CEO until Malcolm Turnbull made a successful cash offer for the party in late 2008.
6. Kevin Rudd. More work is required on the voice, the rhythm and the content but otherwise the Obama impression is coming along nicely.
7. There were two deliberate mistakes in the announcement: 'Bailout' and 'Property Developers'.
8. False. There were only seven wonders of the ancient world and Rex Hunt was not one of them.
9. False. It is not an inventory of Scottish vegetation. He played The Joker in *Batman*.
10. False. It is not because he can't get another job. It is due to a self-less obsession with representing the good folk of Higgins.
11. False. George W. Bush had no second language. His first language will be known when the CIA files are opened.
12. False. Hussein is the name of the Jordanian royal family. Usain Bolt is a rapid pedestrian.

13. True. When Jelena Dokic appeared at the 2002 Australian Open she was booed. When she appeared at the 2009 Australian Open she was photographed wearing a flag and her opponent was booed. The media were present on both occasions.

14. False. Melbourne's Public Transport system is not a raffle. A raffle doesn't get cancelled twice a week, catch fire, bend, buckle, break, melt, or require a billion dollars' worth of infrastructure.

15. True. Work stopped on the desalination plant in winter because the site was underwater. (This only happens every year.)

16. False. John Brumby is not an acknowledged international expert on water management.

17. Ron Walker. The Grand Prix. $45 million a year.

18. Andrew Symonds. All the others are boofheads.

19. No it does not sell toilets. A convenience store is so called because its prices are sufficiently high to make it convenient for the owners.

20. The Liberal Party. The Brady Bunch fell apart when the ratings dropped.

21. The Howard Years. *Paradise Lost* is a poem by John Milton.

22. Peter Garrett. Everything Midas touched turned to gold.

23. Philip Ruddock. The others are all garden ornaments.

24. Kevin Andrews. Dr Haneef will see you now.

25. Jeff Kennett. Ivan the Terrible was called Ivan.

26. Tony Abbott. The Victoria Cross is a bravery award.

27. George Pell. The others are Darth Vader and Anna Wintour.

28. Farnsie, Barnsie, Warnie, Tubby, Boonie, Buddy, Gillie and Punter. Ian Frazer is an immunologist, best known for his work on the development of a cervical cancer vaccine.

29. False. There is an economy. It comes down the chimney once a year if you believe really hard. Perhaps if all the children join hands.

30. Correct. Hedge funds are monies collected in order to facilitate the purchase of herbaceous borders.

November 2010

We had a fantastic response to our last quiz and we thank everyone who entered. The winner was Violet Town, of Violet Town. For the record, the answers were as follows:

1. True. Penny Wong agrees with the ALP's policy position against Penny Wongs.

2. True. John Howard was surprised that the African and Asian countries didn't want him as Vice President of the International Cricket Council.

3. False. The ABC is a non-commercial network. The man who is still in awe of the sea, the conductor of coloured bubbles and the woman who pretends to be a novelist are not commercials. A commercial has a purpose.

4. False. It is not The Dill Solution. It is called The Dili Solution. It is essentially the Pacific Solution but with auto focus, image stabilisation and a better zoom.

5. False. The World Giant Slalom Title has never been held at Etihad Stadium. The event on 23 July was a football match.

6. The Tour de France. It is a cycling race over 3600 kilometres through towns and cities which have in common that Justin Madden was not their planning minister.

7. Ben Cousins. He described lying comatose for a day and a half in intensive care as a wake-up call.

8. False. The twenty-six homeowners and eighty-four businesses to whom Premier John Brumby apologised for failing to mention that their properties will be bulldozed for a regional rail link were not in Toorak.

9. Kevin Andrews. A petard is small bomb.

10. For Sale. Rugby League. Restump, rewire and restore or demolish and redevelop as units. STCA. Entire sporting code. Must go. Suit handyman.

11. False. Paying off part of a mortgage before full term is called principal reduction. Bill Shorten is a politician.

12. Docklands. Now that it has been there for ten years, some thought is to be given to its appearance, design and utility. It has even been suggested the whole area be converted into a human community.

13. Mother Teresa of Calcutta. All the others are from the New South Wales Right.

14. The photo shows Tony Abbott, trouser icon and leader of the federal opposition. Isn't he gorgeous?

15. True. The Australian media made it abundantly clear that Kevin Rudd's downfall was inevitable. For reasons of space, their very lucid explanations were held over until after the event.

16. True. Victorians speak a form of English. Doggies Fly, Dannii Ethan Drama, Fev Brownlow Shocker and Logie Tweets are all key phrases and should be committed to memory. European Economy, Environmental Crisis, Rational Discourse and History of Ideas mean nothing. Concentrate on the important stuff.

17. Clean coal, friendly fire, arts funding and customer services. The unicorn might turn up.

18. False. Melbourne rail commuters emerging from a tunnel on foot does not mean the transport system doesn't work. It means we lead the world in tunnel-walking.

19. False. The purpose of the AFL is not to give young people access to drugs in a supervised environment. It is to govern and manage the popular sport of Australian football.

20. *Midsomer Murders.* It is a British TV series. Inspector Tom Barnaby arrives in a village to investigate the apparent suicide of a man who is found hanging from a windmill during a Michaelmas celebration. While Tom is investigating what he suspects is actually a murder, nine other murders are committed and a barn catches fire. Eventually even Tom works out that the

only person left in the village is the murderer. His assistant, who is even stupider, is amazed.

January 2011

We had a fantastic response to our last quiz and we thank everyone who entered. The winner was Bonnie Doon, of Bonnie Doon. For the record, the answers were as follows:

1. True. Each year in Melbourne on the final Saturday in September, there is a huge event known as Possibly the Grand Final. Two football teams meet at the MCG and play their hearts out for two hours. The following week they do it again until someone wins. This pattern has been broken only three times; once between 1902 and 1947, once between 1949 and 1976, and once between 1978 and 2009.

2. True. The atmosphere at a grand final is unbeloyable.

3. False. The AFL does not have a GDP greater than that of Belgium.

4. True. When it is completed, the desal plant will produce rain quality water using only a billion mega-nargs of electricity per day. Construction is behind schedule and somewhat over budget because of flooding due to almost continuous heavy rain. This could not have been predicted since it has never happened previously throughout the winter in the Kilcunda area.

5. True. The desal plant will cost Mr and Mrs T. Payer $18 billion. This is $16 billion over budget. It will then be owned by someone else. This deal was negotiated by Mr and Mrs Payer's carefully selected representative, Mr J. Brumby, a fifty-seven-year-old male Caucasian, of Melbourne.

6. False. The plant cannot be converted into a luxury facility for changing the names of women called Sally. This can already be

done by deed poll and would in any event, not be a cost-effective use of governmental hubris.

7. Steve Fielding. A nation mourns.

8. False. The answer is not to call the show *Australia's Two Next Top Models*. The answer is to get the result organised before announcing it.

9. False. Oprah Winfrey does not receive more government funding than Opera Australia.

10. The Grand Prix. The DJs claim was only $37 million. And only once.

11. False. At no stage did Mary MacKillop play a few games in the back pocket for Collingwood.

12. It sounds like a fan belt problem although check the radio. It could be that Christopher Pyne is being interviewed.

13. Max Markson. Excema is a skin condition.

14. False. The purpose of the Commonwealth Games was to highlight the sport, not the seating.

15. True. Valium is a benzodiazepine. (*The Bill* is a television programme.)

16. False. Andrew Robb's challenge for the deputy leadership was not a scratching. It was withdrawn at the barrier on the vet's advice, due to bleeding in the off foreleg.

17. Correct. Channel 7 regularly purchases the right to broadcast live international rugby union. Nobody knows why.

18. False. The 2010 Australian Swimming Championships were not held in Delhi.

19. The mine was in Chile. It doesn't matter where Chile is and it is not known whether it was a coalmine, a tin mine, a goldmine or a diamond mine. It was a mine for goodness' sake and we had pictures of it.

20. True. Jeff Kennett claims he was shot at. Four and a half million people are believed to be assisting police with their enquiries.

September 2011

We had a fantastic response to our last quiz and we thank everyone who entered. The winner was Sandy Point, of Sandy Point. Excellent work, Sandy. For the record, the answers were as follows:

1. True. Hugh Hefner's sex life is a key narrative in high-end Australian media.

2. False. James Murdoch is not available for functions.

3. False. Bernie Ecclestone doesn't own the Victorian government. He doesn't need to.

4. True. The federal government has some work to do in the mountains. There is no time-trial stage in the carbon debate.

5. True. Despite their differences on economic policy, social policy, international policy and the future of the planet, Julia Gillard and Tony Abbott are at one on the big threat facing Australia. They're both boldly opposed to gay marriage.

6. The photos show Clint Eastwood and Charles Bronson. Wayne Swan doesn't wear a poncho or a hat pulled down over his eyes. Nor does he sort things out quite so effectively.

7. False. Andy Coulson has not been cleared to play for the Brisbane Lions.

8. True. The world still somehow has news despite the fact that *The News of The World* is no longer published.

9. True. Cadel Evans has announced he will defend his Tour de France title although this does not constitute recycling within the meaning of the legislation.

10. Christine Nixon. Her assertion that the media hounded her out of office because she is a woman is understandably offensive to the media, since they hounded her successor Simon Overland out of office too and he is a man.

11. James Magnussen. He is called The Missile because he follows The Thorpedo and swimming commentators are not yet tested for steroids.

12. The Head of FIFA has been returned to office in a genuinely democratic, completely open and independently supervised ballot due to be held next April.

13. The US economy. Either it is the most successful in the world or it is $4 trillion in debt. You were asked to tick only one box. It is no use trying to borrow more boxes. There aren't any more boxes.

14. False. 37.11.233 is not a secret code or a mysterious theorum. It is a nice afternoon out in the Geelong area.

15. False. The habit developed in the media of labelling a story Something-gate in order to indicate its level of intrigue and importance ('Carbongate', for example) is not known as Drivelgate.

16. Incorrect. Robert Doyle is not the coach of Melbourne. He is the lord mayor.

17. The Australian dollar. For the next four nights it can be seen, with a powerful telescope, high in the eastern sky, between Sirius and Uranus.

18. False, the Big Bash League has nothing to do with football. It is a cricket competition and promises to be most exciting. Anyone who'd like a game, call Andrew Hilditch by Thursday.

19. Dean Bailey. Mike Rann was removed by covert activity within his own leadership group.

20. Wivenhoe Dam. It is built above the residential areas it is designed to supply with gravity-fed water services. This works well so long as it doesn't fill with water.

Election 2013

We had a fantastic response to our Election Special Quiz and we thank everyone who entered. The winner was Trent Ham, of Trentham. Well done, Trent. For the record, the answers were as follows:

1. True. Australia is a democracy. Some conditions apply. Please note the position of the exit nearest your seat.

2. False. The people cannot vote for the person they want as prime minister. They must vote for a candidate in their electorate. Party leadership is a matter for the parties themselves. This is going well.

3. True. The best way to ensure the defeat of the party you least prefer is to vote for the other one. This is called 'choice'.

4. False. Neither of the parties is led by the preferred prime minister. The preferred prime minister is Malcolm Turnbull. One of the reasons he is preferred is that he cannot become prime minister.

5. False. You cannot vote for Tony Abbott's daughters or for Thérèse Rein, Jessica Rudd, Antony Green, Dami Im or Cyril Rioli. They are not candidates.

6. True. The first week of the campaign was between Kevin Bloke and Tony Knackers about who is fair dinkum. The second week was about the economy, which is run by Treasury. Since then it has been about remaining awake.

7. This was a trick question. In fact they are all true. Tony Abbott won a Rhodes Scholarship, Bill Shorten expects people to vote for him and there is a car called a Range Rover Evoque.

8. True. In one 24-hour period, Tony Abbott confirmed that no one is the suppository of all knowledge, that a female candidate he supported had sex appeal and that allowing people to marry on the basis that they wanted to would be too radical a change to existing laws. These were the playful errors of a man abundantly qualified to run the country.

9. True. Kevin Rudd is The Labor Party. There are apparently some local members but Kevin is the founder of the party, owns the copyright and holds all the portfolios in the federal cabinet.

10. True. There were two days of the campaign on which Tony Abbott did not mention asylum seekers. He wasn't well. Happily, he's feeling much better now.

11. True. Climate change is effecting the global environment, except in Queensland and Western Sydney.
12. True. ALP strategists got rid of Kevin Rudd because the polls had collapsed and then got rid of Julia Gillard because the polls had collapsed. Their current problem is that the polls have collapsed.
13. True. Sophie Mirabella has been to her electorate on many occasions.
14. True. Both parties waited until the electorate was suffering from drivel-fatigue and then launched their campaigns.
15. False. Bob Katter was not in *Dirty Harry* although his hat was nominated for an Emmy for its performance in *Gunsmoke*.
16. False. Tony Windsor is not a member of the royal family.
17. True. There is a new TV show called *Eden-Monaro*. It premiers on Sunday and will be heavily promoted after the polls close tonight. All TV election coverage will be peppered with presenters on all channels repeatedly saying 'Let's go to *Eden-Monaro*', 'I'd like to have a look at *Eden-Monaro*' and 'Can we get *Eden-Monaro* on this thing, Antony?'
18. True. Other new TV shows also set to be shamelessly promoted throughout the election-night coverage include *Robertson, Dobell and Lindsay* (comedy/drama about three cops with only one bicycle, trying to bust a drug-ring), *LaTrobe and Deakin* (a spoof news panel show) and *Greenway, Banks and Corangamite* (reality show in which fifteen dozen *vol-au-vents* must be prepared in a house containing only a toaster and a vacuum cleaner).
19. False. Clive Palmer does not actually face Queensland when he speaks.
20. True. Media coverage of this election has been uniformly excellent.

Budget 2014

We had a wonderful response to our bumper post-Budget quiz and we thank everyone who entered. The winner was Jan Juc of Jan Juc. And our congratulations go to you, Jan. For the record, the answers were as follows:

1. True. The picture shows Treasurer Joe Hockey picking up his parliamentary entitlements. This is an example of heavy lifting. Note that he bends at the knees.

2. False. There is no plan to privatise HECS debt. The reason Christopher Pyne is shifting universities to the 'interest-free for six months on all whitegoods' model, is simply a concern for quality in tertiary education.

3. False. The fact that Tony Abbott has promised something does not mean it will definitely not happen. Try to remember whether the promise was written down, whether it was a 'solemn' promise, whether it was 'fair dinkum', whether he has 'moved on', whether it was 'fundamentally honest', whether it was a promise he was 'determined to keep', whether it was broken 'temporarily' and whether or not there was an election on.

4. True. Joe Hockey and Mathias Cormann were given the task of leaking the budget and marketing its underlying agenda. The cigars were a masterstroke.

5. True. The national audit of Australia's fiscal position did not include a discussion of the government's income.

6. True. Joe Hockey's response to the state of the Australian budget when he came into office was to give $9 billion to the Reserve Bank and announce an inherited liquidity crisis.

7. True. Tony Shepherd is a corporate leader with particular expertise in running businesses which used to be government infrastructure. His recommendations included the sale of more government infrastructure. This was completely unexpected.

8. False. When the national audit was announced, Joe Hockey, Tony Shepherd and Mathias Cormann were not laughing at the content of the report and the effect it would have. They were remembering a very amusing story which they'd been told some days previously.

9. False. It is not true that when Arthur Sinodinos remembered his name during the ICAC hearing, the New South Wales Bar Association rose to its feet and sang the 'Hallelujah' chorus.

10. False. The photograph shows Clive Palmer. Jupiter is a planet.

11. True. In the city of Melbourne, the streets are available for use by the public provided this wouldn't cause any inconvenience for property developers, crane operators or construction companies.

12. True. The finding of the International Court at The Hague was that the Port Adelaide football team is not using opposition sides for scientific experiment. They are simply killing them.

13. False. It is not possible to obtain results from next season's cricket fixtures by calling Cricket Australia.

14. False. Barry O'Farrell still cannot remember being the premier of New South Wales. He stressed that it's quite an important job and if he'd ever done it, he's pretty sure he would have remembered it.

15. False. The photo was not taken during a school outing. The person grinning in the cockpit of the Joint Strike Fighter aircraft is the prime minister, Tony Abbott.

16. False. George Pell has not been put in charge of rearranging the tables of the money-lenders at the Vatican. He's gone there to help clean up their finances.

17. False. There is no connection whatever between the involvement of Denis Napthine in anything and his connection with anything else. He has never met anyone and did not know of his own involvement or that of anyone else in whatever it was.

18. False. 'You know nothing, Jon Snow' is a line from *Game of Thrones*. It is not the advice of Mr Snow's barrister at the ICAC

hearings. There is no Mr Snow at the ICAC hearings. If there were, he would know nothing, although the blood would drain from his face slightly when the documents were tabled.

19. You were asked for the next name in the following sequence: Aristotle, Copernicus, Galileo, Issac Newton and Albert Einstein. The answer, of course, is Cyril Rioli.

20. False. The photograph shows a Sesame Street puppet called Beaker. Christopher Pyne is the education minister.

2014 in Review

We had a gratifying response to our Year in Review quiz and we thank everyone who entered. The winner was Glen Huntly of Glenhuntly. And our congratulations go to you, Glen. A mighty effort. For the record, the answers were as follows:

1. True. Joe Hockey has announced he is using the budget as a shock absorber. The government is also expected to confirm that Tony Abbott is using it as a tie rack and Mathias Cormann is using it as an ashtray.

2. Correct. There is to be a referendum on whether or not the Constitution should recognise Indigenous Australians. Further referenda are expected to determine the religious denomination of the Pope and to ascertain whether or not the toilet arrangements of bears have any impact on wooded areas.

3. True. The G20 leaders greatly enjoyed the lecture given to them by Tony Abbott about what he has done in government. On the downside, however, the world's leaders are now aware of what Tony Abbott has done in government.

4. True. The ALP hates the Greens because the electorate is concerned about environmental issues and although the ALP's environmental policy includes a formal acknowledgement of

photosynthesis and comes in an excellent folder, the mustard remain uncut.

5. True. The reason the Oscar Pistorius trial received blanket television coverage in Australia remains a mystery. Shots of people we don't know milling about in a courtroom in another country were broadcast around the clock. We might just leave it there but we'll go back as soon as any development appears likely.

6. False. You are perhaps thinking of a urinary tract infection. Sepp Blatter is the head of FIFA.

7. True. Malcolm Turnbull interpreted Tony Abbott's promise of no cuts to the ABC or SBS as not really a promise because the context had changed. Mr Turnbull later retired hurt.

8. True. Treasury's income assumptions were reported missing in the ACT in July and search teams are expected to continue combing the area with sonar equipment, until March.

9. False. Bronwyn Bishop is not a bouncer. She is the Speaker of the House of Representatives. A bouncer throws out anyone he doesn't like the look of.

10. True. George Pell discovered that the Vatican's fortunes are in much better shape than expected because hundreds of millions of Euros were hidden in accounts in various banks. For some reason these accounts were not officially recorded. Thankfully George has found no evidence of wrongdoing.

11. True. The best performers in the federal government are said to be Andrew Robb and the man who bangs on the parliament door with a big stick.

12. True. Nick Xenophon is an anthropologist. He studies human behaviour in the Australian senate and has his own documentary series called 'The News'.

13. True. Clive Palmer has described Barnaby Joyce as a fat red-faced man who is under terrible pressure. The kettle was not available for comment.

14. True. Joe Hockey will remain as treasurer until every comma in the budget has been removed, changed, denied, reversed, inverted or interpreted to mean its opposite.

15. False. The term 'hospital pass' is used in sport to indicate that someone has been set up by his own side, to be thumped. Malcolm Turnbull was put in charge of snookering the NBN and reducing the ABC and SBS because of his experience in the communications industry.

16. False. It was an impertinence and an insult to the Abbott government for President Obama to make a speech about the importance of finding alternative sources of energy. A spokesman for the planet was not available since he was making a speech about the importance of finding alternative sources of energy.

17. True. Christopher Pyne voted to reduce the ABC's funding and then petitioned the government in which he is a minister to prevent ABC funding from being reduced in Adelaide. The coroner has yet to release a report but police say there are no suspicious circumstances.

18. True. Nobody knows how the Abbott government got in. It is now thought that aliens may have neutralised the brains of the Australian population on 7 September 2013. The four Australians who actually voted for Tony have all now come out against him in their fiercely independent newspaper columns.

19. False. Greg Hunt.

20. False. When the Essendon football team plays next year, the TV coverage will not be out of focus. The blurry effect is just used in news footage, in case anyone finds out what the players look like.

21. True. When the new rules come into force, Adam Scott will have to get rid of his putter. (Lord, hear our prayer.)

22. False. The picture shows Eric Abetz. The Grinch who stole Christmas is a fictional character.

23. Correct. The Age of Entitlement is over. (There are some

exceptions to this. Please check your postcode.)

24. True. Because of a downturn in iron ore prices and a blowout in Australia's deficit projections, the February Unemployment Number will jackpot to April, the May Economic Statement will move to June, the panic set down for July will be rescheduled for late August and the September claim that it's not Joe's fault will become part of the October austerity measures.

25. True. Australia's commitment to foreign aid has been buried at sea following a private ceremony. Our hearts go out to no one.

Saint Paul's Letter to the Electorates

The electorate beareth all things, believeth all things,
hopeth all things, endureth all things.

Chapter 1

i) And so it was, after the time of John, that Kevin went out to meet the enemies of his people. For their enemies were numerous and the people were sore afraid. For the money-lenders had put their own house asunder and the crops faileth in the field and drought was upon the land.

ii) And the people looked at Kevin with confusion in their hearts and they sayeth each to the other. 'He is only a boy. And surely he will be done, yea, even unto a dinner.'

iii) But Kevin raiseth up his hand and he calmeth his people, saying, 'Listeneth thou to me,' and he then spoke for some time and he laid out a plan. And the people were greatly relieved and they offered up praises and hosannas saying, 'Go Kevin.' For the plan was good. And this was reflected in the polls. For they went nuts.

iv) And Kevin putteth the plan into action. And he said unto Wayne, 'Mate, poureth thee thy money into the marketplace.' And Wayne betook himself into the desert, where he sat alone for a long time, looking at the surplus. For he was wrestling with his soul.

v) And at this time in the land, the Pharisees met and lo, he that was called Brendan was sacrificed and a new leader was anointed. And his name was called Malcolm. And Malcolm sayeth as follows: 'Although I am opposed to Kevin, for he is not top drawer, Kevin is correct on this matter of the ETS.'

vi) And chief among the Pharisees was Nicholas. And Nicholas looked upon Malcolm and liked him not. And Nicholas bideth his time.

vii) And Kevin sayeth to Penny, who was in the senate, 'Penny, the crops withereth away and the sun beateth down upon the face of the earth and it raineth not. Therefore buyeth thee back the rivers, prepareth thee thy ETS and packeth thee thy bag. For verily, this is a problem for all the world and we are the hope of the side.'

viii) And it was so. For Kevin and Penny travelled for many days and many nights to the land that is the Mark of Den. For the heads of many tribes were also gathered there. For they saw that the earth was getting warmer. And they knew not what to do.

ix) And Kevin and Penny took neither rest nor sleep. For they worked XXIV/VII and took they no respite. And they told the other leaders of their plan. And the other leaders shaketh their heads. And unfortunately they shaketh them not up and down but from side to side.

x) And lo, Kevin and Penny returned to their people saying, 'We have tried everything. We cannot get agreement from these bozos. For they all agree, except about doing anything.'

xi) And the people said, 'Where is our ETS?' And Kevin replied, saying, 'Holdeth thee thy horses. Seest thou this in some context. Fixeth we not the economy? For it was laid waste and now is the envy of the world.' And the people looked and saw that it was so.

xii) 'Very good work,' they said. 'But where is the ETS?'

xiii) And Malcolm agreed with the people, saying, 'Though I speak with the tongues of men and of angels and have not a carbon market, I am as a sounding brass or a tinkling cymbal.'

xiv) And the Pharisees met again for a second time and there was a mighty racket and lo, he that was called Anthony spoke to the people, saying, 'Malcolm chooseth to spend a little more time with his family. For I, Anthony, am now your leader and the ETS is as ordure upon the face of the earth and will not pass, for we will prevent same in the senate.'

xv) For Nicholas lineth up Malcolm and he smote him hip and thigh. And there was a miracle. For Julie voted for both sides. And there was a great sadness. For Joe stood also, and Joe corketh his thigh in the engagement.

Chapter 2

i) And it came to pass that in the time of Kevin there was peace and prosperity in the land. And the people offered up thanks, saying, 'Blessed are the relativists, for Kevin is better than the available alternative.'

ii) And Kevin travelled widely throughout the land. And he carried with him many shekels and wherever Kevin went, he pressed shekels upon his people saying, 'Take this. And buildeth thy house and bungeth thee thy insulation in the ceiling.'

iii) But there was a problem with this. For it assumeth that the cost of insulation is in shekels. And it was not so. For there was a human cost, and there was weeping and a gnashing of teeth. For perhaps the bunging was insufficiently regulated.

iv) And came there a man called Peter. And he was a maker of music and a dancer, although he was rather jerky in this latter discipline and it maketh complete sense that he got out of that line of work. For he was now with Kevin and was among his people. And was charged with matters relating to insulation and the bunging of same.

v) And Peter spake. And the people lost all hope. And their eyes glazeth over, and their heads droopeth and in some cases they slippeth into repose. For Peter lacketh brevity. And there was great disappointment in the land. For Peter seemeth to say, 'Am I my brother's keeper?'

vi) And the people said, 'Verily, thou art thy brother's keeper. For that is thy job, Peter. And the buck stoppeth with you and your kind.' And Kevin rose up before them and said, 'My people, cavil ye not. For I have brought you through the valley of the shadow. Therefore go forth with confidence and spend the shekels I have given you.'

vii) And the people said, 'No worries on that issue.' For they had spent the shekels on the pod that is called i and the pad that is called i and the phone that is called i. And Kevin said, 'Be comforted, then, for thou art blessed, for I am thy leader.'

viii) And the people said unto Kevin, 'Bloweth thee not thine own trumpet too loudly. For the walls that come tumbling down might be thine own. And where is thy ETS?'

ix) And Kevin replied, saying, 'It is on the back burner. And incidentally, Peter decideth to spend a little more time with his family.'

x) And Anthony saw a great light. And he gathereth up his tribe, who were opposed to Kevin, saying, 'Brethren, and you other lot as well. Seize the day. For lo, Kevin struggleth, and he manageth not. And I cannot afford to bide my time, for I have one shot at this. So let's go.'

xi) And his tribe spoke, saying, 'How will it be?' And Anthony told them his plan, which was as follows: 'Kevin is a tin man, but I am an iron man. For I have smugglers of many colours. And they lack not brevity. And my body is full and ripe and a thing of great loveliness.' And the people looked upon Anthony and upon his body, and they saw that it was so.

xii) And Anthony said an ETS was like unto many cubits of dung. And the scribes went to him and they asked him about this, and he denied it three times, saying, 'Forgive me. For I know not what I say. For my words are not what I mean. For sometimes I engage in rhetorical hyperbole.'

xiii) And the scribes said, 'Dost thou bear false witness?' And Anthony was greatly troubled, for he knew his problem was words, and he restricted himself to the use of one letter. And it was the letter R, which he repeateth a number of times.

xiv) And the people shook their heads and said, 'Truly, he is a very limited unit.'

xv) And Anthony said, 'The truth is written.' And the people said, 'Yea. Whatever.'

xvi) And there came a great change in the land. For while the Kevinites and the Anthonites were fighting, there was yet another tribe and its name was called Green, and its leader was called Brown. And they had many tents and were numerous. For they had gone forth and multiplied.

xvii) And there were among the Kevinites those who studied the signs, and they said, 'The position is not good. For Kevin looseth the plot, and must be replaced.' And their names were called Arbib and Shorten, and there were others with them and among them, and they counted up the numbers. And they spoke not to the scribes but went to Julia, and they anointed her, saying, 'It's your job to tell Kevin. We'll hold your coat.'

xviii) And so it was that the time of Kevin ran out, and though it shitteth him, he saw that it was so. And the leader was Julia. And Julia looked to the factions, whence cometh her help, and said, 'Placeth thou thy trust in me, moving forward.'

xvix) And it was on for young and old.

Chapter 3

i) And at the time of the Assumption of Julia there was rejoicing. And there was also some confusion. And these in equal parts. For within the duration of one day the people were vouchsafed two leaders. And they knew not how to judge the quick and the dead.

ii) And Julia calmed the people, saying, 'We are found who had lost our way.' And she brought forth a plan, and it was three-fold, saying;

iii) 'Blessed are those who dig in the earth and profiteth from the treasure therein, for they shall see me afterwards.

iv) 'Blessed are those who hunger and search after a carbon price, for to them it shall be given.

v) 'Blessed are the fearful and those who would deny succour to the persecuted, for they shall be put on a committee.'

vi) And some of those who were called Green began to leave their tents to follow Julia. And some of those who were created equally with men began also to follow Julia. And there was movement across the land.

vii) And Anthony became greatly distressed, and cried out, 'They are murderers who have done this to Kevin, for Kevin was good.'

viii) And the people said, 'Dids't thou not declare against Kevin and avow oaths against him, and spit upon him and call him an abomination? And dids't thou not also murder Malcolm and usurp his crown?'

ix) And Anthony said, 'Thou must not take any notice of what I say. For I am fair dinkum.' But there was yet disquiet about the spilling of Kevin, for it was done by the factions. And they were faceless, and it was done with great suddenness and it was done in the deepest dark of night.

x) And there were in the land many scribes and their importance was beyond estimation, for their columns were manifold.

xi) And when Kevin was vanquished and his body removed from that place, the scribes spoke, sometimes through a glass or two, darkly, saying, 'Julia must make atonement. For Kevin hath led his people out of the wilderness and is now despised and rejected of men, and behold, and see if there be any sorrow like unto his sorrow.'

xii)　And they went to Julia, and asked her how it was. And she looked also upon Kevin in his grief, and said, 'I do not wish to canvass with you now, at this time, the events that occurred on the night prior to my Assumption.' And the scribes were discontent, and busy in their minds, for that is the way with scribes.

xiii)　And Julia stood before the people and told them of the tradition.

xiv)　'For Gough begat Malcolm and Malcolm begat Bob. And Bob begat Paul, although this was attended not by the cherubim or the seraphim but by both argy and bargy. For Bob stayeth somewhat upon his leaving and Paul requireth the heavy artillery to come into his estates. And Paul begat John. And in his time, John begat Kevin. And this is the tradition of our people.'

xv)　And there was one among the leaders called Lindsay, who was a Tanner and whose father was a Tanner before him. And he had apparently long harboured a desire to spend a bit more time with his family, for he draweth stumps and leaveth by the first donkey. And his place was taken by those that were Green.

xvi)　And the scribes were now turned on Julia and wrote many Jeremiads recording the fall of Kevin. And time pressed sorely upon them as they wrote their lamentations. And they were not able to record that they had opposed Kevin and mocked him and called him a dullard and a buffoon and a dissembler.

xvii)　And Julia spoke to the people, saying, 'There will be a mighty reckoning between the tribes. Therefore enrolleth thee thy name in the lists and firmeth up thy judgement. For it is the law.'

Chapter 4

i)　And a time had been set down for the reckoning, and the people girded up their loins, and began to prepare. For there was much to consider.

ii)　And the scribes assembled, in their place, for Julia appeared at the club which was called Press. And there was a time to every purpose; a time for taking bread and a time to drink, a time for speaking and a time to refrain from speaking, a time for listening and a time for asking questions.

iii) And there was in that assembly one whose name was called Oakes. And he rose to ask a question and, seeing this, the room fell still, for there is also a time of foreboding, and for wondering what will happen next.

iv) And this was a sign, and they witnessed the sign. For it was a long question, and it had many parts and sub-clauses and subjunctives and room for a pool with a sundeck cantilevered out over the lawn.

v) And although Kevin was cast into outer darkness, the words of Kevin seemeth to come through the Oaken one. And the voice of Kevin was vengeful.

vi) And the scribes looked each at his neighbour, saying, 'Behold, the voice of Kevin is manifest. And this lowereth the tone somewhat but we will go with it.'

vii) And Julia looked upon the multitude and said, 'Joy of joys, the Oaken one moveth among us. But he bringeth the gift of doubt and of vengeance; and doubt feedeth upon doubt, and vengeance destroyeth all things. And let us therefore set these matters aside, and languish not, but move forward.'

viii) But the scribes heeded no longer the policies of Julia and nor yet the policies of Anthony, but told they the people that the voice of Kevin liveth, and it was vengeful, and it speaketh through the Oaken one.

ix) And the Anthonians gave thanks to the blessed St Kevin, the martyr, for they loveth his work.

x) And there was a debate between Julia and Anthony, and when the people saw it they said, 'Where is Bob, who is Green? For he hath the balance of power, and yet we hear him not amidst the tumult. Callest thou this a debate? Thou cans't not be serious.'

xi) And the first thing Anthony said during the debate was that he had taken to him a wife, and they had been blessed with progeny. And in coming days there were further revelations. For it transpireth his wife was a woman, and his daughters also were women. Lo, even his mother was a woman. And this was remarkable.

xii) And the people were astonished, for Anthony previously appeareth coarsely made and was an hairy man and showeth himself in the smugglers, although he possibly misconstrueth the meaning of the tabernacle.

xiii) And still the scribes hammereth on about the Oaken one and Kevin's voice. And the voice spake again, and this time it spake about support for the little children, and the voice said there was one who was opposed to support for the little children; and it was Julia.

xiv) And Julia was angry and they asked her, 'How can it be that all this stuff leaketh?' And she replied, 'I know not how this cometh to be. But when I find out, stand ye well back, for there will be smiting, and I mean that most sincerely.'

xv) But the people were not satisfied, for although Kevin hath one voice, they hath many and could speak volumes. And they saw not their concerns represented, and they saw not leadership and they asked again, 'Where is the ETS?' And answer came there none.

xvi) And the people were cast down, and they referred to the sacred texts, which said 'omg, wtf' and 'lol'. And many of the texts also said 'cul8r'.

xvii) And those who were Green went back out of Julia's tent and Anthony rose up in the polls. And it was a time of confusion. For there were dogs being whistled all over the place. And it degenerateth into farce.

Chapter 5

i)   And so it was that the people found themselves in the desert, and were desolate, and they knew not what to do.

ii)   For they had elected Kevin, and Kevin was sacrificed.

iii) And they witnessed the Assumption of Julia, who had attended upon the sacrifice.

iv)   And the scribes cursed both he who was sacrificed and they who did the sacrificing. And the people looked upon the scribes, and saw that they haveth it both ways.

v)   And the people saw also Brendan sacrificed and Malcolm sacrificed, and they observed the rise of Anthony, who was locked up by his minders in case he said something, for he faileth to meet the KPIs in certain crucial respects.

vi)   And there were doubters among the people. And they called out, saying, 'Why endureth we these stories, when they are told to us by seed spillers?'

vii) 'And why witnesseth we a presidential campaign, when we have no president?'

viii) 'And why chooseth we one of two, and yet there are three?'

ix)   'And for the Cth time, where is the ETS?'

x)   And there was a rumbling sound and the Earth trembled and there was a celestial light. And there came before the people a man of seraphic appearance, and he was fair of hair and somewhat circular of dial, and the people rubbed their eyes. And the man spoke, and they knew him.

xi)   And they said, 'It is Kevin!' And verily, it was Kevin.

xii) And they said to him, 'Is what we see before us a resurrection?' And he said, 'No, it's just the way I'm standing.' And they said, 'Where hast thou been?' And he answered, saying, 'I was unwell in the viscera.' And they said, 'And was thou shortened again?' And he said, 'I'll do the jokes thanks. I was shortened once and it will never happen again. What occureth the second time was a cholecystectomy.'

xiii) And they said, 'And will'st thou be working with Julia?' And he said, 'I'm not sure 'with' is quite the term we're searching for there, but I'm here to help, for the barbarians are at the gate.' And they said 'Even after she performeth a Kevinectomy?' And he said, 'The past is another country. They do things differently there.'

xiv) And the Earth trembled once more and the people looked up in wonderment, for another familiar figure appeared. For lo, John stood before them at a lecturn, with both arms in the air and Asian motifs in the background.

xv) And the people looked at one another and said, 'Hast thy deja just become vu?'

xvi) And there was a roaring sound, as of madness, and the seas parted, and thence came Mark. And Julia had not time to prepare. But it did not matter, for Mark barketh, 'I am Mark. Look upon me, for I am Mark. Observe thou the Markness of me, for I am me, which is Mark,' and this requireth little by way of response.

xvii) And Julia sayeth to herself, 'Giveth me strength. For there is a plague on my house, like unto locusts, which arrive in their season and darken the air and consume every herb and nourishing thing.'

xviii) And then the Oaken one also appeareth, saying Mark was bitter, and disruptive, and should be cast out. And the people said, 'Like, Hello.'

xix) And Anthony had a launch, and spake unto the people, using many adjectives. But he keepeth well away from policies, for this was the danger area.

xx) And the polls indicateth a nip and tuck affair. And there were twelve days and twelve nights to go.

Chapter 6

i) Now, after the afflictions of Mark, which were grievous, and the agonies of the Oaken one, which were piteous, and the intercession of Barnaby, which beggareth belief, and a special guest appearance from Andrew, which surpasseth all understanding, the people began to prepare for the counting. For the reckoning was imminent, and the polls were undecided.

ii) And there came forth a messenger, from Babylon, saying, 'Rejoice, for Kevin has received preferment and walketh into some big job at AllTribes.' And this was a healing balm, for Kevin cometh off a run of outs following a shock departure in the heats of the Internecine War.

iii) And Julia went up to the mountain, which was called Q'anda, and there she stood alone and was questioned by the multitude.

iv) And there were those who looked kindly upon her and there were those who looked ill upon her and she played each delivery on its merits, and the selectors were impressed, and she was installed in the Book of Likelihood at $1.20, in from $2.65.

v) And there came forth a priest, whose name was called George, and he stood in full raiment before the people, and he raised up his voice, saying, 'Giveth not thy support to those who are Green, for they are camouflaged poison and many are Stalinists supporting Soviet oppression.' And the people were greatly amused, and rolleth on the ground, clutching their girth, slapping their thighs and calling for oxygen.

vi) And the church leaders looketh at each other, saying, 'And we wonder why the numbers are falling off.' And they moveth away, and distanced themselves from George, who was a bull, and who taketh the precaution of bringing his own china shop.

vii)   And there was brought forth a proposal. Each of the three leaders except one, would appear before another multitude, at the Hill of Rooty. And proceedings would be recorded by the dock of myrrh, whence cometh fairness and balance.

viii) And it was so arranged, and the people gathered, and their questions were the voice of sweet reason, and those who wished to see it looked to the firmament, for coverage was exclusive to the sky.

ix)   And the oracles read the signs, and were divers in their judgements, and they reproached one another, saying, 'thy figures are wrong, for thy sample is wanting in magnitude,' or, 'thou asketh the wrong question, of the wrong people, in the wrong province.'

x)   However, the people placeth not their trust in oracles, for they knoweth that a swing may not be uniform, and they were watchful.

xi)   But the oracles continued to make pronouncements, after their kind, for that is the way with oracles. And the scribes seizeth upon anything at this stage.

xii)   And the people looked at what lay before them, for in five days and five nights they must choose. And this in every family and in each generation and in all parts of the promised land.

xiii) And the books were divided. For Julia hath Timothy and Chronicles but she hath not Solomon.

xiv)   And Anthony hath Acts and Revelation but he hath not Ruth.

xv)   And Bob hath Proverbs and Lamentations but he hath not Numbers.

xvi)   And the people, who had endured much and had suffered much and were weary, looked up with hope in their hearts.

xvii) For there was light at the end of the tunnel.

Chapter 7

i) And Anthony in his turn went also up to the mountain, which was called Q'anda, and showed himself to the multitude.

ii) And those who toil and spin taketh him aside beforehand, saying, 'We have looked upon the multitude, and it is not all alien corn. Keepeth therefore thy straight face when the Kevin lookalike gets up, and remember thy lines.'

iii) And it was so. And the people brought forth questions for Anthony, and he responded, for responding is easier than answering. For it revealeth not thy real position, assuming thou hast one.

iv) And they had many questions, and were respectful, and even when Anthony faileth to grasp the occasional point, such as the broadness of band, they showed him great kindness.

v) And there rose up among them a man, and he had fought in battles for the nation, and had returned home and taken to him a wife and they had children. And the man loveth his children, and was proud, but was also troubled. For his own begotten son was different, and the law was opposed to difference.

vi) But the father so loved his son that his understanding grew and he asked Anthony why he, too, did not allow his understanding to grow.

vii) And Anthony touched another man on the arm and laughed. And Anthony denied the man, and denied his son.

viii) And the people saw that Julia also baulketh on this issue.

ix) But the people baulketh not, except in Baulkham Hills, Baulkington and Upper Baulkwood, all of which were marginal, and swingeth in very light zephers.

x) And the people asked Anthony also about economics and health and education, but he troubleth not the scorer, which was good for Anthony. For with Anthony, nothing is a real cool hand.

xi) And so the lines were drawn. And Julia stood with her forces, who arrangeth for Kevin to walk the plank and playeth into the hands of the scribes and dissemblers, who looketh like a circus but turneth out to be four horsemen.

xii) And Anthony stood with his forces. And they repeateth day and night that they were not Julia. For such was their confidence in the ability of the people to grasp complex issues.

xiii) And Bob, who was called Brown, and who was Green, also stood in the field, but the scribes saw him not, nor counted his people nor asked questions of Bob. And this was remarkable, for Bob would control the senate.

xiv) And the people took up their staff and their rod, and they went to the place where the booths were arranged, and they stood in little cardboard alcoves, with pencils and pieces of paper. For that is how these miracles are performed.

xv) And it was done.

xvi) And they gathered in their houses, and they took wine and food.

xvii) And they waited to see what they had done.

xviii) For how could they get out of this with a halfway sensible result?

Chapter 8

i) And it was written that on the day before the Sabbath the people would gather together in a public place and accept burnt offerings, tip tomato sauce down their fronts, cast their votes and return to their homes. And when the darkness had fallen, and after they had uncorked their evening meal and begun to engage in wassail, there came the sound of a great counting.

ii) And as the counting advanced there emerged a pattern, and it was like unto that established by Noah. For the votes came in two by two, one of each kind with one each of the other kind, until the Ark was full.

iii) For the people had chosen equally, and by close of play neither Julia nor Anthony could rule in the land. And so it was that the result hung in the scales of balance for many days and many nights, and was undecided.

iv) And calls were made to the uttermost parts of the land, including to Solomon, who was wise, for this would make a nice change.

v) And there were those who lacked dependence, but gaineth much, and were not part of the tribes of neither Julia nor Anthony. And they carryeth all before them in the counting and were victorious, each in his area and after his kind. And they were agreed on one issue. And it was Barnaby. For they haveth no time for same.

vi) And they were courted by the Julianites and the Anthonites, yea, even as the counting was done.

vii) And the scribes looked at the figures and they all agreed that they had seen it coming, and were not surprised, and had predicted exactly this result, for it was always on the cards and was inevitable for the following reasons, which they listed. For the scribes see all things, and hear all things, and know all things.

viii) But one factor sneaketh up even upon the scribes. For Bob, who was Brown and who was also Green, turneth out not only to control the senate but to have a big romp downstairs as well. For those who were Green had gone forth and multiplied. And this was a feature of proceedings.

ix) And after a time, late in the evening of the counting, Julia came forth and spoke to the multitude, and they called her name. And although she had suffered losses in all parts of the country, she calmeth the people, and pointeth out that according to law she was still the caretaker leader, or janitor.

x) And Anthony came forth also and the multitude called also his name, and his wife's name, for the wassail was well in hand by this stage and the people were up for anything they could dance to.

xi) And Anthony acknowledged his triumph, and explained how he had done this remarkable thing.

xii) And this was unusual. For he had not won.

xiii) And Kevin spoke also, and as is indicated in the form guide, he spoke for some time and was fulsome in his praise for his own efforts and for his many qualities. And the people were pleased to see him up and about again, although this was a good time to put the kettle on.

xiv) And Bob, who was Brown, calleth it a victory for those who were Green. And it was so. And Bob was most excited, and fighteth the urge to pull his top up over his head and run around the field with outstretched arms.

xv) For there was a large swing to Bob.

xvi) And there was another swing which was even bigger than Bob's swing, and it was a swing to informality. And those with long white beards stroked them at this point, saying, 'Yikes. A great many of the people have lost interest in these matters.'

xvii) And messengers were sent out by the Julianites and the Anthonites to their imaginary friends at the Oakshottery, and in the House of Windsor and among the Kattermites. And they were experienced, and they understood, and were responsible, and they all spoke of the need for stable government. And the leaders agreed, saying, 'Absolutely. Now, how about some steak knives?'

xviii) And the people waited, for there was nothing else to do, and they were getting quite good at it.

Chapter 9

i) And so it was that the moon grew full in its season and the people brought their cattle in for shelter, and their sheep and their goats also. And at sunrise they went out once more, putting their animals to graze in the field. And they did this many times, for such was the diurnal round. And the moon waned in its turn, and still the counting went on.

ii) And in the tents of the leaders there were talks with those who were brought forth by the people but lacketh affiliation. And they were divers in their opinions and spake sometimes jointly and sometimes severally and in the case of colloquy with Barnaby, sometimes not at all.

iii) And there were some who looked upon the confusion and said, 'From chaos comes order, and this is good.'

iv) And there were others who thought the people should be sent back to the booths. 'For the Julianites and the Anthonites haveth each many times the support of the unaffiliated, and it is not mete that the tail waggeth the dog.'

v) And Bob who was Brown and was also Green was not of this view. For he playeth a blinder in the previous round and he expresseth his view at the time. And it was, 'Thank you linesmen; thank you ball boys.'

vi) And the scribes began to write the history of the time. And they were greatly troubled, and reported a plague of cynicism and shallowness, and of narrowness of issues, and of slogans and trivia. And they were sore distressed, for their intellectual rigour was offended by the shambles they saw before them.

vii) But what the people had done was simple, and they understood it, for it conformeth with the tenets and the teachings. And these underpinneth the laws and provideth the foundations of justice.

viii) Thou shalt not identify a great moral challenge and put off dealing with it.

ix) In a system where the people choose the leader, thou shalt not topple the leader without consulting them.

x) And generally speaking thou shalt not consort with faceless geezers hiding in the drapery with sharp objects.

xi) And most importantly thou shalt not toss the mortal remains of a former leader out in the street the next morning and invoice the people for the cleanup. For there will be retribution, and it shall be in spades.

xii) And ask not upon whom the retribution shall be visited. For it shall be visited upon thee.

xiii) And while I've got you all here, thou canst not logically remove thy leader on the basis that he knoweth not what he is doing, if thou art helping him do it. For this will blow up in thy face.

xiv) And so it was that the Julianites lost those who were green and those who were blue. And were themselves lost.

xv) And thou shalt not look upon the dryness of the land and the rivers, and say to the people who live on that land and have not water, 'This is not happening. Look over there. For we are being invaded by boats.'

xvi) Thou shalt make sense in thy utterances, for people like that sort of thing.

xvii) If thou damneth those who assassinate their leader, be not the beneficiary of assassinating thy leader. And if thou pointeth out that thine enemies are made up of factions, haveth not thine own divisions so deeply riven that they produce the independents, for they may control thy destiny.

xviii) And so it was that the Anthonites lost those who were green and those who had grown to adulthood. And were themselves lost.

xvix) And after many days the tent flap opened and out stepped Julia and Bob, who was Green and whose dentist will be very pleased, and they waveth a piece of paper saying, 'Peace in our time.'

xx)   And on this same day, there also emergeth officials from Treasury, who were skilled at calculations, and were particularly adept in the area of addition. And they also carried a piece of paper. And they said, 'Anthony. Joseph. Headmaster's office. Now.'

xxi)   And the tent flap rustled again a third time, and there came forth Andrew whose name was called Wilkie, and he singeth a song from the double white album. And it was 'Julia'.

xxii)   And then there were three. And the moon rose again in its season. And the people looked at each other and said, 'Can't be long now.'

Sporting Heroes

Terry Lineen

In Palmerston North in the winter of 1959, I sat down and wrote to an All Black. I was ten years old and the letter was in my best handwriting.

The letter was to Terry Lineen, the All Black second five-eighth who could float through gaps which he identified using radar. He was elegant and gifted and as Red Smith once said of a pitcher in American baseball, 'He could throw a lamb-chop past a wolf.' The next player who combined strength and subtlety in this same way was Bruce Robertson, who drifted upright past opponents who seemed to accompany him and offer whatever assistance they could. It was ridiculous and it looked easy and no one else could do it.

In those days there were four tests a year rather than one a week and they actually mattered. Nobody sang the national anthem and if a player scored a try he returned to his position in solitude and waited until the fuss died down. Nobody got paid. The players all had other jobs. Like Ed Hillary, who climbed the highest mountain in the world, but was really a beekeeper.

The only way to watch rugby at that time was to be at the game or hope that a few seconds of a test match appeared in newsreel footage at the pictures.

For the kids of Palmerston North, however, there were the All Black Trials, matches between the Possibles and the Probables, imaginary sides made up of real players. Squadrons of us primary school kids would fill the Manawatu Showgrounds and watch our heroes before sprinting into no man's land after the match and getting everyone's autograph.

The national selectors should have paid more attention to us at these fixtures. We were good. We went for balance in a side but we rewarded flair and our selections stand up well to this day. Basil

Bridge and I picked Kel Tremain a year before the selectors did. Kel ran flat; nothing deceptive but he processed things fast and he was up on the opposition like a writ. The selectors ignored him until the Lions scored four great tries against us in the first test in Dunedin and the NZRFU referred to our notes and popped Kel on the side of the All Black scrum for the next eight years. That first 1959 Lions test match was the Dunkirk of New Zealand rugby. On the one hand firepower, élan, tactics and quick thinking. On the other hand (ours) Don Clarke kicked six penalties. As Churchill said at the time, 'We must be careful not to assign to this deliverance, the attributes of a victory.'

Observant kids on bikes who had been in attendance at the Manawatu Showgrounds had sensed this would happen. We'd made a few changes but they hadn't been introduced. We'd picked Red Conway for example. How he'd missed selection for Dunedin we couldn't understand. He'd come down from Taranaki and he'd taken the Trial match apart. He was all over the paddock and was one of the first forwards we'd ever seen turn up among the mid-field backs looking for part-time work.

We'd also earmarked the big Waikato lock Pickering. I was so confident I got his autograph twice. He said, 'You've already got mine,' but I wasn't convinced and he gave it to me again. I may be the only sixty-year-old kid in the world with E. A. R. Pickering's name signed twice, one above the other because he was right and because he was genial, in my autograph book (I'll leave it to the state. It's an important record. It's not just mine. It belongs to the nation).

A lot of people think selection is easy. It isn't. We had our difficulties. We were troubled by the Briscoe/Urban question at halfback and we didn't spot Ralph Caulton, the Wellington winger who looked as if he'd arrived to check the gas meter and then zipped over for two tries in a dream debut in the second test at Athletic Park (I was there that day and Keith Quinn was a ball boy. After the match Keith got the ball from the final kick and returned it to the kicker, Donald Barry Clarke, the famously accurate porpoise from Morrinsville whose brother Ian was still propping the New Zealand scrum at 112. Don thanked Quinnie very much and, recognising a good keen man, gave him a pie).

Terry Lineen wrote back to me.

John Clarke
18 Milverton Ave.
Palmerston North.

The letter thanked me, encouraged me and thought perhaps I might be interested in the signatures of the All Blacks who played in the third test against the Lions (which we won 22–8). These were all on a separate sheet. Each player was named and each had signed next to his name.

I still feel good about this letter.

When Fred Dagg first appeared on television in the 1970s, he got letters from kids all over New Zealand. Every kid who wrote to Fred Dagg received a reply. The reason Fred wrote back to all these kids is that Terry Lineen wrote back to me.

Murray Rose

In mid-July 2011 I met the Olympic swimmer Murray Rose at the North Bondi Surf Club. Our small film crew was setting up to record an interview with him for a documentary about the importance of sport in Australia. Meeting at North Bondi was Murray's idea. He loved the place.

He remembered being a small boy, arrived from England and living near the Sydney beaches. One day he was playing on the shoreline when his small toy yacht drifted beyond his reach and began to bob further and further out to sea. A man in a rowboat saw this happening and rowed over to the little yacht, picked it up, brought it back in and handed it to the boy. 'Here you are son,' he said. 'Can't you swim?' 'No,' said Murray. It was at this point he decided to learn.

15 July 2011 was a dirty day in Sydney, wild and squally. Rain drummed on the surf club windows and lanyards beat on flagpoles. When Murray arrived he showed me around the upstairs room where they keep the photographs of surf lifesavers going back fifty or sixty years. Murray knew who they all were and remembered what they'd done. Murray was one of the greatest swimmers in history but he wasn't just a pool swimmer. He loved the sea and these were his people.

I'd spoken to Murray a couple of times on the phone and we'd discussed what we might talk about in the interview. His areas of expertise ranged across the history of Australian swimming, the Olympic movement and its ideals, drugs, suits and technology, broadcasting, literature, other swimmers, coaching, psychology, the feeling of being in the water, strategy, bodysurfing, philosophy and self-reliance. His voice was soft, with a slight accent from his years in America. He saw the universal and the particular as Astaire and Rogers. His memories were well formed, his manner was relaxed and easy and his point was always clear. He knew what he thought and he wanted to get it right.

When he worked out that I came from Palmerston North, Murray recalled swimming there, at the Municipal Baths, in the late 1950s (I was there, with some other local squirts watching these tall, blond, actual Greek gods swimming in our pool). He explained how, in the relay they'd rustled up an Australian team by instructing the team manager to go and change and swim the first leg. (They won by so much it wouldn't have mattered if the manager had swum in a full dress tartan. We were so impressed we ate a lot of ice-cream.)

Murray's favourite event was the 400m freestyle, which he won in Melbourne and again in Rome. It was tough and required sprinting speed but was long enough to be a tactical race, which he liked. His early hero was John Marshall, who broke twenty-eight world records and was killed in a car accident in his twenties. Murray said he tried to swim like John Marshall until one day his coach asked him what he was doing. 'I'm swimming like John Marshall,' said Murray. 'No you're not,' said his coach. 'You'll never swim like John Marshall because he's unique. But so are you and if you swim your own stroke, one day you'll swim faster than John Marshall.' Be yourself. Know yourself.

Murray's father had grown up with rheumatic fever and had to be careful with his health. He found a vegetarian diet at one stage and started eating cereal and vegetables. Murray went along with this and quickly developed a reputation for having a very weird diet, which in some versions of the story consisted largely of kelp. By this stage Murray was a competitive swimmer and he let the story circulate because it helped other swimmers create a reason he might beat them.

Swimming has changed a lot. In 1956 there were no goggles and no tumble turns. Murray and Dawn Fraser shared the distinction of having their Olympic careers cut short by buffoons in admin. They both kept swimming, of course, and at the age of about forty, Murray started doing tumble turns and his times started coming down. He was swimming faster than he had in Rome. At seventy-two he swam the Hellespont and he wanted to do it again. When we met, he'd been reading Byron, a previous titleholder in the event. Murray still swam most days, often in the sea, at Bondi.

One of the significant examples of the value of the Olympic movement at its best is the story of Murray and the Japanese swimmer Tsuyoshi Yamanaka. Here is Murray:

'When I was growing up, when I was three or four, I was part of a propaganda campaign for the Australian war effort. And the head-line was something like "Will the Japs Come Here With Their Big Ships, Daddy?" And it was a fairly intense campaign. Fast forward a few years and I'm swimming at the Olympic Games and my main rival and competitor is Tsuyoshi Yamanaka and we happened to meet each other in every heat and every final. And by the time we got to the last swim we'd developed a pretty healthy respect and friendship. The last individual event at the Olympics in 1956 was the 1500m. And then after we'd finished we embraced across the lane line and a photograph of that moment was taken and was picked up by newspapers all over the world. For one main reason. The date was 7 December 1956; the fifteenth anniversary of the Japanese attack on Pearl Harbour. So it became symbolic of two kids who'd grown up on opposite sides of the war, had come together in the friendship of the Olympic arena.'

Here are two more extracts from near the end of our conversation:

'I'm still learning about swimming technique. Every time I go in the water I'm conscious of my technique and I'm looking at new ways of relating to the water, and learning, as the elite swimmers and elite coaches are today. They are still learning. We're not done with this. You never become a master, until you're able to go out there on Bondi and watch and be a dolphin, which we do sometimes.'

'We had an experience one day last year; there was a fairly big surf coming in and the sun was shining, the wind was coming off shore and we were looking for waves. And then a rogue set came up from the back, so we swam pretty hard to make sure we got over it. And half way up the face of the first wave I knew that I was going to make it. So I just relaxed and streamlined, and the power of the wave just shot me almost up to my ankles out of the water because it was a fairly big wave. And the spray was being blown by the wind and it caught the sun and I was literally flying in a rainbow.'

Murray Rose (1939–2012)

Marjorie Jackson

Marjorie Jackson is about my mother's age and the people in photos of Marjorie when she was younger look like the people in my mother's photos. The photos are in black and white and a lot of them are taken at beaches and other places where young people met, looking good, possibly for mating purposes. A noticeable feature of these photos is that there's nobody obese or overweight in any of them.

In June 2011 I met Marjorie at her daughter's house, where we'd arranged to discuss her remarkable sporting career for a documentary.

Marjorie was about to turn eighty and looked very fit. She was courteous, quick and lively, and her memory was excellent. In later years she was the governor of South Australia and she served in many national and international roles, but it was in talking about the world she grew up in that she located the values she has lived by all her life.

Her story is a famous one. She came from Lithgow and was the first Australian woman to win an Olympic gold medal on the track. When she was a schoolgirl champion, her father had got a local man, Mr Monaghan, to coach her. Mr Monaghan had been a runner and they trained in the evenings after they'd both finished work. When it got dark Mr Monaghan would park his car at the end of the track with the headlights on and sometimes, when it was foggy, Marjorie wasn't sure exactly where the car was while sprinting directly towards it.

'How I didn't break a leg or something I'll never know.'

Marjorie's father sent away for a pair of running shoes. They cost five guineas and were so precious he built her a pair of protective rubber soles into which she could sit the spikes, so she didn't damage them while walking around. A couple of times when we were talking about her childhood and these teenage years she looked away and shook her head slightly. 'We were so poor,' she said. 'We really did have nothing.'

The big star of the 1948 London Olympics was the Dutch sprinter Fanny Blankers-Koen, who won four gold medals. In 1949 Fanny came to Australia to run in some exhibition races against local opposition. Marjorie was seventeen and she travelled down to Sydney to compete in the first of the three races. To Fanny's very great surprise, Marjorie won the first race in a time that would have won her the gold medal in London.

When she arrived at the track for the second race, Marjorie was told she wasn't allowed to run. When her coach found out about this he insisted that she go back and run, so she returned to the start line. At this point Fanny withdrew from the event. In the third and final race, Marjorie got away well and although she felt the Olympic champion on her shoulder at about the sixty-metre mark, she won again without much trouble. Fanny said there'd been a pothole in the track but the journalists who went out and searched the track reported that they couldn't find one. After the race Marjorie realised she'd forgotten to remove the protective rubber soles from under her shoes. She'd been running without spikes.

Marjorie was getting pretty famous by this stage and when they heard that the Olympic Athletics track in Helsinki would be made of cinders, the people of Lithgow took up a collection and put in one lane of cinders at the local grass oval, for her to train on. When she went down to Sydney to compete in the New South Wales championships, where she hoped to qualify for the Olympics, the car she was travelling in was hit by a truck and rolled over and Marjorie was taken to hospital. The women's sprint events at the New South Wales championships were postponed that year because the other women refused to run until Marjorie was well enough to compete. Marjorie's voice went a bit soft when she was describing this, which she said was one of the greatest things that happened to her in sport.

The 1952 Australian Olympics team flew to Helsinki in a plane. The trip took a week. The first stop was in Darwin. After a couple of days team management said, 'Get up and move around. Go for a walk. Change seats. Introduce yourselves to each other. You'll be sitting down for a while.' Marjorie found herself sitting next to a cyclist from South Australia. They got on very well and by the time they got to London, he'd asked her to marry him. 'I only knew his name,' she smiled. 'Didn't know anything else about him. I thought, fancy waking up with this gorgeous hunk.' Team management were appalled and counselled caution but Peter Nelson and Marjorie Jackson were a match for life.

Marjorie won both the 100 metres and 200 metres in Helsinki, broke world records in both of them and set a new standard for Australian track athletes.

I'd watched both these races on YouTube and observed that she'd won them by a good margin.

'Really?' She said.

At this point our sound operator got his phone out and found the 1952 Helsinki Olympics Women's 100m final on YouTube. 'Here we go,' he said.

An enduring memory of this wonderful day is watching a small group including Marjorie and her daughter, crowded around watching this great race on a very small screen. 'Oh yes,' conceded Marjorie after the race had finished. 'I did win quite well.'

After we left, Marjorie asked her daughter if the 200m final would be on YouTube. It is, and they found it on the computer and watched it together. Marjorie won it by miles. She turned to her daughter Sandy and said 'Do you know why I ran so fast in Helsinki?'

'No, Mum,' said Sandy. 'Why did you?'

'Because I'd just met your father. And I knew he was there, in the crowd.'

When she returned to Australia, the aircraft flew low over Lithgow on its way to Sydney and when it banked Marjorie could see the people of the town lining the streets to greet her. She would not be there for many hours. The honour of making these people so proud was a considerable reward for Marjorie.

Also in Lithgow that day were her parents, of whom she spoke with admiration and gratitude. She misses them still. She wishes they'd lived to see more of the lives of their children.

Marjorie's mother never saw her run.

Peter Thomson

After the Christchurch earthquakes the Australian golfer Peter Thomson contacted the Shirley Golf Club and arranged to come over and visit the course. He wanted to know how he could help. He has friends there he has known for fifty years.

Peter won the New Zealand Open golf title nine times. When I was growing up, you knew it was summer when there were nectarines on the ground and pictures of Peter Thomson in the paper. He looked elegant, compact, determined and ironical. I've played a bit of golf with Peter over the years and have had the opportunity to study him at close hand. He is elegant, compact, determined and ironical.

After winning the British Open five times Peter retired and came home. He became an excellent writer and commentator, flirted with politics and now runs a successful international business designing golf courses.

I asked him recently if he'd always been competitive. 'I think I've always been pretty competitive, yes,' he said. 'I had brothers and we were all competitive.' Then he thought for a moment. 'I'll tell you how competitive I am,' he said. 'My oldest friend in golf is Kel Nagle. I've played golf all over the world with Kel. We won the Canada Cup together. We've been through a lot and he's a great friend. And it has occasionally occurred to me that Kel would be a nicer bloke if he didn't putt so well.'

When the Presidents Cup was played at Royal Melbourne in 1998, the first ball hit down the first fairway in the first match on the first morning was hit by a New Zealander. The Presidents Cup is between the USA and a team of Internationals. The captain of the International Team that year was Peter, and he'd selected two New Zealanders among his twelve players. They weren't ranked in the top fifty in the world but Peter thought they could do some damage. He was later asked by the media why he'd sent the New Zealanders out first. 'New Zealand is two hours ahead,' explained Peter. 'They're awake a bit earlier.'

And so it was that Greg Turner and Frank Nobilo went out and beat Mark O'Meara and David Duvall who were ranked second and third in the world. Greg's brother Brian and his wife and I had followed them around the course and as Greg came off the eighteenth we considered the prospect of lunch. 'No,' said Greg, who was pretty pumped at the time. 'Let's go out to the eighth and cheer Ernie and Vijay through. If we can get away to a start today we might get amongst it.'

So we walked out to the eighth and at about driving length on the eighth fairway, sitting on his own with his feet up on the dashboard of a buggy with 'Presidents Cup Captain' written on it, was Peter.

'Hello, Greg,' said Peter. 'You and Frank played very well. I thought you two might do that. Good on you.'

'Yes. It was good,' said Greg. 'I don't think you've met my brother Brian and his wife Barbara.'

'Nice to meet you,' said Peter.

As they said hello, Brian congratulated Peter on his excellent speech at the opening ceremony the previous evening.

'Thanks,' said Peter. 'That's very kind of you.'

Brian is the senior Turner brother. He's a fine poet, a mountain man and a wily judge of sport. He captained the New Zealand hockey team, caddied for Greg and plenty of others on the tour and he sometimes tosses up between a cup of tea and a bike ride around the South Island.

'Yes, I thought your speech was excellent,' continued Brian, warming to the task. 'Telling the Americans they were the greatest assembly of golfing talent ever to come to this country. That was brilliant.'

'Thank you, Brian,' said Peter. 'I've actually just been sitting here thinking about what I might say at the closing ceremony.'

'Have you worked it out?' asked Brian.

'Yes,' said Peter. 'I thought I might thank them for coming.'

Writers and Artists

Seamus Heaney

(Review: *Stepping Stones: Interviews with Seamus Heaney*, Dennis O'Driscoll, Faber, 2009)

When Seamus Heaney came to Melbourne in 1994, he had not yet won the Nobel Prize and could still play an away game. He participated in three memorable events and was responsible for deep enjoyment among those present. As he talked and read from his poetry, its themes opened up and the tone of his voice provided a sense of the weave and heft of his writing.

'When you write,' Heaney says in *Stepping Stones*, 'the main thing is to feel you are rising to your own occasion'. Marshalling the strength, memory, belief, shyness, humour and philosophy required to do this, is what *Stepping Stones* is about. A roughly chronological record of Heaney's life and work, the book takes the form of a series of interviews conducted with fellow poet and friend Dennis O'Driscoll, whose excellent map of the territory gives the book its structure. Most of the questions, responses and exchanges were written rather than spoken and there has been some criticism of this from the Lilliputian cavalry on the basis that Heaney could have been put under more pressure by direct confrontation. Pay no attention. Heaney has long needed to find safe ground for open, relaxed and generous discourse. And incidentally, even when putting the shutters up, Seamus will go very nicely. At a full house session in Melbourne he was asked how he would define religious poetry. He leant into the microphone as if he were at the House of Un-American Activities hearings and explained, 'Religious poetry is that poetry in which the exclamatory particle "O" figures considerably.' No trouble.

Seamus Heaney was the eldest of nine children in a nationalist Catholic Ulster farming family. At the age of eleven he won a scholarship, which took him away to boarding school and by twenty-two he had a first-class honours degree. The farm that had given him his bearings was behind him and the pull of home was moving from his life to his poetry. He writes of this realisation in an early poem, 'Digging':

> But I've no spade to follow men like that.
> Between my finger and my thumb
> The squat pen rests.
> I'll dig with it.

Heaney's beautifully remembered South Derry childhood nevertheless provides the historical nucleus of his life and work. In 'Digging' we hear the tribal vernacular he has kept in an inside pocket at all times. The circumference of his life has since widened to embrace other languages, work at Berkeley and Harvard, acclaim at home and abroad. But he still holds a poetry book the way a farmer holds an almanac of cattle prices and crop yields. He is practical, friendly and weather-wise and when amused, as he often is, his eyes close with pleasure. The Heaney nucleus also features an instinct for the resolving chord in things; for finding the balance in words and ideas. In another early poem he sees the military disparity of the 1798 Irish Rebellion, in which the French arrived too late to help and were given an ice cream by the English and sent home, while the Irish rebels were slaughtered. Still in his twenties, Heaney's impulse was not to rail against injustice; that would be rhetorical. It was to find, in the real story, an image which was as sure as the rhythm of the seasons. The Irish soldiers, ill equipped and hungry, were given a handful of barley to put in the pockets of their greatcoats.

Heaney's first Faber book of poems, *Death of a Naturalist* (1966), was an immediate success. He was twenty-seven and working as a teacher. His next books were also successful and he was increasingly sought as a speaker, lecturer and professor. In 1972 Clive James recognised the power in Heaney's verse and in 1975 Robert Lowell described him as 'the best Irish poet since W. B. Yeats.' He was hailed, feted and wreathed in prizes. This led to the usual trouble. It was all happening to him too early, some said. It would fade, they predicted. 'Famous Seamus' they joked. He couldn't keep it up, they agreed. The next book would be a dud, they reasoned. But they were not really talking about Heaney. He did not heap these garlands upon himself. And it wasn't happening fast; it was just happening. And actually, there was plenty in the tank. His reading was wide and deep and, all through this book, Heaney illustrates with examples, images, metaphors and quotations from other writers. He was also learning to trust his personal experience, to write out of his own places and people and to invest intimacy in the language itself. One thing is very obvious about Heaney; he is patient. He has never forced the pace. The writing that interests him is not a race. It'll happen or it won't.

It did happen. The books continued to come; poetry, criticism and translations. In 2000 he published his translation of *Beowulf* from Old English. It was a sensation, enriching the language at its source. In doing this work Heaney used words we use now but only those that come directly from Old English. Old English words are short, strong, stalwart, conveying meaning, not flourish. He gave as an example the section from the Churchill speech, which begins 'We shall fight on the beaches' and ends 'We shall never surrender'. The only word in it which does not come from Old English is 'surrender'.

Throughout *Stepping Stones* the reader is surfing in language. Heaney can lilt from a serious point to a softening aside or another thought without losing 'the whole thing.' His English is assured, exhilarating and colossal, but not complex. He returns often to Robert Lowell's landfall line, 'Why not say what happened?' It is never unclear what Heaney is saying and his poetry is able to be read by anyone. When his mother died he wrote a sequence of short poems called 'Crossings.' Read them when your mother dies. When his father died he wrote a sequence called 'Clearances.' When his children were born he wrote about it. When his country was in turmoil he wrote about it. When he and Marie were young marrieds living in a country cottage he wrote the 'Glanmore Sonnets' (1979). When he wanted something new, he journeyed to the bogs of Jutland, digging again but in an older place.

At the heart of this book is an investigation into what Heaney thinks matters and how to say it. In *Preoccupations: Selected Prose* (1980) he asked, 'How should a poet properly live and write?' He found some of his answers in Eastern European writers who were 'keeping on', who prevailed through horrors; the Czech Miloslav Holub, the beguiling and deadly Joseph Brodsky and the man Heaney describes as 'the giant at my shoulder', Czeslaw Milosz. Read Heaney on his admiration for Joseph Brodsky and Czeslaw Milosz. Read him also on his fellow feeling for Ted Hughes or the playwright Brian Friel. Read him on his aunt Mary, on Elizabeth Bishop and on Yeats. When Heaney speaks of the ways in which people have helped him in his poetry, he is not always talking about an insight into where he could tighten a stanza. Often it is a kindness, some support, a wink.

Ulster humour is dark, nutritious stuff. When Heaney showed his friend John McGahern the house he had recently purchased, McGahern pondered upon it. 'Well,' he announced, 'you've bought the coffin.' When Heaney had a stroke, from which he has now recovered, Brian Friel visited him in hospital. Friel had had a stroke himself a few years previously and comforted his friend with the insight, 'Different strokes for different folks'.

If you like poetry or think you might, if you are a writer or might be, if you value place, memory and language, you might enjoy this remarkable book.

W. H. Auden

Across southern Australia there is a beautiful tree called leuco-pogan. If you google it and find a picture, you'll realise you know it quite well. The leucopogan seed can germinate only once it has passed through the gut of a bird. The bird eats the seed, softening it through digestion, so that when it drops on the ground, it can open and grow. Twentieth-century poetry is the Leucopogan tree. W. H. Auden is the bird. Next slide please.

Another natural history lesson includes the maxim that in polite company, you should never discuss politics, sex or religion. Auden was cleaning this theory one night when it went off. Almost everything he wrote about, and he wrote about almost everything, was politics, sex or religion.

It was Auden who said that you don't read a book, a book reads you; a description of the way the creative impulse communicates itself in art. From an early age he himself was read by a lot of history and literature. He was multilingual, saw world events very clearly and he wrote all the time. He also smoked all the time, read all the time and talked all the time. He published verse, prose, criticism and lyrics. He wrote letters, gave lectures and kept a journal all his life. He wrote about love, death, fear, hope and gossip. By the time he was twenty-five a large queue had already formed behind him, waiting to see where he would go next. He pulled journalism into poetry. He pushed politics and ethics into forms previously used only once a week to drive to church. He wrote with such ease and covered such ground that he ran most of his generation out in the heats. People are still copying him and there are strong traces of him even in writers who claim they never touch the stuff.

I have only one small window on all this. In 1966 I was wandering around my school in Wellington with a book of Auden's letters tucked into my belt in order to ward off evil spirits. My

English teacher took me aside and explained the following: When Auden was a young man, the First World War had just blown everything apart. It was no longer possible to write about daffodils or the skylark; the only legitimate subject was the war, the mindless carnage and waste. So Auden and Louis MacNeice, who could not write about the war since they were too young to have been at it, and could not write about anything else since only the war was a proper subject, decided to embark on a venture that was uniquely theirs and out of which they could write. So they went to Iceland with a friend who was a teacher and was taking a party of boys up there on a walking tour. They wrote throughout the trip and eventually published a book about it called *Letters from Iceland*. 'And,' said my English teacher, 'I was the schoolteacher. So if ever you'd like to read any of Auden's real letters, let me know. I have boxes of them.' And so it was that I spent some time reading Auden's rather chatty letters to Bill Hoyland. The handwriting was small, upright, swift, assured and fluent, in a blue fountain pen, with no corrections. I had no knowledge of Auden, of course. The person most illuminated for me here was my English teacher. He told me that Auden's two grandfathers, MacNeice's father and many of the Hoylands were churchmen, and that during the 1930s the young men had sought a way of investing Christian ethics in secular society. Hoyland, a Quaker and our school chaplain, never spoke of scripture. His sermons were about philosophy. So were Auden's.

Wystan Hugh Auden was born in 1907 in York and grew up in the Midlands where his eyes swallowed the limestone country and where he expected to go into the lead mining business. When he got to university he studied English instead and became a prodigiously gifted shambles at the centre of a group that included MacNeice, Stephen Spender and Cecil Day Lewis. Like them, during the 1930s Auden wanted poetry to be a force for change. He was to be disappointed, 'For poetry makes nothing happen.' But he certainly changed poetry. Even his rhythm was new. It sometimes doesn't look like rhythm at all. It looks like talk.

> About suffering they were never wrong,
> The Old Masters: how well they understood
> Its human position; how it takes place while
> Someone else is eating or opening a window or just walking
> dully along

On the real events of his time, Auden is deadly. Here he is in 1939, in a poem officially about Yeats:

> In the nightmare of the dark
> All the dogs of Europe bark,
> And the living nations wait,
> Each sequestered in its hate;
>
> Intellectual disgrace
> Stares from every human face,
> And the seas of pity lie
> Locked and frozen in each eye.

A lot of Auden's poems read like this. He's not a performer; he's a writer who is thinking aloud. The poet's project is himself.

Auden and Christopher Isherwood (see *Cabaret*) left England for America in 1939. Auden married Thomas Mann's daughter Erika, to get her out of Germany, and accepted American offers to lecture. Debate has raged about this ever since. The English establishment disliked Auden because he had sided with the left in Spain in 1936. The left disliked him because he changed his mind after going to Spain in 1937. George Orwell criticised him for writing that during war we all acquiesce in 'the necessary murder'. Orwell called him 'a gutless Kipling'. Auden thought this was unfair and, upon reflection, so did Orwell. Auden also agreed with Orwell, disliking some of his own writing of this period and pulling it from his collections.

One of the criticisms made of modernism is that it was essentially selfish; clever and exciting by all means and for a while there the arts were very cool. But modernism did not warn of the two great monsters, Hitler and Stalin. What use is art if it doesn't pop up a signal before 50 million people get killed? Why should we listen to artists if they don't have a problem with fascism, racism and mass murder? As Auden himself pointed out, his writing didn't save a single Jew. This wouldn't have bothered a lot of poets but to Auden it was a significant moral failure and must be acknowledged. This is a very honest man. Reading him is like being in the disinterested but clever company of a big man who'd have been happy to be small, a famous man who'd have been content to be anonymous and a somewhat distant figure who desperately wants to be close.

The More Loving One

Looking up at the stars, I know quite well
That, for all they care, I can go to hell,
But on earth indifference is the least
We have to dread from man or beast.

How should we like it were stars to burn
With a passion for us we could not return?
If equal affection cannot be,
Let the more loving one be me.

Jane Austen

When I was at university the form guide provided to students of the novel was produced by the Cambridge flat-earther, F. R. Leavis, who named the great novelists as George Eliot, Henry James, Joseph Conrad, D. H. Lawrence and Jane Austen. Lawrence was probably an honest mistake and rehabilitating George Eliot after the Dickens/

Thackeray boom was at least courteous but what Conrad was doing in the side no one knew and selecting Henry James was obviously a cry for help.

It was some time before I returned to reading of any kind and it took decades before I could get near Jane Austen, approaching only at night, through biographies.

During the 1990s, however, many of Austen's works were adapted for the screen and it was possible to actually respond to them rather than be told what the examiners would be looking for.

The novel I knew best was *Pride and Prejudice*. (Discuss. 30 marks).

In the BBC adaptation it is observed that if the writer's asides to the reader are removed from a novel, what is left is the plot. Beefing this up and pouring music through it can elevate it slightly but the writer has gone and in the nineteenth century, before the writer was the subject of the novel, the relationship between the writer and the reader is the key part of the arrangement.

In the TV version Elizabeth is beautiful and her mother is a neurotic shrike who insists that her daughters marry the richest men they can find. Elizabeth then marries the richest man she can find, a smouldering stallion she can't stand until she sees the size of his huge house. In other words we are invited to view Mrs Bennet as a hysterical peabrain with the values of a provincial snob and to imagine somehow that Elizabeth undercuts these values by fulfilling them. This is not terribly ironical and diversionary tactics are employed by the BBC to distract us; extra scenes are added which are not in the novel, such as Darcy peeling off a few laps in his own personal lake and then wuthering off through a Constable landscape.

The main problem here is not the silliness of Cartlandising the story but a misreading of Elizabeth through the removal of the writer. Like Anne Elliot in the more faithful movie adaptation of *Persuasion* beautifully written by Nick Dear, Elizabeth Bennet is not conventionally beautiful any more than Jane Austen was. She is wise and perceptive and she sees folly in idle foreplay, manipulation and dissembling.

In *Persuasion*, the Elliots' house is being rented by an admiral and his wife, who talk to Anne about being at sea together. Jane Austen had two brothers who became admirals and most of the men in *Persuasion* are in the navy, so she knows whereof she speaks. The wife of the admiral tells Anne what it's like going all over the world together, making a life, charting a course, defining a relationship outside the conventions of English society. Anne listens with keen interest and is persuaded. Like Elizabeth Bennet and Emma Woodhouse, Anne is rather assured, so when she behaves badly or makes a mistake, she does it in spades. Hence the self-knowledge lesson, when it comes, is exemplary.

The movie *Clueless* catches this better than the film version of *Emma*, the novel on which it is based, because it doesn't mistake film for a visual medium and it concentrates on the language of the central character and narrator. So we hear the mockery, the fun, the difference between what is said and what we see. In the BBC *Pride and Prejudice* there is no narrator, no irony, no Austen. And to save you the trouble of reading Leavis, it's not the stories; it's the way you tell them.

Ray Parkin

Ray Parkin told stories, real stories, non-fiction, and he didn't tell them to amuse or to entertain. He told them to record. Ray wanted you to understand, to know how it was. This was interesting to me because I knew nothing about the Japanese war, or the navy. I was at his place with my daughter one day when a bird tried to fight another bird. She drew his attention to this and Ray said: 'You should have seen it this morning. That big one came flying out of that tree straight at the honeyeater and he got her athwartships.' I was learning these stories and I was also learning the way they were told. I was learning a new language, a new terminology.

Laurens van der Post wrote in his foreword to *Out of the Smoke*, the first of Ray's three books about being a prisoner of the Japanese, that he had read much of the story years before. This was true. Ray was sitting down drawing in Bandoeng camp in Indonesia one day when van der Post, a fellow POW, introduced himself. He asked Ray who he was and how he came to be there. Ray told him the story: he'd been at the wheel of the HMAS *Perth*, it was sunk in battle, he and some others got to shore, rigged up a lifeboat, headed for Australia, hit a typhoon and were blown down to Tjilatjap, on the coast of Java, some eleven hours later.

'That's a great maritime war story,' said van der Post. 'You should write it down.'

'Yes, I've written it down,' said Ray.

'I mean it should become a book,' said Laurens.

'Yes, it is a book,' said Ray.

'How can it be a book? We've only been here a week.'

'I met a bloke the other day who was a bookbinder and he bound it.'

It was written in pencil on small individual sheets of shiny toilet paper. When Ray was moved from camp to camp it fitted in his shoe, down behind his heel. Van der Post explained that he had published books, and he undertook to introduce Ray to his publisher once the war was over. Years later Leonard Woolf, Virginia's husband, rang Ray in Melbourne. Ray went to England and Hogarth Press printed his book. Cecil Day Lewis was his editor.

'Wasn't he the poet laureate?' I asked, impressed.

'Yes he was,' said Ray. 'But he didn't change anything in the book.'

I learnt that Ray had been through a great ordeal. And I learnt he was not a racist. He did not hate the Japanese. 'That was one of the *causes* of the war,' he said. 'It cannot be the result.' Ray, like Weary Dunlop, was influenced by the East, by the place and the ideas. I sometimes saw Ray asked about his experiences by others, and his responses were seldom what they expected.

'The Burma–Thailand Railway, The Speedo, Hellfire Pass— what was that like?' they'd ask.

'The flowers in that area are among the most beautiful I've ever seen,' Ray would reply. 'We were lucky to be there at that particular time of the year.'

I asked Ray questions, too. I learnt more things. I learnt the reason Australians survived better than others in the camps was not that they helped each other and were mates. Ray said the best thing you can do for anyone else in a situation like that is to be completely self-reliant. A few years ago he fell in the garden; it turned out he had a neurological virus with a French name. He couldn't walk. He couldn't write. He went to a convalescence place. Then one day he told me he thought he might come home next week.

I said: 'Do you want to come home next week?'

He said: 'I'd want to know I could walk four kilometres, up to Ivanhoe shops and back, so I can do for myself.'

'Do you think you can do that?'

'Well, I can do three and a half.'

'How do you know that?'

'I measured it out around the hospital and I've been doing it for a fortnight.' Very self-reliant.

Ray wrote and did drawings all the time he was in captivity. The penalty if you got caught was death. Dunlop, a surgeon, hid a lot of this material inside his operating table and gave it back after the war. One thing I asked Ray about was a series of little drawings of merchant ships. 'Oh,' said Ray, 'there was an English bloke in one of the camps. He'd been in the merchant navy before the war. After lights out we'd lie there and I'd get him to remember ships he'd seen. Sometimes I'd seen them myself, before the war. Sometimes they were ships I had never seen. I'd ask him to describe the details. Where was the funnel? What colour was it? And then I'd draw it. And then I'd show him the drawing and he'd look at the drawing and he'd say: "Yep. That's it."

The drawings were beautiful. The war finished. The camp was liberated. The authorities came around and asked the men to fill out forms naming the commandants and guards who had done these terrible things. Ray called it 'name your war criminal'. Anyone listed in the forms was going to be charged with war crimes. 'We won't be here,' thought Ray. 'These people will be charged and we'll be back in Australia. They'll have no defence. They can't cross-examine us.'

Ray thought the commandant of this last camp had shown them kindness. Instead of marching them down the beach before they went into the coalmine, he let them walk. Ray was able to pick up flowers and leaves and butterflies. One day the commandant summoned Ray to his office, sent the guard out of the room and gave him a small tin of children's watercolours. This meant he knew about Ray's drawings—a summary offence. Maybe it was a trap. But Ray trusted him and took the paints. The commandant made Ray put the paints in his pocket before calling the guard back in and dismissing Prisoner Parkin. Later this same commandant had the prisoners dig a big pit in the yard, but he didn't shoot them. Each day he'd get them to re-dig it, or to dig an extension on, or something. But he didn't shoot them.

So when they were liberated, Ray didn't fill out his form. He drew a picture of the camp and gave it to this man, and he wrote: 'To commandant X, with thanks for his kindness, Parkin.' The commandant was later charged with war crimes. Unlike a lot of the others, he wasn't executed. He had one piece of evidence to present in his defence.

Another thing Ray told me about was Captain James Cook. Ray was a great admirer of Cook's seamanship and gifts as a navigator. Ray's neighbour Max Crawford, a history professor at Melbourne University, had asked him various questions about the ship and Ray knew so much about Cook and his voyage that Crawford encouraged him to write it down. He did, recording everything in big foolscap books, each day of the voyage: Cook's log, Cook's diary, what Banks wrote, what Parkinson wrote. Then Ray wrote what the ordinary person on board would have experienced that day. Then there were all the exquisite drawings of sails and ropes and equipment, all the charts, all done by Ray.

I said: 'This should be published.'

'If you can get it published, good for you,' Ray replied.

H. M. Bark Endeavour was eventually published by The Miegunyah Press, an imprint of Melbourne University Press. In 1999 it won the New South Wales Premier's Book of the Year award. Ray, who was eighty-eight by this time, enjoyed his success.

After that Ray began to write about his philosophy of life. He saw the world as a whole thing. One day he told me he felt particularly close to Thelma, his late wife, in a couple of places in the garden. I asked him where he met Thelma. 'Do you see the way the river comes around that corner there?' he said. 'And that bump there, and that tree? Thelma was sitting under that tree when I first saw her.'

'Is that why you bought this piece of land and built the house here?'

'Of course it is.'

Ray searched for a way of understanding the world and the things he'd seen and experienced. He arrived at a Taoist philosophy and a deep respect for nature. The way a tree knows. Where the sun is. Where water is. He remembered being in the small park over the road from the house where he grew up, in Vere Street, Collingwood, and seeing a dragonfly under a leaf, hiding from a bird. They have knowledge, he said. 'We have knowledge too, in each cell. We should listen to that knowledge. Not be fooled by desire for things we don't need.' Scattered among the things he wrote are ideas from the books he read: the Bible, Plato, Freud, Jung, Spinoza, Kant, novels, political works, philosophy. I once asked him what he needed. He said he needed good food twice a day and it was good if he could sleep dry.

A couple of other things gave Ray satisfaction. When he led the Anzac Day parade in Melbourne a few years ago they asked if he wanted a jeep to ride in. 'It's a march,' he replied. 'I'll march.' But he wanted a navy uniform; he didn't want anyone thinking he was army.

'They won't give you a uniform,' his son John told him.

'Why not?'

'They gave you one in 1928 and you lost it.' He got one in the end, and marched all the way.

Another satisfying moment came in 1967 when they found HMAS *Perth* in the Sunda Strait. People had been looking for it for years. They consulted Ray. It was where he said it would be.

'Is there anything you'd like from the ship?' asked Dave Burchell, the diver.

'Yes,' said Ray, and he asked for the save-all from the wheel-house, where he had been standing during the battle. The save-all is a little scallop-shaped metal holder in which a bosun's whistle or keys might be put for safekeeping. Burchell did the dive, found the save-all, brought it back and it sat on the wall of Ray's study. A place for everything. And everything in its place.

Ray Parkin (1910–2005)

Paul Cox

When Paul Cox was moved from hospital into palliative care, we prepared ourselves for tough news. Paul was getting smaller and weaker, his voice was in retreat and family and friends had attended his bedside to say their goodbyes. His siblings flew out from Europe. I didn't expect to see him again.

A week or so later, Paul decided he was going home and explained to the palliative care people that although he loved them dearly, he would not be dying just yet. He travelled home in a Popemobile-shaped taxi and began blessing people as he passed them in the street. This cheered him up enormously and when we saw him a few days later he rose to meet us, offered us coffee and sat rather grandly in a chair, chatting for hours with a keen emphasis on the future. His voice was stronger, his memory was wonderful, his manners were elegant, his talk was clever and in some cases what he said was astonishing. At seven o'clock each evening, for example, he went out on to his little balcony in Melbourne and raised both arms high in the air in order to receive healing waves being beamed to him by a woman in Uzbekistan. Paul was very amusing about all this but as he said, 'At this stage I believe in nothing and everything.'

A few years earlier, the first time he was going to die, he received a liver transplant and, in a state of profound gratitude, he continued writing and making films. Last year he made a movie in which David Wenham played a man who has a liver transplant and falls in love. Paul met his partner, Rosie, when they were both receiving liver transplants. He was in his late sixties at the time and she is a beautiful Balinese woman of somewhat more tender years. 'I know what you're thinking, Johnny,' Cox said to me when he introduced us. 'Rosie is much younger than I am. But I want you to know, Johnny, my liver is younger than Rosie's.'

Half a lifetime ago Paul and I wrote some films together and we've always stayed in touch. I'd never written a movie before and I quickly learnt it was no use suggesting to Paul a thematically consistent sequence involving sport, for example. That wouldn't fit in a Cox film. Too healthy. And there wasn't much interest in men who fixed cars and called each other 'mate'. Paul's films looked like Dutch interiors with dappled light playing through the window and they were full of urban characters who were ill at ease, often slightly wounded or suffering from incongruity of some kind. As with many collaborations, we wrote by talking a lot together and then writing separately. Paul's house was always full of good conversation. At one stage Werner Herzog was living in a shed in the backyard with a dingo. Peter Watkins also lived there at some point, while he and Paul were discussing a film project. Peter had made the brilliant 1964 docudrama *Culloden* in which 1960s British journalists report live from a battle which occurred in 1745. This strategy of anachronism was new in 1964 and the effect in *Culloden* was terrifying.

Paul's public presentation was that of a serious artist, but he was nevertheless given to fits of amusement which produced a snuffling and rumbling sound such as might occur if a badger were attempting not to explode. When he regrouped, he expressed matters once more in his formal mode, which was not unlike an antiques catalogue. A suggestion which would solve a problem was 'good', a great idea for a scene was 'fine', and if he completely approved of a whole section of plot and dialogue he would pronounce it 'very fine'; as in, 'I read that section again last night, Johnny. That really is very fine.' When *Lonely Hearts*, the first film we wrote together, was about to be released thirty-five years ago, Paul wrote me a letter which I have always kept. In the last line of the letter he said he hoped that having worked on this film together and seeing it come to fruition, would 'strengthen our shy human friendship'. It did.

Having received blessings from Uzbekistan, Paul announced he was going to America. The only people who thought this wouldn't happen were those unfamiliar with Paul's willpower. The doctors wouldn't allow him to fly across the Pacific for fourteen hours so he'd negotiated overnight stays in Bangkok, Dubai and Frankfurt and then a trip across the Atlantic to Chicago. His film *Force of*

Destiny was to play at the Ebert Film Festival and Paul had been invited to speak. Rosie would go with him and make sure he rested, ate the right food and took his tablets. The couple left on April Fool's Day and that night Rosie, whose canonisation is imminent, sent a message reporting that Paul had gone out to dinner in Bangkok. This was probably a PB for the palliative care unit at the Austin but Cox was just limbering up. After Dubai and Frankfurt the official party arrived in Chicago and Paul made a gracious, honest and very engaging speech to an audience who couldn't believe quite what they were watching. Following the festival, Paul and Rosie made their way home and Paul was planning another movie. The fact that he died on Saturday will probably slow him down a bit, although I expect he'll call sometime during the next week or so with a revised schedule. 'I'm still going to do it,' he'll say. 'Why not? I have some good ideas. I want to talk about it. Come to dinner.'

Paulus Henrique Benedictus Cox (1940–2016)

Memories and Reflections

A while ago I received a letter from Susie. When we were very young and she was Susan, we were in the same class at primary school. I rang her at the gallery she was running in Northern New South Wales, to thank her for the letter, to say hello and to ask her a question.

Susan had been in a memory of mine for sixty years and I'd always wondered whether the memory was accurate or whether, over the years, I'd edited it anecdotally to the point where, like Captain Cook's axe, it had six new heads and nine new handles and no longer bore any necessary resemblance to Captain Cook's actual axe.

I told Susan this and asked if she remembered an incident which might conform to these general guidelines. She thought for a minute but sadly she didn't. I told her that was OK and she asked me if I could give her a clue. I told her I didn't want to give her a clue because I wanted her memory to exist on its own so I could check mine against it.

'I'm sorry,' she said. 'I don't think I can remember it. We were only in the same class for a year.'

'It didn't happen at school,' I said.

'Really?' she said, more deeply mystified. 'We didn't know each outside school, did we?'

'It's OK,' I said. 'It doesn't matter.'

'Where did it happen?' she asked.

'It happened at a birthday party,' I said.

There was a pause.

'Oh my God,' she said to her own considerable surprise. 'It was at David's birthday party.'

She then described a memory which she didn't know she had, and which was almost a complete facsimile of my own. We were seven or eight years old and there were a few of us looking at an old shipwreck on Waiterere Beach. Susan and I and a couple of others were on the seaward side of the vessel when a very large wave came in and swept us out to sea. David's older brother ran into the sea, yelling, 'Who can swim? Who can swim?' Susan and I both yelled out above the roar of the sea that we could swim and he rescued the other kids first, running into the waves again and again, fishing kids out and getting them to shore. In my mind Susan and I were just off the coast of Peru by the time he got to us but in fact we probably weren't far out. I felt no panic or fear and I remember being comforted to see Susan's head bobbing in the sea. She had big hair and she was to the north of me and we were both bobbing in the enormous sea.

By the time we came in there were some very concerned adults on the beach and we were put into dry clothes and we ran back along the beach to the house. For some reason the song 'Hi-Lili Hi-Lo' ran all the way back to the house, in my head, in time with my feet on the wet sand. I've never heard that song without the feeling that I'm running along that sand in the late afternoon in a big man's jumper. And I've never thought of Susan without the idea that she and I are together, bobbing along, and that we'll be fine.

⌢

The sparkling Christine Collins was a gifted actor with a particular understanding of the voice. She became an acting and voice coach in London but for many years before that she worked in Beckett plays, often as second voice with Billie Whitelaw as first voice. Many of these productions were directed by Beckett himself and Christine told good stories of working with him. One of my favourites concerned a meeting at Beckett's seventieth birthday party which was held at Beckett's apartment in Paris. Christine had met many of the guests before; they were academics, Beckett scholars, publishers or broadcasting and theatre friends. But she got talking to a very interesting man in the kitchen, whose understanding of Beckett's work was remarkable. He seemed to have seen or read almost everything Beckett had done and seemed to have a been a friend of Sam's forever.

'When did you first meet Sam?' asked Christine.

'The first time I saw Sam,' said the man, 'he was sitting in a railway carriage between Foxrock and Dublin. He was trying to read and there was a lot of noise in the carriage, schoolboys and so on; so I went over to him and said, 'Excuse me. If you're trying to read, you might like to come with me. It's a bit quieter in the next carriage,' and I took him into the first-class carriage. There was no one in there and he had the place to himself.'

'And where do you work?' asked Christine.

'Oh, I'm retired now,' said the man.

'I see,' said Christine. 'And where were you before you retired?'

'I was a porter on the Dublin railways,' said the man.

'So you've known Sam for a very long time,' said Christine.

'Yes,' said the man. 'Except for the war I've been to every one of Sam's birthdays since he was nineteen.'

When Beckett was a young man he studied languages, experienced matters of the kind described in his story 'First Love', was mentioned in *Wisden* (Dublin University v. Northamptonshire, left-handed batsman, left-arm medium-pace bowler) and went to Paris, where he met James Joyce and other exiles. Joyce was a generation older and his eyesight was problematic, and Beckett became an amanuensis. Much of what Joyce wrote in this period was dictated to Beckett. When asked many years later what the difference was between the two of them, Beckett said Joyce was a synthesiser whereas he was an analyser. In his own writing, he said, he tried to reduce things to the essential, whereas Joyce wanted to include everything; every sensation, every sight, every sound, every thought and feeling. As an example, he recalled that Joyce was dictating

Finnegans Wake one day when a man arrived to see him and Joyce said, 'Come in.' When Beckett was reading this section back, he got to 'come in' and Joyce stopped him and considered the merits of a completely extraneous phrase. There followed a brief discussion and Joyce decided to leave it in.

Beckett had earlier appeared in a celebrated court case in Dublin in which the surgeon, athlete, senator and pilot Oliver St John Gogarty had been successfully sued for libel. When they were students, Joyce and Gogarty lived together in a Martello Tower and Gogarty appears as Buck Mulligan in *Ulysses*. The book begins in the tower with Buck Mulligan gently mocking Joyce while shaving and looking out at 'the snotgreen scrotumtightening sea'.

Many years later, when Gogarty was a senator, he was captured by IRA gunmen and only escaped by diving into the River Liffey and swimming across. In one version of the story he was shot in the arm while swimming and when he turned up in the senate the following day with his right arm in a sling, he was questioned by opponents about what had happened. He reported that he had sprained his wrist falling from his bicycle and wanted to keep it immobile. When questioned further he removed the sling and rolled up his sleeve. There was no bullet wound and the matter was dropped. Gogarty had in fact been shot in the other arm.

While he was swimming across the river that night, Gogarty promised the Liffey that if he survived he would bring it a gift, and years later he and Yeats and President Cosgrove were photographed on the riverbank where Gogarty released two white swans, from whom the white swans on the Liffey today are descended.

When I was even younger than I am now, there was a book in our house called *Plutarch's Lives of the Greeks*. I was a bit busy being a child at the time and didn't read the book but a few years ago I bought a spoken word version of it and I listened to it in the car. As I drove, a world opened in my head.

Plutarch was a Roman and was writing about what we can learn from ancient Greece about how to run a society. Each chapter describes a particular individual contribution to the rise of ancient Greece. Themistocles for example. Themistocles's response to the impending attack of the enormous Persian army was to order the construction of 200 ships. He sailed the ships across the Aegean to Persia and made loud and offensive threats before turning and sailing back toward Greece in full sight of the Persians who changed their plans and put their very large army on ships and set out after the Greeks. The Greek ships led the Persians into the narrow straits of Salamis where the smaller Greek vessels were more manoeuvrable and where the much smaller Greek army was positioned on the hills to welcome any Persians who managed to get ashore. The Persians were comprehensively defeated and Themistocles remains an example of how superior tactics can triumph over superior numbers.

This lesson was not lost on Alexander the Great, who was waiting in the wings of history. Before he was great, Alexander was nevertheless thought to be heading in that direction. One day his father Phillip of Macedon was presented with a magnificent, huge, strong and beautiful horse. Unfortunately, at the presentation the horse was wild and unmanageable. Alexander was twelve or thirteen but he demurred and said it hadn't been established that the horse was unmanageable. Phillip snapped at his son and the conversation went something like this:

'Alexander, since you're such an expert, would you like to have a crack at riding the horse?'

'Happy to, yes, by all means,' said Alexander.

'It's an easy boast, Alexander,' said Phillip. 'Talk is cheap. What will you give us if you can't ride the horse?'

'How about I give you the value of the horse?' said the boy, who didn't have the money.

The horse was then brought out again and Alexander walked out to the horse, talked to the horse, stroked the horse, got on the horse and rode the horse, to amazement on all sides.

Asked later how he did this, he said that when first presented, the horse had been petrified. There were people yelling all around his head, robes flapping and men pulling him this way and that. Even more terrifying to the horse was an enormous monster moving about on the ground. Realising that this was the horse's own shadow, Alexander dropped his robe and turned the horse to face the sun. The enormous monster disappeared. Alexander was given the horse, which he named Bucephalus, and together they conquered the known world.

⌢

I watched a movie called *Clueless* the other night. I've seen it before and it's twenty years old but it still holds up as an amusing cautionary tale about a pampered young woman with nothing better to do but manipulate the lives and feelings of her friends in the belief that she is assisting them to find love, about which she knows nothing. In order to enjoy the movie you don't need to know that it is an adaptation of Jane Austen's *Emma*, (and a very good one, too). I also recently watched a movie called *The Queen*, a drama starring Helen Mirren, about the behaviour of the queen at the time of the death of Princess Diana. I struggled not to see this as *Toad of Toad Hall*. The queen, who is Toad, lives in an enormous house and is tolerated only because in the English social structure it is a sustaining pleasure for the poor to look upon the wealthy with love and admiration, as is also the case in Australia and in many other egalitarian nations. When the queen/Toad behaves badly however, Blair/Badger needs to go and say, 'Excuse me. What the hell do you think you're doing? You're in a fabulous position and everyone wants you to stay there but if you're not interested, the media/stoatsandweasels will completely take over and tear the place apart. Do exactly as I say or you'll have this whole thing in the ditch'. The queen then does as she's told and Badger goes out and deals brilliantly with the stoats and weasels. Nothing changes. Reform has been averted. Big win for Badger, who wins the next election going away. Diana is nationalised as 'The People's Princess' and Ratty and Moley go back to buggering about on the river.

A few weeks ago I took some photographs of shore birds, many of which are migratory and fly to the arctic in our autumn to breed. Some of the godwits I photographed had orange leg tags and when I zoomed in I could read the letters and numbers, so I reported these on a website that tracks migratory birds and which tells me these birds were tagged one year ago, in exactly the same place. This means that during 2016 they flew from here, up over the South Pacific and southern Asia to China where for millions of years they have fed on the mudflats in the Yellow Sea between the mainland and the Korean peninsula. Then they fly further north to either Siberia or Alaska. And after the breeding season they fly all the way back. Recently a small transmitter was put in a godwit which flew from Alaska to New Zealand in one go without stopping to eat or rest. As a result more research is being done about how the birds sleep. We used to think that each godwit would take a turn at the front, go like the clappers for a while and then slip back into the peloton for bit of a rest while fresher godwits moved forward and took over. Not the case apparently. Microsleep is the current wisdom. Exactly how they do this, and here's an ornithological term, is anyone's guess. Godwit numbers are down this year and the curlew sandpiper and eastern curlew numbers are so far down both species are now classified as critically endangered. The reason is that the birds can no longer feed on the mudflats in the Yellow Sea on the flight north. The mudflats aren't there anymore. Despite international agreements on the crucial importance of the feeding grounds of migratory birds, the area has been reclaimed for housing.

For some reason I've been to a few florists lately. Last week I went into one about an hour out of town and was having a look around when a man came over and asked what I'd like. I said I wasn't quite sure and he said that was fine and he pointed and said he'd be over there if I wanted any help. I thanked him and in fairly short order I moved away from the arrangements and settled on some fresh flowers. I caught his eye.

'Worked it out?' he asked, coming over.

'Yes, I believe I have,' I said, indicating my choice, 'I think I'll just have a swag of these.'

'Lilies,' he said. 'Yes, beautiful. Good choice.' And he collected a generous handful and we went over to the counter where he began to wrap them.

'You've been out of the florist game for a while, haven't you?' he said.

'Yes, I have,' I conceded.

'Thought so,' he said, and continued wrapping. 'We've pretty much given up the term "swag" these days.'

'Really?' I asked. 'What expression do we use these days?'

'Oh,' he drawled, in what A. A. Milne would call a wondering kind of way. '"Bunch", mostly, these days.'

'Is that right?' I said. '"Bunch" of flowers?'

'Yes. A lot of people call them bunches now.'

'Goodness,' I said, and I paid him and left.

I'll be going back there. He's good.

∽

A friend's house was burgled the other day. A couple of replaceable modern devices were taken and a small amount of cash but the main contribution to her sense of shock and violation was that there was stuff everywhere, books pulled out of bookcases, accounts and professional records tipped out of folders, the filing cabinet upended and the contents tossed about and clothes hauled out of wardrobes and cupboards and thrown all over the floor. All the king's horses and all the king's men were quickly on hand and eventually order was restored.

When she was explaining the drama to her neighbours, one of them reported that his brother's house was completely cleaned out while he was away over the summer. Everything worth anything was stolen in broad daylight. The police investigation revealed that entry was effected by jemmying the back door open and the rest of crime was committed as follows: a large van was backed up to the front of house at about 9.30 in the morning and for the next hour or so, several men carried things out of the house and put them in the van while another man mowed the lawn.

∽

In 1972 I was driving a delivery van for Barkers, which was a titanic London retail institution in Kensington until encountering an iceberg one night in dense fog about a decade ago. Some of the people to whom we delivered were very grand and a bit Miss Havisham but a great many of them were kind and interesting.

Lady Fremantle, for example, was about eighty-five and she had a maid who was hot on her heels, so when I arrived with the week's groceries I'd carry them through into the kitchen. We'd often have a chat and on a cold day we'd sit at the table and have a hot chocolate. If they needed anything shifted, lifted or removed, they'd ask me but 'only if it would be no trouble' and if anything needed to be posted, I'd drop it in the mail. Lady F was from a naval family and hanging in a slightly askew frame on the wall was the first order Nelson had written with his left hand after he'd lost his right arm. There was also a couple called Lord and Lady Graves, who were in films and were stars on the London musical stage and to whom I was delivering one day when I was invited in. 'Come in,' said Peter Graves. 'I'm Peter Graves. You're a New Zealander, aren't you?' I said I was and he said, 'Yes, please come in. We're very sad today. It's the anniversary of the death of our dear friend Inia Te Wiata. We're just going to have a quick drink. It would be great if you could join us.'

A bottle of whisky was produced and Peter spoke about the great baritone and we had a quick drink. They then both told some excellent stories and we had a couple more quick drinks before speaking of a great many things and there was some very enjoyable singing at some point and I think we had some salmon as a few more quick drinks were put away. I then left and continued my delivery round, of which I have no clear recollection.

During the 1980s I worked on a television series on which one of the senior writers was James Mitchell, who'd written *Callan* and *When the Boat Comes In*, and whose experience in writing series television was very considerable. After the first script meeting Jim came over and said, 'We've worked together before, haven't we?'

'No, I don't think so,' I said.

'Yes, we have,' he said. 'I've seen you before.'

'I used to deliver your groceries, Jim,' I said. 'You live in Bedford Gardens.' James was a working-class Tory and was inclined not to speak to people who delivered things, but he was always very nice to me after that first script meeting.

One advantage of the Barkers job was that if I wanted to go somewhere in London, to the National Gallery or to the Tate or to the V and A, I could drive up to the front door and, provided I left one of the back doors of the van open to indicate I'd just ducked in to deliver something, I could park there as long as I liked.

Long before winning the Nobel Prize, Seamus Heaney was aware of the danger of allowing oneself to be elevated by others. He told the story of Antaeus, a great warrior in ancient Greece, enormously strong and born out of the earth itself. Antaeus would challenge his opponents to a wrestling match in which he would neutralise them, wrap his arms around them and crush them to death. Antaeus was eventually defeated by Hercules. Hercules was a famous warrior too, but he was also very smart and he'd been studying Antaeus. He had worked out that when an opponent threw Antaeus down on the ground, it made Antaeus stronger because he drew his strength from the earth. So when Hercules and Antaeus fought to the death, Hercules defeated Antaeus by lifting him off the ground and holding him up.

Something else we get from ancient Greece is the story of Narcissus, although perhaps our understanding of it has drifted slightly from its mooring.

In a nutshell, Narcissus is out hunting one day when Echo sees him and falls in love with him. She follows him and talks to him. She has never seen anything as beautiful as he is and she declares her love for him. When Narcissus rejects her, Echo is brokenhearted and disappears, leaving only her voice.

Then Nemesis, the goddess of revenge, punishes Narcissus by leading him to a pool in which he sees an image so beautiful he becomes enchanted and visits the pool each day to gaze at it. Ultimately he realises that the image cannot love him and cannot even exist independently of his act of looking at it. As with Echo, Narcissus's love is obsessive and unrequited, and he kills himself.

Oscar Wilde, who was a Greek scholar, recognised that characterising Narcissus's obsession as 'self love' misses the fact that what he is enthralled by is a reflection. It is not himself as he knows himself to be. The image is reversed. He is beguiled by a perspective of himself he hasn't seen before.

In order to highlight this otherness, Wilde added an addendum to the story in which, after Narcissus dies, the pool weeps and becomes salty with its tears.

The forest creatures gather around and sympathise. They understand that the pool would mourn for so beautiful a young man as Narcissus.

'No no,' says the pool, and it explains that it mourns because when Narcissus bent over and looked into it, it could see itself reflected in his eyes.

Oscar Wilde's two sons were brought up under the name Holland after the surname Wilde, previously illuminated by one of the greatest gifts in the history of the theatre, had become associated with what was called 'gross indecency'. Both Cyril and Vyvyan Holland served as officers in the First World War. Cyril was killed by a sniper but Vyvyan survived and after the war he worked sometimes as a lawyer and sometimes as a writer and translator. In 1947 his second wife, Thelma, who was from Melbourne and who later became the queen's beautician, was invited to Australia and New Zealand to give a series of lectures on fashion in nineteenth century Australia, and between 1948 and 1952 Vyvyan and Thelma Holland lived in Melbourne.

Among Vyvyan's published works is *Drink and Be Merry*, which, although it is essentially a book about wine, contains a story about the remarkable skill level of the painters Braque and Derain.

The two young men shared a rather long studio and each operated at one end of the room. They developed the habit of throwing things to each other and once they'd reached Olympic standard at hurling and catching any article regardless of shape, they worked out how to throw a carafe full of water underarm the length of the room, spinning it backwards so that the water stayed in it. At the other end of the room the recipient would judge the rotation exactly and would catch the carafe by the neck as it arrived.

At the time it was common to be offered all sorts of wine in a restaurant, but it was difficult to get the waiter to bring water. One evening Derain dressed for dinner and entered the Cafe de Paris at the fashionable hour and ordered a meal and a carafe of water. A few minutes later, after Derain's water had arrived, Braque entered and sat at a table about the distance from Derain's as existed between their easels in the studio. Braque ordered his meal and then stood up and said, 'This is monstrous. I've been sitting here for twenty minutes and I've asked for a glass of water and what do I get? Nothing!'

Those assembled were further astonished when Derain stood up and said, 'You want a carafe of water sir? Voila!' and he spun the full carafe over the heads of diners to Braque, who caught it perfectly, slowly poured himself a glass of water and flung the carafe back over the heads to Derain.

'Thank you, sir,' he said, and both painters sat down as if nothing had happened.

Another admirable piece of spontaneous public theatre was established by the Australian cartoonist Paul Rigby in the late 1950s, through the formation of the Limp Falling Association. Members of the association would gather, often in venues where refreshments were available and would go limp and fall to the ground. This would happen in the middle of a room or along a wall or at a dinner table and in a couple of more orchestral instances, in a group of twenty down a full staircase. At a time when Australia has lost touch with its identity it is regrettable that not only has this tradition been lost but that there is not a Federal Minister of Limp Falling, charged with revitalising an important symbol of folkloric independence. It cannot be that the activity is too absurd. There are many federal ministers engaged in idiocy of a far greater magnitude than going limp and falling to the ground. In fact it might help if some of them made inquiries and joined the association.

Living in London for tax purposes in 1972, I read that Spike Milligan would be signing copies of his new book *Adolf Hitler—My Part in his Downfall* at Hatchards in Piccadilly. I'd never been to a book signing before but Spike was a hero of mine and I arrived early. I lurked near where he was obviously going to sit and by the time he arrived, a long queue spilled out into the street. For over an hour Spike signed books and he was brilliant. A man asked him if he'd please sign a book for his wife.

'Certainly', said Spike. 'What's her name?'

'Elizabeth,' said the man.

'How many times have you been married?' asked Spike.

'Just once,' said the man.

Spike dedicated the book to 'Elizabeth the First'.

Once the shop had run out of Milligan books and Spike was

having a cup of tea I eased a pile of books from a shelf behind me and quietly asked Spike to sign them. In the pile was a copy of every book he had written, plus several extra copies of *Puckoon* for friends. We could all practically recite the whole novel.

'I'm afraid your problem is serious,' said Spike.

The new book *Adolf Hitler—My Part in His Downfall* had actually been released a couple of weeks earlier and I'd already read it. Among a great many delights, the book contains examples of early humour and writing Spike was developing with a friend named Harry Edgington. They'd been in the same regiment and had gone through the war together. As Spike signed the books, I thought I'd ask.

'What happened to Harry Edgington?'

Spike stopped writing and looked up. 'Where are you from?' he asked.

'I'm from New Zealand,' I said.

'Whereabouts in New Zealand are you from?' he asked.

'Wellington,' I said.

'Whereabouts in Wellington?' he asked.

'Wadestown,' I said.

'Harry lives not far from you,' he said and he wrote Harry's address in the front of the book. 'Go and see Harry when you get back to New Zealand. Tell him you met me and get him to make you a cup of tea. Harry is my greatest friend. He's been a rock in my life.'

When I returned to Wellington I didn't have the nerve to go and see Harry but I was in a production of the Spike Milligan/John Antrobus play *The Bedsitting Room* in Wellington and after the opening night I was leaving the building when I heard my name in a deep brown English voice. And there was Harry, still looking very like the army photograph in Spike's book. He told me to keep going as a performer. I thanked him and told him about meeting Spike and he said, 'Spike comes to Wellington from time to time. No one knows he's here. We just talk and laugh and drink and play music. Come around.'

This time I did go. Harry was a photo-engraver for a newspaper and he started work in the middle of the night, so I'd never seen him before these meetings. But his wife Peggy I recognised immediately. We'd often travelled on the same bus when I was at school.

These nights with the pair of them were unique and one year they did 'An Evening With...' concert to raise money for Downstage Theatre. It was not only a fabulous night with the population of Wellington swinging from the rafters, it was full of the private fun the two of them had always had together. Harry sat at the piano. He didn't play it. He just sat at it. He sometimes looked as if he was about to play it, but he never did. Spike was so funny he sometimes had to stop to allow people to breathe properly and when he got spontaneous applause he turned and gestured to Harry, who stood with great dignity at the piano, accepted the applause, bowed and sat back down again. It was like watching excess and restraint dancing together. And maybe Spike's gesture was a truth told generously and maybe Harry's silence was his tribute to his friend.

When I was first appearing on television I'd sometimes get a message from Harry. The more there was a fuss about what I'd done ('Who is this long-haired lout?', 'How dare the NZBC make fun of the government'), the more certain it was that I'd get a message from Harry.

'Good on you,' Harry would say. 'Keep going.'

I stayed in touch with Harry until he died in 1993. I still think of him often. He was a very kind man and he co-wrote some of the early Goon Shows. The origin of 'The Ying Tong Song' was a discussion between Milligan and Secombe about how to pronounce Harry's surname. 'It's not Edgerton. It's EdgYINGton.'

Peggy Edgington still thrives at ninety-six.

It used to amaze me that Spike Milligan was my parents' age and had been in the Second World War. In my childhood head he existed independently of the conventions of time or place and it wasn't until I was about ten that I realised *The Goon Show* had been written, and that he did all that too. And it was decades before I realised *The Goon Show* is essentially a Second World War show. 'How on earth did we win?' Spike used to say. In the show Britain is an outmoded steam-driven shambles hobbled by class and bureaucracy and populated by mountebanks like Grytpype-Thynne and idiots like Eccles and Bluebottle, with a few like Major Bloodnok who fall neatly into both categories. Ned Seagoon is a sort of boy scout, keen but frequently being blown up (as Spike was in Italy) by the incompetence of the system he is fighting to defend. Neurosis and an escape inside the language led Milligan to the laughter he needed but the effort nearly killed him.

In the front of the Adolf Hitler book is the single line, 'After *Puckoon* I swore I'd never write another book. This is it.' This reaches back to Lewis Carroll, who died in 1898, which can't have happened, since he wasn't Lewis Carroll.

The script agency which typed and submitted scripts for broadcast at that time was Associated London Scripts, one of whose founders was Ted Kavanagh from Auckland, who wrote *ITMA*. One of the other writers said Spike's scripts were unique. 'No one else would write the following.' He said by way of example: 'Ned Seagoon is trying to explain the law of gravity to Eccles. "Look, I'll show you," says Seagoon. "You jump up in the air. Go on." Eccles jumps in the air. "Now," says Ned, "you came back down again. Why?"

"Because I live here," says Eccles.'

One day at Associated Scripts Spike came out of the toilets into the large room full of typists and said, 'Who put the tea leaves in the toilet?'

No one owned up and Spike repeated the question. 'Come on,'

he said. 'Someone must have done it. The toilet was full of tea leaves. Who put the tea leaves in the toilet?'

Eventually a timid hand crept slowly into the air. Spike turned slowly to the young woman in question and the room became very quiet.

'You're going on a long journey,' he said. 'And you're going to meet a tall, dark stranger.'

⌒

The other day I suggested that my granddaughter come and help me wash the car. She's four and a half and likes nothing more than helping other adults with important matters of this kind. We discussed how best to do it, I made a few suggestions which were accepted in broad outline and off we went. I designated a cloth for her use alone. (This turned out to be a very good idea, for those of you trying this at home.)

Once we got going it was obvious that she saw her role as the officer with particular responsibility for door handles. She came to me and announced that the door handles were filthy and I saw that she was very busy indeed, so while the rest of the vehicle was being washed, the door handles were being cleaned to within an inch of their lives. When both she and the car had been thoroughly washed, I explained that the next stage of the operation was to have a cup of tea. She announced, however, that there was still important work required on the door handles, so while I went to empty the bucket and put things away, she toiled nobly on.

After we'd both come inside, I looked out the window and saw that she'd draped her cloth over one of the vehicle's side mirrors. I'd been stressing the need to clean up properly after finishing a job so I said, feigning a casual interest, 'Claudia, what did you do with your cloth after I took the bucket of water away and you were still working?'

'Oh,' she said, 'I couldn't find you so I folded the cloth and left it on one of the antlers.'

—

While sorting things out in my office I came across the programme for a concert, in 1989, for Weary Dunlop, the doctor who was the senior Australian officer on the Burma–Thailand railway.

Among the performers at the concert that night was Bill Griffiths, an Englishman who was captured by the Japanese in Indonesia in 1942. Bill was blinded and lost both hands after being forced by the Japanese to clear minefields. When they were moved north to Changi, the prisoners who were very ill or handicapped and would slow things down were lined up to be executed. Bill was heavily bandaged and not very mobile. He was ordered to stand up on the hospital verandah and he became aware that the hospital doctor was approaching fast and telling the Japanese guards not to touch his patient. The doctor was Weary Dunlop. He put himself between Bill and the guard's bayonet and he said quietly to the guard, 'This man is my patient. We have worked very hard to save his life. If you kill him, that bayonet will have to go through me first. Go and get your senior officer.' The senior officer needed doctors more than he needed a problem and Bill spent the rest of the war in Changi. His wounds healed and when he returned to England he went back to the firm where he used to drive a truck, got an office job and ended up running one of biggest trucking companies in England.

He flew to Australia for the celebration of Weary's life and at the concert (military bands, show tunes of the period, etc.) Bill provided the outstanding moment of the night. He was walked out on to the stage by his wife, he stood alone at the microphone and he sang without accompaniment a song called 'Two Little Boys'.

'Did you think I would leave you dying, when there's room on my horse for two,' et cetera. Bill was a wonderful singer and the performance was slow and the concert hall was full and as the song continued, a lot of very strong men developed quite bad colds.

When Bill was interviewed in England about his long association with Weary he said, 'Weary saved my life. He's one of my greatest friends. I speak to him every day. He comes and sits in my den here and we talk. He sits over there in that chair. That's Weary's chair. It's no use saying that Weary lives in Melbourne and can't possibly be here with me. I'm blind. I can't see that he's not here.'

⁓

I was invited to participate in a discussion about the 1916 Easter Uprising in Dublin. I was there to talk about Kathleen Fox, who painted the scene as it was happening and was a relative of my grand-mother, but most of the other speakers were proper historians with actual qualifications and real knowledge. I felt like a pullet at an exotic bird festival and in order to work out an approach I asked the speaker sitting next to me what she'd be talking about. She was a professor of Irish History and a flicker of concern darted across her face.

'I'll be talking about the Proclamation,' she said.

'That'll be interesting' said the pullet. 'I was reading the Proclamation the other day. It's pretty remarkable.' The Proclamation is the document which framed the rebel cause and a public reading of the proclamation marked the beginning of the rebellion.

'Yes,' conceded the professor, 'although there are some difficulties.'

'Really?' said the pullet, to whom life seemed simple.

'For example,' continued the professor, 'Patrick Pearce famously read the Proclamation out on the post office steps.'

'That's right,' I said.

'The post office in Dublin doesn't have any steps,' said the professor.